KADIM
THE LAND
OF
EARTHEN
VESSELS

Master Potter®
and the Mountain of Fire

JILL AUSTIN

Destiny Image Fiction

An Imprint of
Destiny Image₀ Publishers, Inc.
P.O. Box 310
Shippensburg, PA 17257-0310

ISBN 0-7684-2190-X

For Worldwide Distribution
Printed in the U.S.A.

This book and all other Destiny Image, Revival Press, MercyPlace,
Fresh Bread, Destiny Image Fiction, and Treasure House books are available
at Christian bookstores and distributors worldwide.

1 2 3 4 5 6 7 8 9 / 09 08 07 06 05 04 03

For a U.S. bookstore nearest you, call
1-800-722-6774.
For more information on foreign distributors, call
717-532-3040.
Or reach us on the Internet:
www.destinyimage.com

DEDICATION

How do I say thank you to my very best friend, Holy Spirit? What do I love the most about Him? Amazing grace—that's what He gives me. That's how He loves me and how He empowers me. His tender companionship and guidance always points to the glorious Son, Master Potter. Oh, how I love His violent love and insatiable fervency to bring suffering humanity to Jesus. I'm in awe that I can partner with Him to bring in the harvest.

High adventures! Walking with Him daily is never boring! He is not afraid of controversy or exposing religious doctrines and traditions of men. He is dangerous; He is not a tame God. We can't control or manipulate Him. At times He's is like the roaring wind or consuming fire, but at other times He's like the gentle dove.

Our relationship certainly hasn't been meek and mild. Often He is the one who gets me in trouble. Over the last 25 years of meetings I've been more or less the straight guy while Holy Spirit is a wild, heavenly tornado that wreaks havoc, shaking everything that can be shaken. Fear of man? He never has to deal with it; only I do, after He's offended many. But talking and wrestling late into the night I always see His great love and wisdom in challenging people to run for their highest callings.

He fills the lonely places of my soul as His wind blows this traveling vagabond across this terrestrial globe. Always together, He's my confidant, counselor, and strategist. I love how He partners with me in ministry. It's as though He's standing right next to me whispering prophetic words and revelations, which proclaim destiny and birthright to many. He shows me insight into the Word and glimpses into eternity. He makes me homesick to be with Him forever.

This wondrous Person, who is God, is so awesome and yet such an intimate friend. His colorful personality captivates my heart. My comprehension of Him has deepened over the years—never stagnant, forever growing. Amazing grace, that's what He gives me.

ACKNOWLEDGMENTS

T his book was made possible by the prayers, love, and support of many friends, generous supporters, office staff, and intercessors. I can't adequately express my gratitude to everyone who has fasted, prayed, and loved me as I've sat pounding out this book in my basement between rigorous road trips to the nations.

I want to thank all the past and present staff of Master Potter Ministries who have helped me on this prophetic journey. What incredible sacrifices everyone has made. Linda Valen has been my ministry assistant for the last ten years. I affectingly call her, "my valentine," a gift from God. You are truly a woman of excellence and integrity.

David and Tracy Ruleman, Dick and Karen Hol, Michael and Georgette O'Brien, and Rich and Pam Boyer have been friends and intercessors for over twenty-five years. They have stood with me through torrential floods and raging fires as I've ministered the power and demonstration of the Holy Spirit. You are life-long friends, and I love you.

Melody Green, you are truly a sister and comrade in the ministry, standing with me during blessings and adversity. You've always been a strong voice of counsel and wisdom. You're amazing.

Paul and Naomi Beltz and Mary Pedraza you were part of the original Master Potter team and were willing to be radical and on the cutting edge when it wasn't popular. You are truly glorious comrades, still challenging the status quo.

Barbara Fraley, Bev and Steve Bartlett, Lawrence and Pamela Stead, thank you for your friendship, long talks into the night, and many prayers.

To my brother, Jon Austin, who's a great friend of mine and of Jesus. I love you!

To Nettie Clevenger, who is like my little sister. I love your courage and loyal friendship.

To Andre Ashby, you are an awesome spiritual son, psalmist, and prophetic preacher. I believe in you!

Mike Bickle, your intercession, love for the Word and for the Holy Spirit still inspires me. Your humility in the midst of outstanding revelation is astonishing. Thank you for believing in the call on my life and being an encourager. I love your abandonment for Jesus.

Thanks to the following contributing editors who worked so long and hard with me. Your skill and suggestions have significantly molded this book. What a delight to work with such gifted writers: Madeline Watson, Jackie Macgirvin and Peg de Alminana.

Once again, Destiny Image, you have outdone yourselves. Thanks to Don Nori for birthing such a prophetic publishing company. Thanks also to Don Milam for giving a listening ear and great wisdom. To the rest of the staff—you're exceptionally creative and you really went the extra mile. You're awesome. Thank you.

ENDORSEMENTS

Jill Austin has more credibility when writing about the Master Potter than anyone I know. That's because she writes with clay under her fingernails. I'm sure you will be blessed by this book.

—Tommy Tenney
Author, *The God Chasers*

Master Potter and the Mountain of Fire, is an excellent Kingdom response to the Harry Potter craze and provides a positive, inspirational alternative for the young and the young at heart.

—Dr. Myles Munroe
Bahamas Faith Ministries International
Nassau, Bahamas

The fires of testing that God permits in our lives are often difficult to understand. Jill has the gift of helping us to see that our suffering and heartache are for our eternal glory. The fires of affliction are for the beautification of the soul.

—Gwen R. Shaw
End-Time Handmaidens
Servants International

Jill Austin is a master storyteller, and she has given us a story that will live forever. Why? Because it is the human story. It is your story and it is mine. In Master Potter and the Mountain of Fire you will discover the great secrets of the deeper life as Jill creatively and wonderfully brings spiritual meaning to the pain that inflicts us all, while at the same time she inspires us to continue on.

—Don Milam
VP, Acquisitions
Destiny Image Publishers
Author of *The Ancient Language of Eden*

Jill Austin is a visionary. Using the powerful vehicle of allegory, Jill takes us into the world of the Master Potter—a place all of us have visited but few of us have fully recognized. It is a glorious journey to intimacy and healing.

—George Otis, Jr.
President
The Sentinel Group

Jill Austin has been given a gift by Jesus Himself to enable us to enter a deep spiritual place as we journey with her characters through the Master Potter and the Mountain of Fire. This book calls us to a glorious devotion to our Bridegroom King. The profoundly insightful story provides a map for a deeper life in God. Let the fire fall as you read this incredible book.

—Dr. Heidi Baker
Co-founding Director
Iris Ministries
Mozambique, Africa

Rarely do you pick up a book that fascinates you from the first sentence. In a word, it is as though the Lord is saying to you the reader, "Come on, child, let's go down to the Potter's house." Jill Austin has given us a classic.

—Pastor Cleddie Keith
Heritage Christian Fellowship

Jill Austin is a highly gifted, anointed vessel. She has done an awesome job of revealing and enlightening us in our need to embrace the supernatural presence of the Spirit of God. Your heart will be encouraged as your read Jill's picturesque spiritual journey. I recommend this book to all who have a holy hunger to advance ever deeper in the things of God.

—Bobby Conner
Founder of Demonstration of God's Power Ministries
Moravian Falls, North Carolina

In Master Potter and the Mountain of Fire, Jill captures a vision of the prophetic destiny of this generation and communicates it in a creative and compelling manner.

—Paul Keith Davis
White Dove Ministries
Orange Beach, Alabama

Jill's allegory mirrors what Paul said: "Therefore we do not lose heart. Even though our outward man is perishing, yet the inward man is being renewed day by day. For our light affliction, which is but for a moment, is working for us a far more exceeding and eternal weight of glory."

—Barbara J. Yoder
Senior Pastor of Shekinah Christian Church
Ann Arbor, Michigan
Author of *The Breaker Anointing*
Editor of *Mantled With Authority, God's Apostolic Mandate To Women.*

Jill Austin's sequel to Master Potter takes her protagonist through more refining fire to a place where she even more closely resembles her Maker. If your journey to Christian maturity still includes the mystery of suffering (Isn't that all of us?), you will not only enjoy the tale, but you will find yourself absorbed in the truth that the pathway to a more profound revelation of God's love winds its way through pain.

—Melinda Fish
Author of six books including *Keep Coming, Holy Spirit*
Editor of Toronto's *Spread the Fire* Magazine

Jill Austin successfully answers the heart-felt questions of day-to-day Christianity, all while brilliantly introducing the reader to the wonders of divine Purpose. This whole book works to unveil the mystery of the promise contained in Romans 8:28 "All things work together for good…"

—Bill Johnson
Bethel Church
Redding, California

Fascinating journey! Jill's skillfully written allegory is engaging and creative. I was both entertained and enlightened as one biblical principle after another literally jumped off of the page and into my heart. Awesome book!"

—Alice Smith
Executive Director
U.S. PRAYER CENTER
Houston, Texas

What I love about Jill Austin's book is how well it paints a picture of the journey that any Christian can relate to. It may be an allegory, but it is a true story of God's love for us and His deliverance and healing from anything that the enemy would bring to devastate our lives."

—Cal Pierce
Director
Healing Rooms Ministers

Continuing the allegorical tale begun in her first book, Jill Austin weaves spiritual truth and principles through the charming story of Beloved, Purity, Comrade, and the other earthen vessels in the Master Potter's House. Believers everywhere will relate to the arduous journey the vessels must take through the Mountain of Fire in order to be transformed into beautiful vessels that are fit for the Master's use.

—Jane Hansen
President, Aglow International

Together with the anointing, Jill Austin's words create a journey into the purpose of God, mapping the unseen realms as we go, and telling the true adventure of faith. *Mountain of Fire* is the ultimate adventure-love story, a parable of the believer's transformation from useless lump of clay to glorious vessel. Along the way, self-discovery and universal insight abound. I saw myself and others through Jill's knowledge and experience of the Father's love and wisdom as He works to mold us in His image.

—Dr. Bonnie Chavda
Pastor All Nations Church
Co-founder Watch of the Lord Prayer Movement
Charlotte, North Carolina

CONTENTS

PROLOGUE

But we have this treasure in earthen vessels, that the excellence of the power may be of God and not of us. We are hard-pressed on every side, yet not crushed; we are perplexed, but not in despair; perse-cuted, but not forsaken; struck down, but not destroyed—always car-rying about in the body the dying of the Lord Jesus, that the life of Jesus also may be manifested in our body. For we who live are al-ways delivered to death for Jesus' sake, that the life of Jesus also may be manifested in our mortal flesh. So then death is working in us, but life in you (2 Corinthians 4:7-12 NKJV).

Master Potter and the Mountain of Fire continues Jill Austin's allegorical tale of Heaven's devoted quest to redeem lowly clay and fashion it into finished masterpieces, honored and celebrated by both heaven and earth. There are uncounted varieties of vessels fashioned by human hands—fragile teacups, squatty mugs, slender wine goblets, elegant vases, beautiful perfume vials, and on and on. These many vessels that serve us both functionally and aesthetically come alive in the pen of Jill Austin to portray the great diversity of human ves-sels being fashioned in love to fulfill the purposes of God. The hidden wisdom of Master Potter appoints a unique journey for each vessel that culminates in beauty and honor transcending even the highest reaches of the human imagina-tion. Every step in the potter's process in bringing forth a beautiful vessel is given its spiritual counterpart—from the potter's wheel, to the drying and prun-ing, to the glazing room, and finally to the fiery kiln.

The Mountain of Fire continues the story of Beloved, a little pitcher, once known as Forsaken, rescued from the brokenness and rejection of the Potter's Field and drawn into new hope and joy by the redeeming love of Master Potter. As her story continues, the wisdom of Master Potter slowly discloses by degrees to her sight and understanding the path that will bring her into her destiny. It is a path that leads to the firing chambers, located in the heights of the Mountain of Fire, where vessels of honor are unfailingly produced. Master Potter must un-fold this "vessel of honor" destiny appointed for Beloved in stages and with much patience, because the path must take her through great trial and suffering that will purify her and make her fit for the Master's use. Heavenly callings are costly, requiring a painful cleansing from the marks and remains of sin in our members. Beloved faces some of the deepest places of pain and brokenness in her life as she learns to trust the love of Master Potter.

As our earthenware characters catch glimpses of the road they must travel and the price they must pay to become vessels of honor, they wonder if there might not be an easier way to reach this destiny. Others, however, cling to Master Potter's loving assurances that His refining fire is the only means to true glory and honor. In the end they will wear a beauty that the enemy can only cheaply counterfeit, but never duplicate. They discover, as Master Potter said, there are no shortcuts to the magnificent destiny He appoints.

As the story develops, and the issue is settled as to which path they will travel, Beloved, Comrade, Long Suffering, and the others in their company, begin to discover why it is the narrow, less-traveled way. The road winds through difficult and treacherous places, and even takes them into the valley of the shadow of death. They find themselves more than once in the devastating circumstance of someone deeply loved being ravaged by sickness to the point of death. The pain of these desperate moments stirs fervent intercession for miracles of healing, but Master Potter's responses to their petitions leave them with deep questions and a shaken faith.

What happens when the prayer for someone's healing does not produce healing? Where does that leave us? If we know that it is God's will to heal (see Matt. 8:2-3), and our confidence is that if we ask anything according to His will, we know that He hears us and that we have the petitions we asked of Him (see 1 John 5:14-15), then if we pray for someone's healing, why doesn't it come? If healing is the children's bread (see Mark 7:24-30), and if the Father in Heaven doesn't give rocks when his children ask for bread, but instead gives good gifts to those who ask Him (see Luke 11:11-13), then why if we pray for someone's healing doesn't it come?

Hard questions! And the answers are varied, emotional, and conflicting. The struggle of the vessels with these questions leaves us squarely in the biblical tension surrounding this issue of divine healing.

The biblical boundary lines within which these questions occur are stretched wide in opposite directions. On the one hand, Matthew affirms, quoting Isaiah, that the healing ministry of Jesus was included in His atoning work (see Matt. 8:16-17). The healing miracles of Jesus that flood the Gospel records were foretastes of benefits flowing from His atoning death. Deliverance and healing were released in Christ's atonement as direct expressions of the kingdom inaugurated by His death and resurrection. Just as surely as He forgives sin by His atoning death, He heals our infirmities by the same death (Mark 2:10-11; Psalm 103:3).

On the other hand, Paul informs us that in the outworking of our salvation we yet await the redemption of our bodies (see Rom. 8:19-23). Our bodies are still mortal, and are awaiting the final benefits of Christ's redemptive work. This mortal will put on immortality only in the resurrection, when death is finally swallowed up in victory (see 1 Cor. 15:53-55). The death of death is the climactic work of the Cross in history, and it yet remains to be fulfilled.

What does this have to do with healing? Everything! What must be healed above everything else is our mortality. Only when death is finally swallowed up in the Cross can we claim full and final healing of all our infirmities and sicknesses. All healing that is received now is partial and temporary, and only a token and foretaste of the fuller version that will become ours in the consummation of Christ's kingdom. No miracle of the New Testament was a permanent rescue from the ravages of sin, sickness, and the curse. Even Lazarus was raised only to die again. Christ alone has been raised from the dead never to die again! (see Rom. 6:9) Christ's resurrection alone carries in it the promise of the death of death. His glorious second coming will usher in that promise! Our resurrection at His second coming fulfills the promise of His resurrection at His first coming, and ushers in the full and final release from every consequence of sin by the death of death. "Christ the firstfruits, afterward those who are Christ's at His coming" (1 Cor. 15:23).

These are the outer boundaries that encompass the debate over healing. Like the present manifestation of the kingdom of God in the earth, with the healing question we are living between the already and the not yet. While we are in this processive movement from the inauguration of God's kingdom in the earth (first coming of Christ) to the final consummation of that kingdom (second coming of Christ), we will have events (and non-events), healings (and non-healings) that create questions and dilemmas for which we cannot provide final answers. Clearly, there is a sovereign wisdom that informs all moments and occasions of divine healing, but it is also inescapable that faith receives such miracles, exactly as is true with the forgiveness of sins.

While all the questions and mysteries surrounding healing will never be resolved in this life, there is in the pages that follow a serious attempt to grapple with them at the level of human pain. And the setting for wrestling with the pain is a story with characters that have real emotions and are involved in deep struggles.

What follows, therefore, is not a dispassionate, predictably dull treatise on human suffering and divine healing, but a lively story. Stories touch and stir our emotions. They breathe real life into truth! And as this story unfolds, you will feel the love of God unfettered from esoteric realms. It will become more than mere theological proposition to which you give assent. It clothes God's love in the rhythms of real life that dares the human heart to reach up in faith and embrace this indescribable gift, even while caught in the web of earthly trials. It is a story of love that suddenly breaks in on our fallenness as a consuming fire to burn out everything that stands in the way of communion and intimacy with the Creator, Redeemer, and Lover of our souls.

Like all stories, Master Potter and the Mountain of Fire is an invitation to enter the realm of imagination, which is the growing place of true faith. "Faith is the substance of things hoped for, the evidence of things not seen" (Heb. 11:1). The ground in which faith grows is that vast reality God declares to us that is yet unseen, but which becomes the harbor and dwelling place of our hope. God invites us to meet Him and explore this vast realm of the unseen in the holy imagination of faith.

He has carefully set down the words of Scripture to establish the frame for this imagination that will safeguard it from straying into error and deception. All other stories must be measured by these specially chosen words, ordered, and superintended by the Holy Spirit. Jill Austin's story measures up well by this standard! It provides a safe place for holy imagination to carry us into the length and breadth and depth and height of the love of Christ.

So welcome to the land of earthenware vessels! They, like us, come in all shapes and sizes! Enjoy the journey into the heart of Master Potter, the fashioner of these vessels! Come, see a love guided by unsearchable wisdom! Prepare to be surprised by joy at the discoveries you will make on the summit of the Mountain of Fire!

—Steve Carpenter
Th.M. Dallas Theological Seminary
President of Word and Spirit Ministries

FOREWORD

Everyone at some point in life has experienced the rude awakening of human frailty. Although we are powerful creatures intricately designed to accomplish much mentally and physically, we are still dependent beings. We learn just how fragile we are when we catch a cold, forget something, or make a poor decision. Even the air we breathe, our slightest movements, and what we see and hear are not totally under our control. Let's face it, dependence is vital to our existence. As adults, pride tells us that being dependent upon anyone or anything is weakness. However, the truth of the matter is that strength comes when we are dependent upon someone, namely the Master Potter.

There is no one greater upon whom we can depend than the Master Potter! He is the only one qualified to "put us back together" when we've been damaged. Jill Austin has convincingly conveyed this truth. Her storyline causes the reader to develop an affinity with God as they witness His different attributes during Beloved's journey—His compassion, His father-like nature, His desire to direct and to defend, and His willingness to heal—all of which He chooses to do for "mere men and women." The point most evident in Jill's writings is that God has made the choice to be ALL things to us. This thought alone is mind-boggling! His delight is to usher us through life from beginning to end, concerning Himself with the small and big issues we face.

Master Potter and the Mountain of Fire is must reading for those seeking to be more than just an admirer of God, but who hunger for a life-changing relationship with Him. All elements central to developing an enduring and endearing relationship with the Father are referenced in this book. Read it and share it with a friend. Both of you will never be the same after journeying with the Master Potter!

—Dr. Kingsley Fletcher
International Speaker, Author and Pastor
Research Triangle Park
North Carolina

Greetings From the Author

But we have this treasure in jars of clay to show that this all-sur-passing power is from God and not from us (2 Corinthians 4:7 NIV).

With the world teetering on global warfare, it is imperative that we live supernatural lives! Moving in the Spirit is no longer an option, but a necessity. The Lord has given me a mandate in writing Master Potter and Master Potter and the Mountain of Fire to pull back the curtains of the supernatural realm and use these stories as something of a textbook on the Holy Spirit.

Theses books demystify the supernatural and unravel the mysteries of the glory realm, training you in spiritual warfare, hearing God's voice in every day life, and prayer intermingled with a love for the Word. The cosmic war between the demonic and the forces of heaven is vividly portrayed within the Christian framework and will satisfy your deep hunger for spiritual encounters.

Using the force of prophetic allegory, the Master Potter series deals with real life issues—alcoholism, physical and sexual abuse, divorce, betrayal, adultery, unforgiveness, and spiritual deception. Also, the hard questions of unanswered prayers, loss of loved ones, suffering, and sickness are addressed. This is a powerful journey of faith, a story of redemption, every believer's struggle toward wholeness.

My heart is that these books will transcend the four walls of the church and touch a hurt and dying world that is starving for the supernatural. If the church begins to move in the power of the gospel, the world will not flock to the occult. It is time that the church raises up a standard to the world instead of letting it feed off of fool's gold!

With its biblical foundation, Master Potter and the Mountain of Fire counters the current fascination with counterfeit spirituality—witchcraft, sorcery, New Age, occultism, and demons. I hope that these novels redirect the Harry Potter generation into the loving arms of the Master Potter Himself. It's time someone warns it that the demonic is dangerous to dabble with.

These books are a prophetic journey—not just a story. It unfolds on many levels—the Potter and the clay, the divine and the human, the angelic and the demonic, the good and the evil. The reader engages on a heart adventure through a world of clay vessels who suffer bumps and bruises, which cause cracks and chips. In our moments of brokenness, the world pronounces us "worthless."

It's then that Master Potter rescues us—like He rescued Beloved—and we begin the long and winding road of sanctification (which unfortunately includes those painful firings in the kiln.) If we opt out at any step of the journey because it is just too painful, we miss out on the fullness of the destiny the Lord has for us. But, if we submit and trust the loving hands of the Master Potter, we will eventually go through the Mountain of Fire and end up as a vessel of honor fit for the King's service.

There truly is impartation in these books as the reader identifies with Beloved's struggles toward wholeness, and learns as she learns, that Master Potter desires us even in weakness. Absolutely no one is too broken to be healed and used by God.

My prayer is that the Lord would ambush each and every reader, especially you, and ruin you for the Master Potter—the Lord Jesus Christ!

*O living flame of love that tenderly
wounds my soul in its deepest center!
Since now you are not oppressive,
now consummate! If it be your will:
tear through the veil of this sweet encounter.*

ST. JOHN OF THE CROSS

Settings and Characters

Settings

Kadim, the land of earthen vessels

Comfort Cove, a quaint nineteenth-century fishing village

The Potter's House, Master Potter's home overlooking Comfort Cove

Mountain of Fire, a mountain kiln deep within the Formidable Mountain Range

Formidable Mountains, a rugged mountain range behind the Potter's House

Precarious Pass, a dangerous pass to the Mountain of Fire

Cavern of the Ancient Mysteries, a demonic stronghold hidden in the Formidables

Deeper Life, a religious commune in the wilderness

Gates of Heaven

Throne Room

War Room, a strategic command center

Heavenly Library, records of the past, present, and future

Miracles Unlimited, a heavenly warehouse

Heavenly Courtroom, the judgment seat

Major Characters

Father in Heaven

Master Potter/Bridegroom King

Holy Spirit/Amazing Grace

Satan

Death

Suicide

Beloved, formerly Forsaken, a pitcher

Purity, formerly Promiscuous, Beloved's daughter, a mug

Comrade, formerly Friendless, a mug in Beloved's set

BELOVED'S FRIENDS

Long Suffering, a tall willowy vase
Harvester, a large canister
Sweet Adoration, a delicate perfume bottle
Fearless, a wine carafe
Joyful, a wine goblet in Fearless's set
Golden Incense, a teapot
Tender-Hearted, a saucer in Golden Incense's set
Blessing, a saucer in Golden Incense's set
Steadfast, a large serving platter

BELOVED'S TEAM OF MUGS

Comrade	*Self Assurance*
Purity	*Devotion*
Loyalty	*Champion*
Generosity	*Mercy*
Confidence	*Kindness*

FORMIDABLE MOUNTAIN RANGE

Watchman, the guide for the pottery wagons
Elder, the wagon master

COMFORT COVE

Master Craftsman, the potter from Comfort Cove
Madam False Destiny, a spiritualist and owner of the Inn
Mayor Lecherous, the village's mayor
Pastor Compromise, the pastor of the Country Club Church
Pastor Beguiler, retired pastor of Deeper Life Commune

ANGELS

Valiant, Beloved's guardian angel
Exhorter, Long Suffering's guardian angel
Gallant, Purity's guardian angel
Courageous, Comrade's guardian angel
Rembrandt and Angelo, artistic angels
Guardian of the Glory, Beloved's heavenly guide

DEMONS

Fire Chief	*Religious Ritual*
Fear of Man	*Sickness and Disease*
Law 'n Order	*Lust*

Recap From Book One

Master Potter

Have you ever experienced the deep grief of brokenness? Has your life been ruined by wrong choices, shame, and regret? If so, you will love this allegorical tale. Prepare to fall in love with a broken pitcher and her friends—a charming teapot, a courageous wine carafe, a boisterous canister, a squatty mug, a forlorn vase and others—that will enchant and disarm you in a genuinely delightful way.

One of the most powerful biblical images describing the relationship of God and humanity is that of the potter and the clay. God created us as earthenware vessels so we would realize our weakness and call out to Him. Each of our journeys takes us through much joy and pain—but no person or situation is beyond hope.

Master Potter vividly portrays the truth that no one is too broken to be healed and used by God. There is no situation He can't redeem. He is the God of second and third chances and passionately loves all His vessels. Each one is a beautiful, unique piece of art designed before the foundation of the world and fashioned by His loving hands. He delights in us all.

This charming allegorical tale takes place in Kadim, the land of earthen vessels. A young woman named Forsaken, portrayed as a broken clay pitcher, dwells in a quaint 19th century fishing village called Comfort Cove.

If you've ever felt abandoned and alone, surely you will understand Forsaken's story. Her mother died when she was young and she grew up with an alcoholic father. She never really had a family and never felt as though she belonged. The brokenness of her need and confusion of her hurt led to making all the wrong life choices. She did the wrong things, went the wrong places, was with the wrong men, and, ultimately, ended up in the wrong marriage.

THE JOURNEY BEGINS

Shattered by betrayal, abuse, and loneliness, Forsaken finds herself discarded in the trash heap of a loveless existence. Out of that brokenness and despair this wounded pitcher—who could be you or me—meets Master Potter, the lover of her soul—her Creator. He changes her name from Forsaken to Beloved.

Through a long and often difficult process, her utter despair is transformed into wonderful joy and fulfillment. Come with her and enter into a love that she thought was only possible for others, but never for her.

THE POTTER'S WHEEL

Master Potter takes her to His house where He begins the long, painful process of making her into a vessel of honor. Because of her cracks and chips, He must start all over again. She is crushed and must soak in the healing pools of His love to become soft and pliable clay once again. She learns to trust Him and yields to His gentle hands as He reshapes her into a beautiful pitcher on the potter's wheel.

Remember that Master Potter is an artist, and the designer of your life too. He knows what kind of vessel you are, your unique shape, beautiful colors, and wonderful destiny. He knows every detail of your life.

THE WILDERNESS

Taken from the potter's wheel, Beloved is then placed on the shelf to dry. It's there she starts on a wilderness journey to learn to follow Holy Spirit. But her path is diverted when she takes what she thinks is the easy way out and marries a seemingly godly man. In attempting this shortcut to happiness she ends up losing ten years, her husband, and her children.

Have you, like Beloved, exhausted yourself struggling to get out of your barren, dry wilderness?

Bruised, bloodied, and an emotional wreck, she resumes following Holy Spirit to the Tent of the Lord. She is warmly embraced by Master Potter, who has longed for her the entire time she was away.

ENTERING THE REFINER'S FIRE

Beloved and her friends enter the kiln for their first firing. Master Potter gently walks her through forgiveness toward those who abused her in the past as the fires rage around her.

Do you dream of having your heart reawakened and being able to love again?

When the refiner's fire is over the kiln is opened and the vessels are surprised to find they still need to be glazed and go through a more intense firing in a hidden mountain kiln—the dreaded Mountain of Fire—before they become beautiful vessels of honor and fulfill their destinies.

MASTER POTTER AND THE MOUNTAIN OF FIRE

Becoming a vessel of honor is a painful process that requires dying to self. In Master Potter and the Mountain of Fire, Beloved discovers this high price— as well as unexpected joy.

Hidden in this delightful story of believable characters lies the powerful truth that His authentic love can transform your life. Come along on this journey into the inner recesses of the heart. There's far more than you have ever hoped for in your relationship with God. He wants to fill your heart's desire and draw you into a safe, intimate love relationship. If you long to go deeper with God, then accompany Beloved into the higher fires—inside the Mountain of Fire.

PART ONE

THE GLAZING ROOM

CHAPTER ONE

JILL'S STUDIO

*D*eadlines, deadlines, deadlines, I complained to myself, because no one was there to listen. *Well, at least they're good deadlines.* I carefully moved pieces of bisque ware separating them into sets and individual pieces of art-work. The elation I'd felt over being chosen for a private showing of my work at a local gallery had given way to anxiety. The weekend was coming fast and the next few days I would live in my potter's studio. I remembered my college days in art school when I'd hole up in a studio for and entire weekend making pots on the wheel.

Fortunately, I had all my pieces thrown and two kilns were in their final glaze firing now, but I had several hundred more vessels on wooden shelves lin-ing the studio walls. They were waiting patiently to be washed, glazed, and fired.

I was nearly overcome by fatigue, but I reminded myself that being a free-lance potter was my dream-come-true so I'd better enjoy it. I poured a cup of hot tea from a delicate teapot. *I need caffeine, lots of caffeine!* I glanced long-ingly at my cot, hoping I could spare a few minutes for a catnap later on.

What a blessing to have my pieces become so popular. I cradled a small perfume bottle in my hands, admiring her narrow, sleek lines. *Thank you Lord, for Your favor on my work as a potter.*

My studio was first-rate. Tucked away in the mountains and surrounded by fir trees, the view never ceased to provide creative inspiration. My potter's wheel sat in front of the large window where the early morning sun flooded in, gently warming my face as I spent tireless hours shaping precious vessels.

I'd been working in the studio all of yesterday and most of today and it was almost midnight. It had rained off and on all day, but suddenly I heard a differ-ent sound. I flipped on the outside light to reveal freezing rain and smiled. *Let the elements throw me their worst. I'm protected from the weather, and the rag-ing fire in the kilns will keep me warm all night.*

MUGS AND ANGEL WINGS

A squatty little mug waited on the table to be glazed. He was part of a set with a matching pitcher, and his round, fat belly-like shape made me chuckle. He reminded me of a perpetually disheveled professor I'd had in college who never seemed to be able to keep his shirttail tucked in. Holding the mug up to the fluorescent lights, I gently rotated him and admired my handiwork. *OK, mister, tell me a little bit about yourself? What color do you want to be?*

Sometimes as I pray and worship I catch glimpses of my pieces as finished vessels and know immediately how to proceed. *Thanks Lord, I will do an angel theme on this set. My little mug and his companions will be beautiful with an angel wing painted on their white glazes. The matching pitcher will have an angel with accents of blue and gold filigree adorning her rim.*

I picked up a paintbrush, and after several careful strokes on the mug stepped back to get a long view. *Only seven more mugs to paint and then the pitcher.*

I studied the little fellow, wondering who would buy him. Where would he end up? What would his destiny be? What if someone carelessly dropped him on the floor and he broke? Ouch, that was too painful to even think about.

Since the Lord gave me the vision of Beloved and her friends in Kadim, the land of earthen vessels, I'd come to appreciate how jealous is God, our Master Potter, for all His clay pots. Each one is truly beloved to Him.

TENDING THE KILN

The blaring alarm clock told me it was time to check the first kiln. I pulled the plug out of the spy hole in the door and peered into the blazing inferno. The heat radiated on my face even though I stood a foot away. Several white temperature cones were melted, but several were not, indicating that the kiln wasn't yet hot enough.

Each cone bends at a certain temperature, and when all four are bent the kiln can be shut down.

The four cones in the midst of the swirling flames always remind me of Daniel's three friends, Shadrach, Meshach and Abednego, who were thrown into the fiery furnace by Nebuchadnezzar. There in the blazing inferno they found a fourth man who looked like the Son of God. These cones always present a comforting reminder that, even in the midst of my fiery trials, I'm never alone.

Bending down, I looked through the bottom spy hole, which gave me a narrow view into the blazing kiln. I could see the outlines of vessels glowing white-hot. It was time to begin the heavy reduction firing, so I pushed in the dampers and cranked up the heat. Taking a few steps back, I avoided the scorching flames shooting out the spy holes as the pressures transformed the bright fire into a heavy, black, carbon dioxide fire.

A POTTER'S FASCINATION

I love the raging fire. I've always been fascinated with fire's wild unpredictability. It can provide life-saving warmth, but it's so dangerous it can devastate cities. It's a living substance with a heartbeat and a mind of its own. That's part of what drew me into becoming a potter, my love relationship with this roaring element. Only the fire can bring durability and strength to the clay and melt the glazes. The potter lovingly creates a vessel, but how the pot responds to the fire imprints it forever.

This is the most exciting part of the firing process, when the kiln becomes a blazing, smoking inferno. In this violent heat the intense pressure releases hidden colors and pigments from the clay and glazes. Soft tan clay vessels turn rich chestnut brown, while green carbon dioxide glazes become vibrant ruby reds.

This is so like our lives. There is a mystery to suffering. The Lord allows the fires of real life to bring great depth and beauty if we allow them. Concentrated, painful fires bring forth the character of the Lord in our lives and help us to complete our destiny.

Each firing is so different. Every time I pull open the door of a cooled kiln I find a tantalizing surprise. *What will my pots look like this time? Will the glazes have melted in pleasing patterns? Will the brush strokes have taken on the beautiful depths I intended? Will the iron and other mineral flecks in the clay have combined beautifully with the glazes?*

Everything is so subjective, but that's why I love this creative process. It's full of surprises. What beautiful vessels will await me this time? It's just like every believer's journey; none of us knows what the end result is going to be as we go into the fire.

CHAPTER TWO

ANGELIC INVASION

I reset the alarm for the kiln and settled on my cot for a catnap. The room was uncomfortably warm. I took one last admiring glance at my squatty little mug with the angel's wing before closing my eyes. In my mind, I still pictured my studio and was thinking about the destinies of my other pots. An unusual glow from the kiln drew my attention as several artistic angels stepped out through the kiln wall and began to speak to the pottery pieces inside.

The first angel, wearing iridescent white robes, picks up a large canister and begins to prophesy: "You, my friend, have a great destiny in God. He has made you a pastor, and you will be full of the grain of the earth to feed the poor and needy." The magnificent angel carefully paints royal blue and deep purple on the vessel's rich tan base.

The second angel is busy painting yellow roses on a white china teapot while singing, "Holy, holy, holy …" Holding the delicate little teapot up to the light, he chuckles and asks, "You are quite the little intercessor aren't you? You will be given maps and strategic keys to open city gates."

TEETERING BETWEEN LIFE AND DEATH

I jumped when the phone rang. Glancing at my watch, I realized I'd been asleep for over an hour. I was expecting a call from Jen about Carrie's condition following their car accident. Jen was like my sister, and Carrie was almost like my own child. It'd been almost three weeks since a drunk driver hit them.

Jen was distraught. Through her sobs I understood that the doctors wanted her to make a decision regarding life support. After weeping for the longest time she gained some composure and let me have it with both barrels, "If *your* God really is good, Carrie won't die. You told me before she was born that she had a special purpose and destiny from God. What's her special purpose now, to donate her organs so other kids can live? How can I trust a God who would let *this* happen?"

"Jen, I…"

"I don't want to hear about your God unless He heals my daughter. I don't know if He even exists. My baby is hooked up to tubes and wires that breathe for her..." Jen dissolved into hysterical crying once again.

Each sob was a sword plunging into my heart. I could barely get my breath. I wanted to defend God's goodness even in the midst of her pain, anger, and sorrow, but I knew I just needed to listen. In the midst of Jen's accusations, I thought I heard the Lord's gentle voice whisper to me, "She will live and not die."

Was that You Lord?

Immediately an attacking voice came to snatch away the promise, "That's just wishful thinking. You need to face the truth—she's going to die!"

I didn't have enough courage to tell Jen that I thought I'd heard the Lord say Carrie would be healed. I wasn't sure myself. All I could do was cry with her and beg her to put off making the decision to disconnect the life support equipment.

When she had finished venting I made her promise to try and get some sleep. I gave her my word that I'd pray for Carrie throughout the night. I felt like I was spinning out of control on the Potter's wheel. I couldn't image what Jen was experiencing

WATCHMAN ON THE WALL

I was drawn to the window by the sound of howling winds. The freezing rain had been replaced by snow. Staring into the storm, my eyes did not focus on anything in the darkness. Wild flakes whipped this way and that, buffeted at the mercy of the wind. *Between monitoring the kilns and praying for Jen and Carrie, I guess I'll be a watchman on the wall tonight just like You, Lord. You always intercede for your vessels, especially when they are in the fire.*

Hot tears filled my eyes and splashed down my cheeks. I walked back to the table and picked up my paintbrush in my trembling hand. I sighed, *It's going to be a long night, and I'm exhausted going into this marathon.*

I tried to paint angel wings on my next little mug as I interceded for Jen and Carrie. In seconds my sobbing caused my hand to jerk several times, and it became obvious that I couldn't do detailed work. I washed my paintbrushes in the sink, and turning abruptly I bumped a graceful vase and sent it tumbling to the floor where it shattered.

That lovely piece was going to be prominently displayed at the show. I'd had special plans for her. Certain vessels are showpieces, one-of-a-kind treasures. I love them so much that I price them way too high, hoping that to bring them back home with me. I stared blankly at the shards around my feet, grieving the loss of the beautiful vase.

That's it; I'm worthless. I'm doing more harm than good.

The Dark Night of the Soul

The alarm sounded for the second kiln. I peeked into the spy hole. This inferno had a cooler red and orange flame licking and dancing and embracing the vessels. This huge kiln had about seven more hours to go and wouldn't move into the reduction fire until early morning. I turned up the heat and adjusted the dampers.

Wiping sweat from my brow and tears from my eyes, I moved back to the first kiln and pulled out the spy holes, the final indicator cones showed me the temperature was balancing out. Turning up the heat even higher, I continued to push in the dampers to intensify the pressure and fire on the vessels, subjecting them to a smoking, billowing inferno of flames.

In this crucial phase, black smoke and raging fire tries to escape through every nook and cranny. This time of intense pressure brings out the richest colors from the clay and glazes. I always equate this stage to the sufferings believers endure.

I set the alarm clock for another hour and turned off the studio lights. The glow of the kilns provided enough light to see. Making my way to the corner, I collapsed on my cot, physically and emotionally exhausted. "Lord, that's exactly what Jen and Carrie are going through. They're in a terrible fire and can't even see you in the midst of it. The enemy is trying to steal Carrie's destiny!"

Spiritual Warfare

I tried to focus on my prayers but eerie pictures of Carrie's broken, little, weak body assaulted my mind. I'd never known such agony as I lay sobbing on my cot. I clutched my pillow in a strangled grip. "I break the enemy's power over her Lord. I call forth life and come against the spirit of death. Lord, send your healing power."

The room was sweltering, but I was too tired to get up and crack the window. Every time I closed my eyes I'd see the car wreck over and over. I fought to keep my eyes open, but I was just too tired. Each time it played in my mind I could hear little Carrie's screams over the screeching tires, twisting metal, and shattering glass. I kept trying to shake off the images of the paramedics pulling Jen and Carrie from the wreck.

Evil voices bombarded my mind, "She's going to die. God won't rescue her. What about the great destiny you prophesied over her?"

"Lord, help! I rebuke the enemy's lies. She will live and not die."

Praying and travailing for what seemed like an hour, I tossed restlessly on the cot. I checked my watch—10 minutes had passed. I tried to refocus, but I couldn't stop the enemy's voices or those haunting images of the wreck.

I dozed fitfully, but found no relief. I'd never known torment like this. My dreams were filled with pictures of demons laughing and blaspheming as they pulled the plug on Carrie's life support machines. Once my own screaming voice woke me up.

Bolting upright, the only sounds I could hear were the roar of the kilns and the wind howling outside. I felt like my studio was a big kiln, and I was in the high fires.

"I choose to love You Lord, no matter what. But please, p..l..e..a..s..e don't allow her to die. Who will fulfill her destiny?"

I thrashed on my cot trying to throw off an increasingly claustrophobic feeling. Sweat trickled into my eyes, burning them. I clamped my hands over my ears and cried out, "Jesus, help me!"

TRANSPORTED

In seconds the spiritual atmosphere changed; I was engulfed in a heavy mist of radiant glory. I rolled over and was hit by a blinding glow radiating from a huge warrior angel. His sword was drawn and pointing toward the heavens. His mere presence cleared the room of the demonic. Earthly trappings faded and the Spirit realm emerged. As I pushed myself up onto my elbows a swirling, churning portal saturated with iridescent particles of light appeared. Magnificent angels descended. The room was alive with the presence of heaven.

The angel motioned at me with his gleaming sword and pointed upward. The minute I stood up I was transported into a swirling portal. *This is strange,* I thought, *my anxieties are gone, and I feel totally safe, enveloped in a celestial cocoon.* Wispy ethereal hues, colors I'd never seen on any artist's palate, danced around me. Fiery flames mixed with flecks of glimmering light spun rapidly as far as I could see into the night sky.

I couldn't tell how long it took to get through the portal; it was as though time had stood still. When it faded away I was standing in what appeared like an enormous chamber lit by kerosene lanterns.

I heard a sound and turned. Artistic angels were busy carrying huge bundles of kindling and placing it outside a firebox. Then I realized I was standing in front of a huge kiln. I'd never seen one so massive. It was incredible. It was an entire mountain hollowed out and filled with bellowing flames.

Master Potter was there in his simple brown robes. His rugged features and olive skin were exactly as I remembered. When His warm, tender eyes met mine I was flooded with unconditional love toward His vessels. I was feeling what He was feeling!

"This will be the high fire, the last step in the long process to be a vessel of honor. Here all their dross and their impurities will be removed." He motioned for me to look inside the kiln with all the excitement of a kid on Christmas morning. "I've waited so long to see their destinies come forth," He smiled as He spoke. "They will be my warrior brides. They will wreak havoc on the enemy's kingdom."

As my eyes adjusted to the darkness of this soot-covered room I could see rows and rows of shelves, from floor to ceiling containing about a thousand glazed vessels ready for the high fires.

As I scanned the shelves I saw pots I recognized. "There's Golden Incense," I said, "the little intercessory teapot. And look, three shelves above her is Beloved...."

Chapter Three

MOUNTAIN OF FIRE

Master Potter bricks up the opening of the kiln as Beloved nervously watches her only chance for escape slip away. Sitting on the shelves in utter darkness the vessels are too anxious to even talk among themselves. Each silently wonders if he or she can make it through the high fires of this dreaded, hollowed out mountain kiln—they had heard and thought much about the Mountain of Fire, but nothing had prepared them for what was ahead...

The sound of wood being thrown into the firebox causes Beloved to cry out anxiously. She steps sideways in the darkness until she bumps into Fearless, the courageous little wine carafe. "W...w...will you hold my hand?" she whimpers in a barely audible voice.

To her left, Long Suffering, the tall, forlorn vase wails in the darkness: "I knew this wouldn't have a happy ending, mark my words."

The massive mountain kiln begins to creak and groan as a giant blaze erupts. Terrifying darkness slowly yields as dry kindling cracks and crashes as it burns wildly. Low red flames explode into long, licking orange and yellow fingers that light the shadowy cavern.

DEMONIC ATTACK

Outside, other snow-capped peaks in the Formidable Mountain Range gleam in the morning sun, but there is no snow on this one. Rather, it is scorched black and covered with ashen soot. Barren trees cover its sides like enormous dark skeletons, their bone-like branches pointing toward the sky.

Valiant and the other guardian angels are posted as sentinels on the desolate, singed mountain, watching and interceding as a churning, dense, demonic storm approaches. Valiant, with regal auburn hair and piercing blue eyes, was assigned to Beloved the day she was born. He is dressed in a white tunic shimmering with light and glory. In his left hand he holds a glistening silver shield. His sword is sheaved to his side. Pulling an ancient silver shofar from his golden belt, he sounds a mighty blast, summoning reinforcements.

Magnificent, fierce warring angels, with eyes set like flint, arrive just as a dark, greenish, demonic cloud engulfs the quaking mountain. Lightning strikes the barren trees. Thunder rolls across the mountain range, reverberating through the firing chambers and causing Beloved to shutter.

With a holy, violent determination to protect the vessels, the angels wildly shout their battle cry: "For the Father, the Son and the Holy Spirit, that the Bride may come forth."

Fully armed and ready for battle, the holy awe and terror of God surrounds them. They wield flashing swords and rejoice in the victory of the Cross, leaving a trail of sulfuric demonic carnage.

INSIDE THE KILN

The ravenous blaze intensifies as heavy pine logs are heaved into the firebox. Suffocating heat and violent flames rip upwards, lapping the walls. Molten shadows from the blaze dance inside the crucible, casting an eerie, otherworldly red hue. Beloved, still clutching Fearless's hand can begin to see around the huge kiln again. Thousands of vessels line the shelves. A few rows from the top Golden Incense and Sweet Adoration are aggressively interceding.

Valiant and the other guardian angels leave the battle and enter the mountain to protect their vessels. Demonic spirits follow, infiltrating the huge cavern. War explodes in the mountain kiln.

"Our God is a consuming fire!" shouts Valiant as he plunges into the demonic hoard with his fiery sword flashing.

Grotesque demonic faces with glowing yellow eyes appear in the flames mocking Beloved with sadistic glee. "You are a fool to have followed Master Potter into the tormenting fires again. He threw you into this inferno and left you to die!" These wicked schemers become drunk with hatred as they smell her rising fear. They attack with murderous contempt, reveling in their depraved plans to bring hopelessness and black despair.

Beloved feels her heart pounding, her breath comes is short gasps. She wants to run, but there is no escape. She bends down and gulps out a desperate prayer, "Help me Master Potter. I can't make it without you."

Demonic spirits lick their drooling lips and move in for the kill. They are eager to win the challenge between the Godhead and Satan for her soul.

Many vessels put on their armor and stand strong; others sink immediately into deep despair. In fear, these cowering vessels struggle with doubt and unbelief, questioning Master Potter's faithfulness.

Meanwhile, Master Potter calmly removes a center plug from the bricked up entrance and looks inside of the mountain kiln to check the temperature.

Nodding in approval, He says, "Stoke up the firebox; it needs to be much hotter." With seemingly little effort, excited worker angels heave massive logs into the fireboxes. They have witnessed the mystery of life emerging from death and are eager to see it again.

LISTENING TO THE ENEMY'S LIES

The ravenous fire devours the dry timber. Sap sizzles and wood splinters in hundreds of ear-splitting explosions, causing Beloved to shutter and gasp. The roar of the fiery blaze drowns the vessels' terrified cries, as it blasts through the mountain and out the top. Like an erupting volcano, the enormous mountain looks spewing soot, flames, and billowing black smoke into the atmosphere.

Inside the belly of the mountain, the acrid smoke and all-consuming inferno make it increasingly difficult for Beloved to breathe. Unrelenting flames and suffocating heat bring back memories of her first painful firing. Claustrophobic terror sweeps over her. *This is just the beginning! It will get much hotter! It will go on for a week! Will I even survive?*

Overwhelmed physically by the heat, she feels she's burning from the inside out. With every beat of her heart her body throbs in pain. Warm tears stream down her face that feel cool compared to the fire that engulfs her. She scoots farther back on the shelf but finds no relief. The hungry demonic swarm slithers after her, lashing at her with their gnarled talons.

The black pungent smoke becomes so dense she can't see the vessels next to her. She is oblivious to the terrifying cries of other vessels. Feeling alone and abandoned, she cries out, "Master Potter why have you left me here to die? Where are you?"

"Well, well, it looks like you're Forsaken once again, aren't you?" a dark figure hisses.

"So how do you like your God's consuming fire now?" taunts a sinister, webbed creature. His jagged mouth spews furious hatred, "What about all those promises that you would become a prophetic voice? Ha! Ha! Ha! What a joke!"

The cruel onslaught of the enemy torments her. "You almost perished in the last fire," comes another hissing voice from beneath her.

"The Mountain of Fire will surely kill you," voices seem to echo, getting louder.

"You are such a fool! Little Beeeelooved…why did you even think you could survive this?" another mocking voice sneers loudly.

Sweat drips into her burning eyes as she agrees with the demons. *Oh, why did I think I could ever survive this?*

CHAPTER FOUR

HOW DID I GET HERE?

As the demons continue to lash out at her, her troubled mind flashes back to the day she made the decision to follow Master Potter into the high fires. Beloved and some of her friends: Comrade, the squatty mug, Harvester, the boisterous canister, Joyful, the wine goblet, Long Suffering, a tall, pessimistic vase, Golden Incense, an intercessory teapot, Fearless, the wine carafe, and Sweet Adoration, a perfume vial, are in Master Potter's fireside room.

Joyful, Sweet Adoration, and some other of the musically gifted vessels grab drums and bugles and sing and play, *Onward Christian Soldiers* as they march on the shelves that line the room. "Come on, everyone join us," shouts Joyful.

"Comrade, you never could keep the beat; pass that drum this way," laughs Harvester."

The vessels are singing and marching when Master Potter says, "Yes, strategic warfare is necessary, but you'll never survive without a deep revelation of My love. I'm calling you to be my warrior Bride."

THE HEAVENLY BRIDEGROOM KING

The room is suddenly transformed as heavenly portals open into realms of glory. Swirling gusts of dazzling brilliance surround Master Potter as He transforms into a heavenly Bridegroom King before their stunned eyes. His humble, brown potter's robe changes into flaming garments of white light. Girded about His chest is a golden band. His handsome and rugged face is like the sun shining in its strength. Torrents of magnificent light reflect from His fiery, eternal eyes. His head and hair are white like wool.

Holy Spirit sweeps around Him in rushing surges of heavenly devotion. The intensity of His presence grows brighter. Glory beyond earthly imagination fills the room.

An angelic processional descends carrying shimmering white wedding gowns draped over the angel's arms, one for each of the vessels.

The lovesick Bridegroom passionately calls out: "I want a deeper intimacy with you. Will you trust Me and come into the high fires? Will you not only be My army, but will you also be My warrior Bride?"

THE BRIDEGROOM'S DELIGHT

Master Potter motions for the enthralled vessels to stand, as a beautifully completed royal purple pitcher trimmed in gold enters the fireside room. "This is His Desire," Master Potter says, beaming with obvious pride. "She is one of my vessels of honor."

The manifest presence of the Lord rests upon her with unquenchable rays of celestial light. She is wearing a stunning, iridescent wedding gown adorned with rare, priceless pearls of suffering. Carrying herself with regal beauty and dignity, she exudes authority and government as she shimmers and blazes with His glory.

As the awestruck vessels watch her, a holy jealousy arises within them. A supernatural, heavenly desire erupts in their souls as they long for their own completion.

Amazed, they question each other, "How did she get so beautiful?"

"Look at her brilliant colors!" says Beloved.

"Great balls of fire," blurts out Harvester, "She must be glazed!"

The intense pleasure of the Bridegroom is obvious as He warmly embraces His Desire before placing her on Beloved's shelf.

It was then that Beloved noticed something in Master Potter's eyes that she had never before seen. It was a fiery, passionate love rising up from the very depths of eternity that flashed each time He looked at her.

INVITATION TO THE MOUNTAIN OF FIRE

Maybe the higher fire is worth it, Beloved thinks.

Gently approaching her, His Desire says, "You have a calling very similar to mine. But one firing isn't enough. Although you are strengthened now, you are still not a glazed, finished vessel. You must go into the higher, more intense fires in order to fulfill your great, eternal destiny." The words echoed through her being.

"I don't know if I can bear the fire again!" wails Beloved. "Isn't there *any* other way?"

His Desire nods in understanding. "I asked the same question. But His purifying flames alone enable a clay vessel to carry His holy presence. I hated the fire and wondered if I would even survive, but it was worth it! I'm more passionately in love with Him than ever before."

"He told us the first fire was called the "refiner's fire." What will happen in the Mountain of Fire? Maybe I can prepare myself if I know what to expect!" Beloved asks hopefully.

"There is no way to prepare to die except to cling to Him. It's because of His great love and mercy that He sends His consuming fire to burn out everything that hinders His passionate love. It's a custom-designed death to work His character in you."

Beloved watches in stunned amazement as His Desire heals the sick and delivers Long Suffering and Sweet Adoration from past traumas. She then gives Comrade, Golden Incense, and Fearless powerful prophetic words delivered from the very heart of the Father.

"I'm ready to go," booms Harvester's loud voice. "Count me in. This is what I was created for. I can feel it in my bones."

"Me too?" says a more hesitant Comrade with his voice wavering and ending in a little squeak.

Beloved watches her two friends as they choose their future and destiny and are carried into the glazing room by guardian angels.

THE COST

The Bridegroom watches His Desire with a passionate look of love in His eyes. Beloved feels she can barely breathe for her desperate sense of longing to have Him look at her in the same way. Her heart beats loudly in her chest. Seeing her lovesick stare, He points to the beautifully glazed vessel and explains, "She paid an incredible price for the anointing."

Beloved turns again and looks longingly at His Desire. "Beloved, I remember being exactly where you are. I was so scared and wondered if it could possibly be worth it. All I can tell you is that it cost much, but it was worth the price."

"I… want to…but I…I'm so scared," says Beloved, ringing her hands.

"Your flesh is always afraid of pain and death; that will never change. If you wait until you're no longer afraid, you'll never do it. You have to make the decision in faith from within your spirit."

"I…I…" Beloved stammers.

WILL YOU BE MY WARRIOR BRIDE?

Stopping in front of Beloved, the Bridegroom holds up a beautiful gossamer wedding gown for her to see and gazes deeply into her eyes. "Are you willing to love Me with an insatiable love, no matter what the cost, even when you don't understand the mysteries of My scorching fires? Only through death can you experience true resurrection life. Will you drink the cup of suffering, as I drank it long ago?"

Beloved's eyes are riveted on the glowing purity and translucent beauty of the wedding gown. Lustrous pearls and opulent embroidery symbolize the future high glories.

"Beloved, are you willing to follow me?" He whispers in His deep, soothing voice.

She looks deeply into the Bridegroom's eyes; they are burning with eternal love for her. Deep yearning erupts in Beloved's soul, a holy desperation. She longs for completion no matter the cost—even if it means her death.

Weeping softly, she pours out her heart, I don't want to sit on the back pew and die. I want everything You have for me. "What was I thinking? Besides, I'm ruined! I've already gone too far. I desperately need You. I've lost my children, my home, my dreams of being happily married—everything! But, as bad as that was, it was not even worthy of being compared to the joy of being loved by You."

LOVESICK FOR THE BRIDEGROOM KING

Envisioning herself clothed in the wedding gown He is holding, she makes the final decision to pursue the completion of bridal love. Her body trembles with fear as she hears her own voice echo throughout the fireside room, "Yes, Lord. Yes, I want to be Your fiery Bride forever." Hot tears flow down her cheeks.

Valiant stands with the other guardian angels watching her like a proud father. He weeps unashamedly as she agrees to give her all to Master Potter. At her declaration, Valiant says goodbye to his cohorts who are left fervently praying for their pots, and he lifts Beloved off the shelf to take her to the glazing room.

MAY I HAVE THIS DANCE?

"Excuse Me Valiant," the Bridegroom says with a large smile on His face. "May I cut in?" The glorious Bridegroom gently takes her from Valiant's loving grasp and sweeps her into a dance. "I knew you would say yes, Beloved. I knew you would."

Suddenly, Beloved is unaware of anything or anyone else. She is lovesick for Him alone. Time has ceased for her as she revels in the Bridegroom's deep love for her. All fear is gone as He holds her in His strong arms. Suddenly, she is aware that she is dancing in His arms on the sea of glass before the throne. She is wearing her shimmering, beautiful wedding gown covered with priceless pearls of suffering. Her hair is swept up on her head and held in place by a diamond tiara.

From the corner of her eyes she catches glimpses of angel's wings; their silvery folds reflect the glorious lights of the blazing lamp stands. Yet, Beloved cannot take her eyes off of her magnificent Bridegroom to look at them.

Dazzling white rays of holiness emanate from the Father on His throne. He is filled with unspeakable joy at the fulfillment of His Son's desire for a Bride.

Lost in their own world, they dance to the celestial music. The majestic Bridegroom stares deeply into her eyes. "I have loved you with an everlasting love, Beloved. I've been waiting, anticipating this sweet moment since eternity past—before the foundation of the world. Your yes means more to Me than you can understand. I gave my life to purchase it. I betroth Myself to you forever, Beloved."

Back to the Fireside Room

Slowly, peacefully, when the music fades her surroundings come back into focus. She looks down, surprised to see she is wearing her regular clothes and is standing at the door to the glazing room.

As she looks into her Bridegroom's deep, loving eyes, He transforms back into Master Potter. Tenderly, He takes her face in His hands and whispers, "I believe it's customary for the groom to carry the Bride over the threshold, Beloved."

Looking into His loving eyes, Beloved whispers, "Yes, Lord."

He gathers her in His strong arms and carries her into the bustling glazing room.

CHAPTER FIVE

ARTISTIC ANGELS

The fire crackles as the heat of the kiln is turned up even higher. Still, the lingering spiritual presence of the vivid vision causes Beloved to feel strangely cooled. The comforting presence increases. Her flashback continues, unfolding into the images of preparation that preceded the great fire....

Master Potter steps from the fireside room across the glazing room threshold carrying Beloved. A radiant cloud of glory overwhelms her. Squinting in the brilliant light, she is able to make out thousands of vessels on wooden shelves lining the walls and arranged on tables.

Surveying the room, Master Potter sees dozens of artistic angels hard at work preparing vessels for the high fires. Each angel is dressed in multi-colored glowing robes of all the vibrant hues of the spectrum.

He smiles and nods approvingly while setting Beloved on a table near the door. She is a little disoriented from all the glory that engulfs the room. He steadies her before letting go. Still lovesick, she gazes up into His tender brown eyes until Harvester, the large canister, swoops her up in his strong arms and spins her around. He erupts in a loud whoop of his deep, booming voice. "I couldn't imagine going on without you, Beloved. It seems that we've been pals forever."

Comrade, the squatty mug, blinks back tears of delight. "We were praying so hard for you," he said. "I could tell it was a tough decision for you to make."

HEAVEN'S CREATIVITY

Two huge, colorful angels, Rembrandt and Angelo, are directing other artistic angels. Some sit on tall wooden stools painting delicate designs on vessels. Others carry large boards holding vases, planters, and mugs. Vessels of all sizes and shapes are being carefully washed, glazed, and painted. The entire room is alive, buzzing with heavenly, creative activity.

Each vessel began its journey as an inspired thought in Master Potter's mind and has been birthed on the potter's wheel and brought to this day of preparation and promotion. The excited vessels revel in the glorious atmosphere, and an even deeper camaraderie develops among them as they reaffirm their decision to go forward together to the next step. They have chosen to journey to the dreaded Mountain of Fire.

The ceiling is supported by huge beams of aged cedar and opens into the heavens. A pillar of swirling fire, which constantly moves around Master Potter's rustic house, is a doorway into eternity. Angels ascend and descend on this Jacob's ladder, which reaches from Master Potter's home into the heavens. This glorious fiery portal and its dazzling display of lights always fill Beloved with amazement.

"Is it just me or are those angels changing colors right before my eyes?" Beloved asks.

"They're kind of iridescent and shimmery. Look how they reflect all the beautiful colors around the room," replies Comrade.

Glorious worship from a heavenly stringed orchestra wafts down through the opening from the very courts of Heaven, drawing the vessels attention upward and awakening hidden destinies.

The celestial music gently floats in the atmosphere and is mixed with harmonious cries of "destiny," "new seasons," "promotion," as well as, "holy, holy, holy" and "worthy is the Lamb." The shimmering artistic angels echo back the refrains as they move vessels from the rows of old wooden shelves to the many tables in the room.

CELESTIAL BLUEPRINTS

Comrade's mouth drops open in unbelief as he jabs Golden Incense in the ribs and points upward. Under the watchful eyes of Holy Spirit, angels descend carrying sparkling gold dust, mother-of-pearl powders, glistening silver, and burnished bronze lusters to mix with the colored pigments. These will be used as accents for the most intricate detailed designs. As these beautiful angels arrive, the vessels are engulfed in the heavy mist of radiant glory, saturated with iridescent particles of gold and light.

Amazed, the vessels catch glimpses of creative images, blueprint plans from the Father's throne coming down to direct the artistic angels on how to proceed with each of their specific designs. As they begin to lovingly paint each vessel, carefully adhering to every minute detail from heaven, the celestial strategy releases prophetic destiny for it. Every brushstroke evokes excitement among them as they paint and praise the Father for His great purposes in each unique life.

"This one's going to be an evangelist. When he comes out of the Mountain of Fire his colors will be bold and beautiful. He can't wait to preach the gospel!"

"Well," says the next angel in obvious delight. "This delicate little china cup named Tenderhearted will sit on the tables of the wealthy to give comfort and counsel. She's going to need some extra luster. Pass down some mother-of-pearl iridescent powders and gold dust for her accents."

Beloved's soul is gripped with the beauty and promise of God's handiwork for her life. *I can't wait to get glazed so I can finally be that beautiful pitcher with blue and gold filigree accents.* In the midst of her joy, Beloved is pierced with another thought: *This would be an absolutely perfect day if only Purity and Crusader could be here with me. In seconds her joy is turned to sadness.*

I can still see the terrified look on their little faces when I was driven out of Deeper Life. The religious commune ended up being such a prison for me. Everybody thought I had the perfect marriage to Pastor Beguiler's son, Enchanter. I still can't believe I caught him having his way with a 14-year-old girl! When I tried to expose him I was driven out of the commune and almost killed.

Beloved is distracted from her anguished memories of her lost children by the sound of the door swinging open again.

MORE FRIENDS

"Look, here comes Golden Incense," Comrade shouts as he slides over to make room for her guardian angel to set down the little intercessory teapot. Taking one step too far, Comrade falls off the end of the table. Before he even has time to cry out, his guardian angel, Courageous, catches him and places him back in the center of the table.

"Thanks," says Comrade with a sheepish grin.

Nervous excitement causes Golden Incense's lid to rattle. "What a decision! I was praying, and the Lord showed me a vision of my matching cups and saucers marching off to the nations without me. I couldn't let that happen!" All the vessels gather around her cheering and talking over each other in a warm welcome.

Steadfast, the talkative large platter, shouts above the celebration: "Hey everyone, I'm here. I bet you didn't think I'd make it. I thought about it and prayed about it. I think that His Desire is right; there's no good way to prepare to die. You just have to do it!"

Harvester gives Steadfast a hug. "Wow, will you look at this place?" declares Steadfast. "There's so much activity, so much glory, so many angels! I can't wait to get glazed and get on with my special destiny."

"Listen! Is that Joyful's beautiful voice I hear?" asks Harvester. "It sounds as if she's coming closer." The vessels hush their chatter, each one straining to hear the distant melody. Beloved grabs Comrade and they jump up and down together as the door opens and Joyful, the wine goblet, is carried into the glazing room singing a beautiful prophetic song. Her guardian angel is smiling widely from ear to ear.

"It sure feels good in here," says Joyful as she is set down on the table amidst her friends. "All this glory makes me a little dizzy—just the way I like it!"

Two guardian angels enter. One carries Fearless, the wine carafe, and the other holds Sweet Adoration, the fragile perfume vial. Fearless is doing his best to comfort her, but when they enter the golden mist that permeates the glazing room all her fears dissipate. She inhales deeply and lets out a sigh of relief. "I made it! I made it!" she squeals with joy.

Master Potter laughs heartily in utter delight as He watches each vessel's welcome into the glazing room. *These little pots will one day be My mighty warriors.*

"Well, I couldn't stay behind. I'd miss you all too much!" says Long Suffering, the pessimistic vase, as she is carried through the doorway by her guardian angel, Exhorter. "...although I know that I'll no doubt regret this decision later!"

Her guardian angel touches her head, and a download of faith flashes through her. "Wait a minute; what am I saying? 'Trust in the Lord with all your heart....' I'm just going to step out on faith and try to trust Him."

The pots all giggle and cheer her declaration of faith—so out of character for her.

"Long Suffering, I'm so glad you're here," shouts Fearless.

CHAPTER SIX

A CHANGE OF SEASONS

A thud on the roof draws the vessel's attention out the back wall of windows. Squirrels scamper across the lacy tree limbs of these ancient giants causing patches of wet snow to fall and hit the roof of this mystical house made of fragrant cedar logs and living stones. Their relentless quest for pine nuts is the only disruption in the tranquil silence of this beautiful snow-covered scene.

They are surprised to see that the season has changed outside as well. The snow-covered branches of the tall trees on top of the cliff sway in the bitter northern winds.

In the distance, Beloved looks out at the snow-capped Formidable Mountain Range and a chill goes down her spine. She twists her hair around her fingers as she worries, *The Mountain of Fire is hidden somewhere among those treacherous peaks. My dad always said no one ever comes back from there.*

Master Potter's joyful laughter booms from behind her as He welcomes another vessel willing to pay the price of the high fires. She scans the room, anxious to find Him. When she finally sees Him, she is reminded of how she loves His strong rugged features, distinct nose, and olive complexion. The melodious sound of His voice is always so reassuring.

SLUMBERING VESSELS

Fearless raises himself up and searches table-to-table, looking to see if all his friends made it to the glazing room. "Hey, has anyone seen Diligence? I know he's kind of self-righteous and obnoxious at times, but I really like him! Where is he?"

"The last time I saw him he was dozing in the fireside room!" says Comrade.

"Didn't anyone wake him up and tell him we were leaving?" asks Joyful.

"You're right. He's not here! I don't see Abundance either!" says Golden Incense.

"I can't leave any of my buddies behind," shouts Harvester. "I'm going back for them! Who'll go with me?"

Master Potter moves closer and puts His arm around Harvester. "You've really got a pastor's heart Harvester, but only Holy Spirit can awaken my sleeping vessels. They are not forgotten, but remain behind until they choose to pay the price of the higher fires. You can't go back for them, but you can intercede."

"Why should we intercede for them; they're probably the smart ones," mumbles Long Suffering under her breath. "We're all going to die." Her guardian angel, Exhorter, touches her again, and a download of faith causes her to blurt out: "Wake up, O sleeper. Rise from the dead, and Christ will shine on you." Exhorter smiles.

Golden Incense, the head intercessor, organizes a group to pray for those left behind. The vessels grieve for their lost companions.

Beloved prays for Abundance and Diligence, but her mind quickly wanders again to her missing children. *God, I can't bear it. Will I ever see them again?* She fingers the small flask of perfumed frankincense on the chain around her neck. She could never forget the day Master Potter gave it to her after she was driven from Deeper Life. She made it to the Tent of the Lord by following Holy Spirit.

There, waiting for her with open arms, Master Potter dressed her wounds and gave her this necklace to remind her not to stop praying for Purity and Crusader. He released an impartation of intercession, and she spent several hours praying for them. Then He opened the heavenly realms to her and showed her angels carrying her precious petitions up to the golden altar where the Father received them. *I wish I could feel that kind of hope again. I miss them so much.* Tears silently glide down her cheeks.

HIT THE SHOWERS

Master Potter slips His old, worn apron over His head of thick brown hair and reaches back to tie it. "It's time for work." After rolling up the sleeves of his simple brown robe, He carries Beloved to a washbasin.

"It's time to get rid of the sooty, black smudges left from the warfare of the past." He puts Beloved directly under the faucet and drenches her with cool water.

"Remember your old friend Soaking Love?"

"Of course I do," she giggles as the cool water tickles and refreshes her.

"This little sponge will have you cleaned up in no time." After a good scrubbing, He places her on the table to dry while He returns for other vessels. Artistic angels sit Harvester, Comrade, Long Suffering, Steadfast, Fearless and

Sweet Adoration—all newly energized from their own showers—down on the table by Beloved. Master Potter returns, tenderly cradling Golden Incense and Joyful in His arms.

"My angelic assistants are mixing glazes of different colors and textures. In a little while they will paint each of you."

Bubbling over, Joyful exclaims, "Oh boy! Another party! It's a glazing party this time. Are there refreshments?"

Sweet Adoration, the worshipping intercessor purrs, "Pour it over me Lord; I'm ready!"

"Count me in!" yells Harvester. "I don't want to miss out on anything."

Golden Incense chuckles and asks, "Is this when I get my hair dyed? Should it be blue or purple?" she says posturing like a fashion model.

"Yes, it is Golden Incense, but even though you get glazed your true colors will not be seen until you come out of the Mountain of Fire. Glaze turns different colors when exposed to the fire. Until then, your hair color is shrouded in mystery," He says with a wink.

"Ohh!" laughs Beloved, inspecting Golden Incense's head, "Only her hairdresser knows for sure!"

THE MYSTERY OF GLAZING

Master Potter warmly says, "That's right, before the glaze is fired it looks like dull house paint. It is lusterless, without beauty or shine. Smiling He continues, "Glaze is made of tiny pieces of silica or glass. Only the mountain kiln reaches temperatures high enough to melt it, resulting in a beautiful, glassy finish, which seals the surface of your porous earthenware vessels. The high fires enable you to hold My golden grains, refreshing waters, fragrant oils, perishable foods, and many other substances."

Long Suffering glances around the room suspiciously, "This glazing room is a setup! We're all going to die in the Mountain of Fire." Exhorter shakes his head and touches her again, and she blurts out, "But of course, if we don't share in His sufferings we won't share in His glory."

Her words bring a hush to the room as the vessels are reminded of one of the lessons they learned—that each choice they make has a consequence.

CHAPTER SEVEN

SEPARATED FOR HIS PURPOSES

In the midst of the hustle, bustle, and laughter of the glazing room, Beloved hears a commotion coming from the next table. She turns to see Rembrandt and Angelo directing the other artistic angels to rearrange the vessels, taking them from their companions and placing them into matching sets.

Cries and moans erupt, drowning out the angelic worship as the vessels protest the reassignments. Teapots, cups, and saucers are collected from different tables and grouped together. Dinner sets with matching salad and dessert plates, along with their cups and saucers, large meat platters, soup bowls, and salad plates are brought together.

Each vessel is arranged according to his or her unique design and the color of glaze to be applied—all for Master Potter's sovereign purposes.

A terrible realization dawns on Beloved and her friends as they look at each other—a wine goblet, a tea cup, a perfume vial, a canister, a tea pot, a platter, a mug, and a pitcher. "None of us matches," wails Comrade. Beloved looks at Steadfast and sees tears begin to well up in his eyes.

"You're the only family I have," laments Beloved.

"What can we do?" moans Comrade.

A group of guardian angels, great friends since ancient times, are gathered together watching their vessels.

"Vessels never understand that this is an important step toward reaching their destiny," declares Valiant.

"It seems like a death to them," says Courageous.

"Excuse me gentlemen, but my vessel needs an infusion of faith," says Exhorter stepping closer to the table.

Harvester, always one for action, barks out commands: "Quick, Sweet Adoration, Comrade, and Joyful, you're small, come hide behind me. Maybe Master Potter won't see you, and we'll be able to stay together."

"Who are you fooling Harvester? He sees everything. I knew that this party wouldn't last," says Long Suffering. Exhorter reaches out to touch her, and she smacks his hand before retreating by herself to sulk.

The other guardian angels dissolve into laughter. "Exhorter," shrieks Courageous, "You need to get control of your vessel!"

BREAKING UP IS HARD TO DO

Rembrandt turns to Beloved's table to separate and organize the vessels for glazing. He motions for an angel who picks up Joyful. She cries out, "I don't want to leave my friends! We've been through so much together! I don't want to start over somewhere else."

"Bring her back," barks Harvester, hands on hips, "Or I'll…I'll…well, just bring her back right now!"

Tears stream down Beloved's face as she watches Rembrandt move toward their table with his gaze on Golden Incense. Beloved jumps in front of her friend. "Wait, please don't take her! I've had enough losses in my life; it isn't fair! What will I do without her?"

"You've always been there when I needed you! Your prayers and prophetic words gave me so much hope. Please don't forget me!" calls out to Golden Incense sadly as she's carried away, cradled gently in Rembrandt's arms.

Master Potter takes Golden Incense from Rembrandt and lovingly tells her, "I know this is hard, but I made you a teapot, and you're going to another table to be glazed with your matching cups and saucers. I have purposefully designed each of you to come together to be a prophetic intercessory team for the nations."

Beloved looks on in dismay as she watches Master Potter carry her best friend to another table. Beloved feels stripped again, aching with the same dull pain she's experienced every day since she lost Purity.

Knowing her deep grief, Master Potter returns and picks her up. "Beloved, do you remember the prophetic word you gave Golden Incense? You said her prayers would open up city gates to bring salvation and deliverance to thousands?"

"Yes, Lord, I remember. But why can't she intercede while sitting next to me?"

"Beloved, she'll never be happy outside of the destiny I have ordained for her—none of you will be."

From Master Potter's hands, she helplessly watches Angelo pick up Comrade, place him on a wooden board, and quickly move away. Beloved wails in anguish when she hears the familiar dear voice of her old friend call out, "Don't worry, Beloved! I'm fine! You just hang in there. Maybe we'll see each other again some day!"

"Oh no! Not Comrade too! What will I do without him? I'm really all alone again!" Beloved puts her hands up to her face to muffle her sobs.

THE HEAVENLY MAP

Master Potter wipes away her tears and walks through the glazing room holding her in His strong arms. Gently, he explains, "I know you're hurting. Change is difficult, and suffering and grief accompany the loss of dear friends. But, you must remember, you are players in an international chess game to save broken lives from Satan's cruel bondage. Let me show you!"

He unrolls a large scroll on the table. "This is one of the maps from the heavenly war room highlighting each vessel's prophetic geographical assignment. My Father in His wisdom brings forth eternal purposes through the strategic placement of His vessels by sending them to the land of their anointing."

She wipes her eyes as Master Potter points to a 12-piece dinner set gathered on the next table.

"Look, there's Steadfast. He's the platter," says Beloved.

"Yes, Steadfast has an apostolic calling; he is a visionary, a builder of foundations, one who puts fresh strategies into place. He will serve my heavy meats along with this team of carefully chosen vessels. Each vessel in this dinner set is an individual and has different callings and functions. Yet, they're part of a greater team."

"Where are You going to send them?" asks Beloved, still sniffling.

"Steadfast and his team will go to the Land of Lost Promises to preach my gospel and plant churches in places where there's great hopelessness and despair."

"What colors will they be?" she asks, as her curiosity takes over.

"This dinner set will be white with red and gold leaves."

"Did you hear that team?" asks Steadfast "We're going to be white with red and gold leaves. And we're going to plant churches in the Land of Lost Promises. I knew a guy from there; he was so discouraged all the time. Let's start praying now for a huge harvest, so when we get there we can go up and possess the land! Who's with me?"

CHAPTER EIGHT

REUNITED!

Master Potter carries Beloved by several other glazing tables. She sees Harvester with a set of canisters. *He's the largest and taking charge of the entire table, as usual*, she thinks, forcing a smile.

Passing the table where little Joyful, the wine goblet, is sitting, Beloved sees that Fearless the wine carafe is her leader. *At least Joyful's not alone; Fearless will be a good companion.*

"Gather round everyone," shouts an artistic angel, as he holds Joyful upside down by her stem. "We're going to have a baptism today." Fearless and the rest of her team clap, sway, and sing as she is dunked into a huge bucket of white glaze. Coming up for air each time, Joyful sings out, "I surrender all!"

"Say amen somebody," yells Fearless.

"Amen!"

"Amen!" they all respond as they sway to the beat and cheer.

Finally Master Potter sets Beloved down on a table next to Comrade. Overjoyed at seeing her old friend, they hug each other and burst into laughter. She tells him, "I'm so glad to see a familiar face again!"

Comrade squeezes her even tighter and jumps up and down with her. "This is just great! This is just great. You won't believe it, Beloved; I've got a surprise for you. There are eight of us wide-mouth mugs, and we've been wondering who would be our pitcher. I was praying so hard that it would be you. Let me introduce you to the rest of the guys, I mean, the team," he says with a mischievous smile.

Beloved is thrilled to be reunited with Comrade, but her delight is mixed with a foreboding sense of dread that she can't quite understand. The move and new location feel uncomfortable.

Except for Comrade, I don't even know these new mugs. I don't want to pour my life into them. I should feel so happy being promoted, so why do I still feel empty? Sighing sadly, she looks down into their upturned, expectant faces. *What if I fail at this too?*

MEET THE TEAM

Holy Spirit hovers over the little group releasing surges of His love and acceptance. As His presence rests upon Beloved, she feels somewhat reassured and comforted.

Comrade is eager to start the introductions. But before he can speak, a mug steps forward, thrusts his hand toward Beloved, and exuberantly gushes, "Hi! My name is Confidence. I'm so excited to be a member of your team. This is my best friend, Self-Assurance. We do everything together." He slaps his friend on the back, and both of them smile widely.

Beloved can plainly see that the two friends are inseparable, and she warmly receives them before moving on.

"On my right is Champion," says Comrade, "He's going to be an awesome evangelist. You should see all the new vessels he's brought to Master Potter."

Champion's face takes on a happy glow as he nods to Beloved and acknowledges Comrade's compliment. "Next to him are two beautiful ladies, Loyalty and Generosity." Both mugs give her a big hug. Unexpectedly, a tiny surge of affection makes its way into Beloved's tightly closed, mother's heart, and she allows their embrace to last a little longer than she'd planned.

She takes the hand of the next mug as Comrade tells her how loving and sweet the shy young lady is. "Beloved, this is Devotion, one of my favorite people." Whispering to Beloved he says, "I know with a little tender love and care from you this one will blossom into a godly woman of wisdom and counsel."

THE BEST FOR LAST

Finally the entire team has been introduced, except for one last mug off to the side with her back to them. "I've saved the best for last, Beloved," he says, almost unable to contain his excitement.

She reaches the mug who is sitting, staring at the ground, just in time to hear her irritably say, "Master Potter said I'm supposed to be on *your* team." For some unknown reason this unhappy little mug stirs Beloved's heart. She seems so sad and alone. Beloved longs to reassure her.

She smiles warmly at the little mug as she affectionately fingers her necklace and tells her, "I'm so happy you're a member of my team. Master Potter really knows how to put people together, doesn't He? Tell me, what's your name?"

The mug takes in a deep breath, and still looking at the floor replies, "Purity." The little mug raises her head, allowing Beloved to see her face clearly for the first time. Looking into familiar blue eyes, her immediate reaction is unbelief.

Beloved focuses all of her energy on maintaining her smile, but inside she goes numb. All of the color drains from her face, and her hands begin to tremble. She excuses herself quickly and runs to hide herself behind a giant lamp base nearly. Covering her mouth with her hands, she muffles her violent sobbing. *Help me Master Potter. I need wisdom!*

Then, summoning all of her courage and strength, she wipes the tears from her face, chokes loudly against the giant knot in her throat, and does her best to compose herself. Still in a state of shock, she forces herself to put one foot in front of the other and return to the angry young woman still sitting in the same place.

PURITY

Silently Beloved whispers a prayer, *Lord, I'm so afraid. I won't be able to bear it if she rejects me?* In that all-important moment, the fruit of all the years of intercession for Purity stand right in front of her.

Nervously she clears her throat and asks, "Purity, where are you from?"

Purity's eyes take on a steely glint as she answers cautiously, "Just a small community, in the middle of nowhere. It's called Deeper Life; most people have never heard of it."

Beloved carefully studies her for a moment. *Does she know who I am?* Choking loudly against the giant knot that is growing larger in her throat, and working too hard to sound light and cheerful, she asks, "Did your family come with you?"

Purity's voice takes on a new hardness, "I lost my family. My only traveling companion was Holy Spirit, I mean Amazing Grace."

Comrade quietly comes alongside Beloved and takes her hand. The rest of the mugs hush their small talk, straining to hear as the tension increases.

Swallowing hard Beloved replies, "I understand how painful that is. A long time ago I had a family that I loved very much and I lost them. I was terribly betrayed, and my children were taken away from me. I was driven into the desert and left to die."

For an endless moment both women stand perfectly still gazing silently into the other's eyes. Beloved dreads the questions she knows are coming, uncertain that she has the answers.

Every nerve in her body is shaking as Purity looks into the same eyes of another's face that she's seen in the mirror throughout her entire life. Spirits of rejection move in. A deep wound opens in Purity's heart, and her steel wall of self-protection cracks. A single tear wells up and rolls down her cheek. "Why didn't you go back for them?"

CONFRONTATION

"I wanted to go back, but they would have killed me. Purity, sweetheart, there was no way I could have rescued you. We both know your father was demonized."

Unable to hold back any longer, color rushes to her face as Purity jumps to her feet and shouts, "So, you left us with a demonized man! Is that what you call love?"

Beloved feels naked and vulnerable, surrounded by strangers who she feels are ready to judge her. She realizes her answers are crucial. She grabs the small vial of frankincense hanging around her neck and begins to silently intercede.

The urgent plea of Beloved's aching heart resounds into the Spirit realm. Praying for the right words, she tells her newly found daughter, "I can't do anything to fix the past. But please believe that I love you Purity; I love you more than life. I prayed every day for you and little Crusader. The anguish I felt can't be put into words. But I'm sure your pain is even greater than mine."

Purity's hard countenance remains unmoved, and Beloved's fears, unmovable. Deciding to risk it all, she takes several steps toward Purity and drops to her knees. The agony of Purity's lonely past breaks through her façade of self-protection. Her pretty face becomes broken and twisted as she bursts into sobs.

"Purity, darling, I'm so sorry. Please understand…"

"No! I don't understand how you could have left us. I…just…don't…understand!

"Purity, I love you. I'm your mom," pleads Beloved. "Please don't do this. You need me. We need each other…"

With an incredulous look on her face, she screams, "You've got to be joking! I've spent the majority of my life without you, and I've done just fine. Why would you think I'd need you now?" She turns on her heels and runs back to the fireside room, slamming the door behind her.

CHAPTER NINE

THE VALLEY OF DESPAIR

As her team members look on, Beloved collapses on the table weeping bitterly. Comrade bends over her gently stroking her hair, at a total loss about what to say or do.

After several minutes of gut wrenching sobbing, she looks past Comrade's shoulder and notices for the first time the rest of her team watching. *I can't do anything right. I just want to die!*

Comrade tells the newly formed team of mugs, "That's Beloved's daughter; they haven't seen each other in years. Please pray!"

"Comrade, help me up," says Beloved. "I've got to go after her. Come with me, please. I can't let her go."

"We'll be right back. Just keep praying for reconciliation!" says Comrade. Taking Beloved's arm, the two slowly make their way back into the fireside room. Beloved's team of mugs kneels and begins to fervently intercede.

IT'S TOO LATE

Purity collapses on the floor, sobbing from the years of rejection. Beloved prays for wisdom, *"Please, please. I'm desperate. I need help. Give me the right words."*

She quietly sits beside Purity and lays her hand on her daughter. Purity shrugs her shoulder and Beloved reluctantly removes her trembling hand. She glances at Comrade and begins to cry as dark spirits of rejection bury their talons in both women.

Purity rolls over and with hatred flashing in her eyes, and with utter contempt starts venting her years of pain on Beloved. The foul spirits dredge up bitter memories of pain, stirring up the deep wounds between mother and daughter.

"So you think that your tears will make it all right? Do you think that you can possibly make up for abandoning Crusader and me?"

"I never wanted to leave you. It wasn't my fault...I..."

"I was just a little girl. I was only ten. You left me with evil people in a horrible situation. Dad changed my name to Promiscuous and disowned me. My life was a living hell. Grandpa turned me into a servant, and I was separated from Crusader, and it's all your fault. You didn't protect me. I'll never forgive you, never, never, never!"

Standing to her feet, Purity turns to leave. In a last desperate attempt, Beloved reaches for her, and Purity screams, "Don't touch me. Don't you understand? It's too late. It's just too late!" She storms outside to the garden.

Unnoticed by Beloved, a beautiful white dove flies after her.

ARE YOU WILLING?

Purity stomps around in the snow, crying and shaking her fists. "I know I'm supposed to be part of my mom's team, but I just can't forgive her. I can't! It's too hard. No, no, I'm not willing!" she chokes.

The glint of white sweeping through the air catches her eye. She watches the dove as it flies near her and whispers into her ear: "If you're willing to become willing…I can help heal your heart."

Suddenly, a warm ray of sunlight bursts through the wintry sky. Purity, face washed with tears, looks up at the light.

CHAPTER TEN

THE BATTLE IS THE LORD'S

Death and Suicide have been watching Beloved with glee. Snorting murderous contempt, Death tells Suicide, "This is the time we've been waiting for." Suicide bows slavishly low, eager to savor his victim's blood.

"I will not fail!"

Death spews, "This is our chance; Beloved is vulnerable. Go to her."

Suicide snickers, "Don't you mean Forsaken?"

"Of course I mean Forsaken," sputter's Death. "She's always been Forsaken, and she will die a forsaken death. Now go!"

PUT ON YOUR ARMOR

Bending over her limp body, Comrade gently touches her shoulder. "Beloved, I'm so sorry. What can I do?"

"There's nothing you can do; it's over. I've lost her for good."

"Help us Master Potter," he prays fervently. Comrade is suddenly aware of another presence, and turning he sees his guardian angel, Courageous, standing close by.

"Comrade, first put on your armor so you can withstand the enemy's attacks. Then help Beloved get hers on."

"Right, my armor. Last time I had it…."

"I've brought it for you Comrade. Here, put it on. Now help Beloved."

"Beloved, don't give up. You've got to fight. Put on your helmet to protect your mind from the enemy's lies."

"It's too late. She's never coming back. It's impossible," she moans while batting the helmet away with her arm.

"Master Potter can win even in impossible circumstances. The battle is the Lord's," says Comrade boldly as he scurries after the helmet.

"Good," says Courageous. "Keep the Word in front of her. Give her shield."

"Here Beloved," says Comrade. "Take your shield." He picks up her limp arm and unsuccessfully tries to get her to grasp the handhold. Her arm thuds back to the floor.

Beloved crumples under a torrent of dark emotions, as she's plunges into a dark abyss of despair. "She's gone. I can't believe Purity's gone from my life again."

HER OLD "FRIEND" SUICIDE

Courageous places his hand on Comrade's shoulder, and the spirit realm opens in front of him. He watches in horror as the snake Suicide slithers into the fireside room leading a multitude of lower-ranking demons. A shadowy, tangible darkness permeates the fireside room.

Demonic imps fling fiery darts at Beloved's broken heart and screech in mocking laughter. Yellow-green sulfur smoke assaults her senses, making her nauseous. Beloved wretches, reeling from hopelessness and guilt over all the wrong choices she's made.

"Put on your breastplate. They're sending arrows into your heart," says Comrade. "Protect your mind with your helmet."

"Leave me alone. It's over."

SUICIDE'S OPPORTUNITY

Suicide slithers toward the emotionally broken heap that is Beloved. With hatred masquerading as sympathy, he hisses, "Beloved, what a terrible situation you're in. I know you have waited, hoped, and prayed over this day. Master Potter is just so hard to figure out. He should have rescued your children a long time ago. How sad for you that He chose not to."

He begins nuzzling with her and whispers in her ear, "After all that you've sacrificed for *Him*, after everything that you've given up, you would think that *He* would have just spoken one simple word or snapped His fingers and reunited your family. I guess you'll never be reconciled with your daughter now. And we don't know if your son's even alive."

"No Beloved," interjects Comrade. "Put on your armor and fight. Here's your shield. Don't listen to these lies." He begins praying in the Spirit and jabs Suicide's thick hide with his sword. "You leave my friend alone!"

With no effort at all, Suicides smacks Comrade with his large tail and sends him sprawling into the far wall. Courageous follows and ministers to the unconscious Comrade.

Beloved, near an emotional breakdown, listens to Suicide's empathetic, soothing voice and feels his gentle touch. She believes she has found a compassionate friend. "You're right. It's over. I prayed and prayed for this chance, and I blew it."

Suicide continues talking as he gently coils around her body like a python. "Not you Beloved. It was Master Potter's fault. Dear sweet Beloved, you love Purity more than you love your own life. You know you would die for her. Master Potter's the one who failed you. He has forsaken you and your children." Beloved sobs again and wraps her arms around her head.

"Why does He let you suffer like this? You weren't even in this much pain when I met you on the Potter's Field."

In total emotional torment she nods in agreement.

"Why did He put you through all the years of sacrifice only to let you end up more broken and in more pain than before? Why would someone who professes to be pure love…? Why would someone who has the power to stop it…? Why did He let this tragedy happen to you?"

Savagely tormenting voices rip at her mind as nauseating dry heaves wrack her body. She is held tightly in Suicide's serpentine embrace of death and yields to his fiendish venom, giving up all desire for life.

"I'm a failure as a mother. Make my pain stop. I can't… I can't go on…I just want to die."

THE BRAVE WARRIOR

With a gentle slap to his face from Courageous, Comrade regains consciousness, and the angel helps him slowly to his feet. Holy boldness overcomes him as he watches the demon ravishing his best friend. "Now you did it," he says under his breath.

"Go get him Comrade. Your sword is the living Word of God. You have all the power of the Cross backing you up."

Charging back into the battle, he shakes her, "Don't give up Beloved. Don't give up. Put on your helmet. Resist the Devil and he will flee. You're listening to the enemy's lies."

"Leave me alone; I'm tired of fighting."

"Use your sword, Comrade," whispers Courageous.

Standing to his feet, he holds his sword above his head and yells, "In the name of the Lord I cast down every high thing that exalts itself against the knowledge of God." Suddenly Comrade's sword comes to life. Tip glowing with white-hot intensity, it grows several times larger than its original size. Comrade grabs it with both hands to keep it from crashing onto the floor. "Oh my goodness," he says in surprise.

Suicide begins constricting the breath out of Beloved's body. "Won't my master be pleased that we will finally win the challenge over this vessel?

Forsaken will be our prized trophy. Satan will love flaunting her decaying body in front of the Godhead."

Two violent flashing swords interrupt Suicide's thoughts. An enraged Valiant and the little Comrade both lunge forward striking the foul serpent. Suicide loosens his hold on Beloved. He recoils and then springs forward once more, only to be deflected by Comrade's glistening shield.

ANCIENT ENEMIES

Ancient enemies of the Cross—Depression, Murder, Betrayal, Deception, and Unforgiveness—swarm into the fireplace room. Spirits of self-hatred strike Beloved as they join Suicide in this diabolical celebration of fiendish joy at another victim's gruesome demise. Completely abandoned to their greedy cravings for pain and destruction, they fight thirstily to secure another victim's death.

"Good one Comrade! Now put those little ones to flight."

Plunging into the fray with his sword flailing, Comrade takes on the smaller demons. "I break the enemy's power over Beloved and her family." His revelatory words of truth pierce the darkness with blazing light and send confusion through the lower-ranking demons.

"Call for more angels to help."

"By the blood of the Lord I rebuke you. Warring angels of the Most High, come now!"

In response to Comrade's words, Valiant gives a blast on his shofar, and the sound of redemption breaks open the atmosphere. Reinforcements from Heaven flood the room. Fully armed and ready for battle, their fiery eyes search out the demonic horde. Vile spirits explode in red sulfuric vapor.

"You've got them on the run Comrade!" shouts Courageous, who can't resist wielding his flashing sword to pierce several demons who strayed too close.

The sounds of swords and ferocious cries from the angelic warriors can be heard once again in the fireside room. The clash of the angelic army and the demonic spirits cause spiritual sparks to fly.

At the height of the battle, Comrade cries out to Master Potter, "We need You, come! By the power of Your shed blood for us, I proclaim that every demonic power is defeated by the Cross."

VIOLENT LOVE UNLOOSED

The door from the glazing room slowly opens. A flood of brilliant, living light invades every corner of the fireside room. Master Potter, face like the blazing sun and eyes filled with fiery love and devotion, steps inside the room. With a deafening roar He shouts, "Enough! I have come for My Beloved."

One flash of the violent force of His resurrection glory instantly destroys the enemy's hold. Trembling, sniveling lower demonic hordes instantly vaporize like wax before a flame from contact with the fiery flame of holy splendor.

Suicide recoils, screeching in pain from the scorching light emanating off of Master Potter. The demon's scaly, black hide begins to smolder and shrivel. He writhes as if mortally wounded, rolling from back to front, hissing and gasping until he abandons the dying carcass and flees.

With a nod of His head, Master Potter signals to the other angelic warriors that they should pursue the vanquished enemies. They will be crushed and destroyed like dust in the wind and poured out like mire in the streets.

Turning to Comrade He smiles, "Well done brave warrior, well done! Return to the glazing room, and keep the others praying."

Comrade, exhilarated from the victory, returns to the glazing room. A smiling Courageous follows closely behind.

Bending down Master Potter tenderly picks up Beloved and settles into His brown leather chair in front of the fireplace. He blows warm, life-giving, eternal breath upon her. Within moments she revives and opens her eyes to find herself staring into His eyes of eternal, unconditional love for her.

"You are and always will be my Beloved. I have betrothed Myself to you forever."

CHAPTER ELEVEN

I WILL NOT REJECT YOU

As Beloved lays her head on Master Potter's shoulder, she realizes that she nearly gave her life and her destiny to the enemy. She averts her eyes in shame.

Beloved, look at me," says Master Potter still embracing her in His arms. He tenderly turns her face back towards His. For a full minute He gently holds her face steady and looks deeply into her eyes. There is only silence.

"Don't turn your eyes away from Me, Beloved. From the day you were born My eyes have never left you. I watched and ached as you made bad choices, but I never averted My gaze. Finally the day came when you committed to follow Me, and through all the successes and failures that have happened since then I continued to gaze on you. I know more about your heart and than you do. Please don't turn your eyes from Me. I will never turn Mine from you."

Overcome by His tender acceptance and unconditional love, Beloved weeps openly.

"When I look in your eyes I see confusion and fear, but when I look deeper I see the yes in your spirit. In the center of your being, at your very deepest core, you are fiercely committed to Me. When I gaze on my Beloved that is what I see. I see you now as you will be in the future—as My mighty, overcoming warrior Bride—such a threat to My enemy's kingdom.

"You will be a prisoner in this earthenware vessel, this body of sinful flesh, throughout this life, but the eternal Beloved is connected to Me through her forgiven, renewed spirit. How I long for you to be secure in My unrelenting, unconditional love for you.

Beloved snuggles deeper into His arms and rests.

PARTNERS WITH THE GODHEAD

"Will she ever come back?" Beloved whispers. "I'm so afraid for my children."

"I will not abandon them. I promise you I will protect them. Your children have a destiny in Me, but you have to trust that I'm going to work this for good.

"The very heart that you have for your children is only an infinitesimal reflection of the vast oceans of love that the Father has for them. Yes, you birthed them, and you'd even die for them. But, He created them, and painted the entire universe just for their pleasure. His love knows no limits."

Taking her face into His hands once again, He solemnly tells her, "You are not in this battle alone. Do you understand that My Father does not take your prayers lightly?" A tear trickles slowly down His face.

Beloved begins to see the anguish Master Potter feels for Purity and Crusader. She realizes they're His precious, loved children, too. She's deeply touched by His sense of grief and begins to realize that this overwhelming challenge is not hers alone to carry. She is in a partnership with the Godhead.

Emotionally spent, she falls asleep in His comforting arms giving her aching mind and body much needed relief. He gently rocks her back and forth. Her dreams are filled with visions of Purity and Crusader.

CHAPTER TWELVE

BURNING COAL OF FIRE

A bitter winter wind swirls through Master Potter's garden. Purity shivers on the bench under the lattice arbor. Last year's rose canes still scramble over the top, but now are brown and covered with ice.

Wavering between anger and despair, she holds her head in her hands and sobs. *You are so stupid, stupid, stupid, stupid. You've been praying for years to reconcile with your mom, and then when you finally get the opportunity you mess it up.*

As another winter blast stirs the snow flurries, the white dove transforms into Amazing Grace, one of Holy Spirit's many manifestations. He stands before her with outstretched arms, looking like a brown robed desert monk from previous centuries.

Sensing a presence, Purity looks up. "Oh, Amazing Grace, You're here. You've come for me," she wails as she lunges toward Him. Wrapping His comforting arms around her, He strongly embraces her. Overwhelmed with grief, she buries her face in the folds of His robes and together they stand in the snow, gently swaying.

"I told you I'd never leave you, dear one," He says gently.

"I know, but I couldn't see You. It felt like You weren't there." She bursts into sobs again. After several minutes, Amazing Grace wipes her tears away and gently sits her down on the bench beside her. "Let's get you warm," He says as He slips off His brown, burlap robe and wraps it around her. Strength immediately flows into her exhausted body as Amazing Grace looks deeply into her swollen eyes.

Whispering words of encouragement, He helps her pour out her anguished heart. A pained expression crosses her face, "Oh Amazing Grace, I do everything wrong all the time. I didn't want to reject my mom. All this anger just welled up inside of me; it came out of nowhere and the next thing I knew I was screaming at her. I thought all that pain was dealt with in the first firing, the refiner's fire. Why did it come back?"

"Purity, healing a wounded heart is a slow process."

"I keep seeing the hurt look on her face. I can't get it out of my mind. I feel like I love her, but I hate her too. I want her, but I want to punish her for hurting me. She never came back for me; she left me with demonized people."

"Purity, after Beloved was stoned by the members of Deeper Life Commune and driven into the wilderness I was with her. She pleaded, she begged, she screamed, she did everything she could to convince Me to let her go back for you and Crusader. I wouldn't let her. Your father and grandfather would have killed her. She prayed every day for you two. She really did all that she could. You need to know that she loves you deeply."

LIFE IS UNFAIR

"But I was just a little girl, and it wasn't fair."

"As long as Satan prowls this world, life will never be fair. All Master Potter's friends left Him when He died on the Cross for their sins. That wasn't fair, yet He chose to love. Always remember, He understands what it's like to be abandoned and to forgive those who abandoned Him."

"I didn't think it was going to be so hard. I thought I forgave everyone. I can't believe this anger is back again."

"You're farther along than you know. You just have to be willing to be willing. Are you?"

Pulling the brown cloak around her for comfort, she silently nods her head yes. Taking her head in His hands and turning it toward Him He lets out a joyful laugh.

"That's my girl. That's what I've been waiting to hear," He says with a twinkle in His eye.

THE GIFT

Reaching in His pocket He pulls out a delicate ceramic jar. As she looks at this beautiful iridescent purple vessel, she says in delight, "It has my name carved on it." Running her fingers over the impression she asks, "Why is it so warm?"

Ignoring her question He says, "I've been carrying this since the day you were born. As you can plainly see, your name is Purity and always has been, even before the foundation of the world. Your name is also your prophetic destiny, your calling."

"I don't understand."

"Purity, today because of the yes in your heart, I get the honor of commissioning you." He gently wiggles the cork free from the opening and turns the bottle upside down over her cupped hands. He shakes the container and a flaming ember tumbles out. Purity jerks her hands away and gasps, "It's on fire."

"Yes," replies Amazing Grace, catching the prized treasure. "This fiery ember, this burning coal will purify your lips and awaken your heart."

Purity's fascination is swallowed up in fear. Her voice trembles, "Is it going to hurt me?"

"Purification can be painful. This coal will burn away your impurities. It will cleanse the words of your mouth and the dark secrets of your heart. Will you accept this fiery stone of intimacy from the heavenly altar of incense? Will you let it do its purifying work in you?"

"I don't want to hurt anymore. Please...I don't want any more pain."

"Purity, the enemy's pain only brings death. But there is a reason to go through God's redemptive pain; it bring healing and life. It's always uncomfortable when He takes shriveled, broken hearts and enlarges and makes them whole."

He reaches out to take her hand. Shaking from fear, she draws back.

"Purity, when you were ten years old your heart shut down as you were so cruelly separated from your mother. It was so traumatic that you vowed to never love that deeply again. But, today I want to reawaken your heart."

"It's too hard to trust people; they just end up hurting me."

THE COURAGE TO LOVE

Holding the flaming coal in His hand, He continues, "It takes courage to love. There are no guarantees you won't be hurt. It's how you handle the pain that makes the difference. It can enslave your emotions and imprison you, or you can choose to forgive. Will you take this fire and let it enlarge your heart to contain more of His unconditional love?

She lets out a whimper as she looks at the flaming ember but manages to nod yes. Amazing Grace moves the fiery coal toward her lips, and she steels herself and closes her eyes. The coal touches her lips and is immediately absorbed.

She sees flashes of how her words have brought judgment to situations and imprisoned people. "Forgive me Lord. Cleanse me." She realizes that words of life need to pour from her lips. "Woe is me! I'm a woman of unclean lips," she cries out.

Laying His hand over her heart, He says, "Awake sleeping princess for your Bridegroom is calling."

The intense burning on her lips moves slowly toward her heart. Emotions she hasn't felt in years surface as she becomes increasingly tender. Purity cries out loud, expelling the pain of the past years. After several minutes the glowing ember awakens her heart, and a warm, contented feeling of peace overwhelms her. She smiles up at Amazing Grace.

"Never again will you receive the false name Promiscuous. I fire brand you the name Master Potter ordained for you: Purity. As the words leave His lips, her name is set as a seal on her heart.

Born for a Different World

Amazing Grace prophetically proclaims: "Blessed are the pure in heart for they shall see God. Read the Word, Purity, and you will develop an insatiable hunger for heavenly things. All desire for things temporal will slowly fade away. You will be satisfied only with living in God's presence, because you were made for the glories of Heaven. You will come to understand this more as each day passes."

"Purity," he continues with a somber tone, "you are a sojourner on a short journey, passing through a foreign land. Make the most of each day and every precious relationship."

Purity is taken aback by His serious look.

"Now, are you ready to resume your journey?" She nods yes as Amazing Grace stands her up, puts His arm around her waist, and walks her back to the Potter's House.

I can forgive my mother, Purity thinks, *I just don't know if she'll forgive me.*

CHAPTER THIRTEEN

ETERNAL ADORNMENT

Beloved wakes in the morning still in Master Potter's arms. When she opens her eyes the first thing she sees are His eyes gazing lovingly into hers. After receiving ministry and encouragement from Him, somewhat reluctantly she follows Him back into the glazing room to resume control of her team.

Still embarrassed, she gathers them around and says, "I know by now you have heard that I lost my children. Needless to say it's the most painful thing in my life. I had hopes and dreams of what reconciling with Purity would look like and obviously, yesterday wasn't it. I would value your prayers on her behalf.

"I understand if you no longer have faith in my leadership. You probably could get reassigned to another set. No hard feelings if you want to talk to Master Potter…"

"Who's leaving? I'm not leaving!" says Comrade standing to his feet. "You're an awesome leader, and I'll follow you anywhere."

"Master Potter designated you as leader of our set. You'll help me reach my destiny. I'm not settling for second best," Champion says.

"Me too," says Generosity. "We were all placed here together because of our different strengths and weakness. We all need to be here to function as a team."

One by one the other members pledged their determination to stay.

"We need to pray for Purity's return. We're not complete without her," says Comrade. The seven mugs gather round Beloved and pray for her and for Purity's safe reunion.

Master Potter watches from a distance like a proud Father. *That's how my teams function and become family!*

PROMOTED

A little later, Beloved takes Comrade aside. "Thank you for being there for me."

"It's not over yet, Beloved. I'm still believing she'll come back."

"You've been such a good friend through thick and thin. I want to ask you if you'd like to be my second-in-command? I love and trust you."

"Oh Beloved, I'm honored to be your assistant."

Calling the team together again, she announces: "We have a reason for celebration. I've just promoted Comrade to be my second-in-command. Anytime you can't find me, you may go to him. I trust him, and I know he will help us to complete our journey safely."

WHO'S FIRST?

Master Potter surveys His glazing room where thousands of vessels are being prepared for the high fires. He nods approvingly. Rembrandt, one of the head artistic angels, walks up to their table, stretches his beautiful, golden wings and says, "It's time for promotion and celebration! Who's first to be glazed?"

Beloved musters her courage and volunteers. "All right, watch closely so you won't be afraid when it's your turn," she says, her voice shaking.

Rembrandt picks her up and pours a white milky glaze inside her vessel. She feels it swishing around and coating her inside as she's turned in his hands. Her head spins as the motion continues. Then he empties the excess glaze back into the container and wipes her rim clean.

"This glaze looks like dull, matte house paint when I apply it," says Rembrandt holding Beloved up. "It's only after the glass or silica particles melt in the high fires that your true colors will come out. Then you'll be beautiful!"

Before she has a chance to say thank you, Rembrandt holds her by her foot, turning her upside down, and pours glaze all around the outside of her vessel. Cleaning her foot of excess glaze, he then sets her back on the table to dry.

She encourages her team, "That was wonderful! It's a little disorienting, but not painful at all. I can't wait to see what Rembrandt will do with each of you."

Comrade shouts, "I'll go next and show you guys how it's done! Hey, Confidence and Self Assurance, I'm one step ahead of you. How do you like my leadership style?"

Honoring his request, Rembrandt picks up Comrade and begins to glaze him as he cries out to his friends below, "Look guys, I'm flying!" The angels smile at each other, amused by the antics of the little mug.

All the vessels eagerly line up waiting for their turn to receive as they watch the others getting glazed. The joyful vessels sway and sing and clap as each one returns. Their guardian angels all join in the celebration.

MUGS AND ANGEL WINGS

Using brushes loaded with colored pigments, the artistic angels hand paint beautiful borders and designs. Intricate flowers, birds, and nature scenes are meticulously applied according to Master Potter's individualized plan for each vessel.

Dipping various paintbrushes into the colorful pigments, Rembrandt dabs gold filigree trim around Beloved's top and carefully paints an angel on her side. Using delicate strokes, he releases eternity onto the dull matte glaze. Each stroke leaves an invisible trail of dazzling brilliance. Setting her aside to dry, he meticulously paints angel wings on each of the seven mugs.

A mysterious and profound secret is taking place as eternal adornment is applied to each of His creations. The vessels can neither see nor comprehend the splendor and glory that covers them, but hidden in their glaze is the immeasurable depth and fiery passion of the Bridegroom for His Bride.

Master Potter and His angelic team work diligently until they have completed their tasks. Each vessel is positioned according to his or her sovereignly-appointed purposes and covered in His veiled glory.

The Father looks down at the glazing room taking great pleasure in the beauty of His handiwork manifested in them.

CHAPTER FOURTEEN

WHAT DOES THE FUTURE HOLD?

❦

Beloved and her team of mugs are placed on a board and carried to an empty shelf at the end of the glazing room. A blast of frigid winter wind draws their attention back to the windows and the white, lacy snow flurries outside.

The vessels are thrilled to finally be glazed, even if it doesn't reveal the ultimate color of their final destiny. They wonder what will happen to them next as they look down row upon row of shelves. Each row is filled with recently glazed vessels chatting with one another about their new appearance.

Comrade and Beloved look across the shelves with excitement as they see their old friend Joyful surrounded by other goblets. Comrade calls out to her, "Joyful! Over here! It's me Comrade! You look great! I love that grapevine design. It's really slenderizing. Look who I have with me."

"Look at the awesome team Master Potter set me in." She gestures toward Fearless. "He's my team leader! Isn't that great? Who would have thought Master Potter would put me with an old friend?"

Fearless looks up and waves at Beloved, but before he can say anything, the vessels hear whistling from across the room. Beloved's eyes light up as she recognizes the shape of a familiar teapot now glazed white and painted with roses. "Golden Incense, over here, it's me."

All the vessels chatter loudly and excitedly about their commissioning and glazing. As daylight fades into night, hundreds more glazed vessels are placed on the shelves and join the festivities.

Master Potter lights brass oil lanterns, which hang from wooden posts throughout the room. The artistic angels continue to glaze and paint beautiful designs until each vessel has been completed.

WILL WE SURVIVE?

In spite of Comrade's snoring, the other vessels doze off. Beloved is awake, longing for Purity and beginning to feel apprehensive about the high firing ahead. "Lord, will we survive? What if I don't make it or can't lead the others through it?"

In answer to her prayer, she feels the warm breath of Holy Spirit covering her like a feather comforter. He gently reminds her of Master Potter's prophetic words of destiny spoken over her life. Her mind travels back in time to the fireside room where Master Potter transformed Himself into the Bridegroom.

Re-entering this holy visitation, deep love is reawakened in Beloved, driving out all fear of the dreaded high fires. She sees the shimmering wedding gowns covered in pearls and the burning passion in His fiery eyes for her. With renewed courage mixed with a tinge of sadness, she again accepts the invitation to be His warrior Bride and finally falls into a deep, peaceful sleep.

PART TWO

THE FORMIDABLES

CHAPTER FIFTEEN

THE POTTERY WAGONS

E arly the next morning, Rembrandt shouts the order to open the massive wooden doors at the end of the glazing room. Cold winter wind rushes in and startles the vessels out of their cozy sleep.

Huge Clydesdale's snort their hot breath into the frigid morning air as they back the pottery wagons to the door. The creaking of wheels and the driver's voices calling out signals add to the clamor. Horses stomp their white tufted hoofs, stirring up the rich odor of damp, leather harnesses.

The drivers climb down, taking off their heavy winter work coats and rolling up their sleeves. They join in the hustle and bustle of the angelic workers loading the wagons.

RISE AND SHINE

The half-asleep mugs begin grumbling about all the noise and cold wind blowing through the shelves. Cranky, Comrade yells, "What's all the racket about? What time is it anyway?"

Harvester complains, "No one in his right mind should be up at this hour! And from where did those horses come?"

Comrade shakes his buddy, "Hey, Fearless, it's time to get up!"

Wiping sleep from his eyes, Fearless says excitedly, "It's about time we got our marching orders! This is what we've been waiting for!"

Golden Incense whimpers, "Did anyone put the tea on? I'm so cold my teeth are chattering."

"Are we really going out in this blizzard?" asks Comrade.

Beloved tries to encourage her team, "Listen, soon we'll be beautiful glazed vessels on our way to the nations, and this will only be a memory."

Long Suffering, hidden on a back shelf, complains to no one in particular, "Well, it's either boiling hot or freezing cold around here. I wish they would make up their minds!"

"Hey Joyful, get your boots on and let's get going, the guys are already up," whistles Golden Incense.

ELDER, THE WAGON MASTER

The old pottery wagons were once beautiful forms of art. Carved out of oak, their sides depict ancient victories over the enemy. Hundreds of vessels ride on wooden boards slid onto shelves attached to wooden frames and anchored to the wagon beds. Beloved and her little group are the last vessels to be loaded on the lead wagon.

Master Potter strides purposefully toward a man whose kind face is weathered and deeply creased with wrinkles. It's hard to guess his age, but Beloved believes he must be in his late sixties. His hair, once coal black is now peppered with gray, as is his beard. His long, calfskin coat gives him protection from the harsh winter wind. His khaki pants are tucked into boots, and an old, slouched hat tops off his rugged appearance.

Settling into their new surroundings on the wagon, the vessels ask Rembrandt, "Who is that talking to Master Potter?"

"That's the wagon master, Elder. He's worked for Master Potter for years and made this trip hundreds of times. He knows the mountain trails and passes like the back of his hand."

Beloved looks up into the clear winter sky and notices a giant eagle gliding effortlessly high above their heads, encircling them and covering them with his expansive wings. The large shadow of those great wings falls across the wagons.

PREPARING FOR BATTLE

The vessels strain to hear as Master Potter draws Elder close for a private talk. They keep their voices low. The vessels lean forward afraid they might miss something. Pulling out a detailed map, Master Potter discusses the dangerous trail Elder will be taking. "Due to the heavy storms, Precarious Pass is the only opening through the Formidable Mountain Range."

Elder replies, "The pass is really dangerous. The last time we went through there I wasn't sure we'd make it, but somehow we did. The warfare is becoming more intense every time we take the trip, and we've lost some vessels."

Putting His arm around Elder's shoulder, Master Potter says, "My friend, I have faith in you to deliver these precious vessels safely to Me at the Mountain of Fire, but we both know this is a treacherous journey. I'll be interceding for them as usual."

Pointing on the map Master Potter discusses possible avalanche areas and places where thieves might hide along the trail to capture the wagons and take the vessels. "And, of course, Elder, you must be alert for demonic attacks everywhere."

The vessels are alarmed as they hear snatches of the conversation. "Precarious Pass?" says Comrade.

"Demonic attack?" chimes Loyalty, swallowing hard. They huddle closer together and Beloved prays, asking the Lord for help. Her heavy responsibility for her team members is starting to dawn on her.

WATCHMAN

Master Potter raises His voice as He tells Elder, "Here comes our faithful friend, Watchman. He'll ride shotgun as usual and guide you through the Formidables. He specializes in dangerous situations and will be invaluable." They both smile as they hear a big sigh of relief from the eavesdropping vessels.

Beloved sees a tall, lean man walking toward the wagon. He is dressed in a leather duster and carrying a rifle over his shoulder. A wide-brimmed hat is pulled over his sandy hair partially hiding his piercing blue eyes. He enthusiastically greets Master Potter and Elder.

He seems familiar thinks Beloved. *But I know that we've never met before.*

Barrels of water and supplies are attached to the sides and backs of the wagons. Elder heaves a weathered tarp over the wagon, startling the vessels. Their view is obscured as the drivers tie down the tarp to protect them from the winter elements. They huddle together as they are left in the darkness.

A sudden movement of wheels jolts the vessels as they leave the threshold of the massive cedar doors. Beloved's wagon stops abruptly, waiting for the others to be loaded and pulled in behind.

Finally, with a great jolt and a screaming chorus of squeaks and creaking, the wagon train sets off for the mountain pass.

Far out of Beloved's sight, Master Potter hurries to the last wagon, carrying a small, recently glazed vessel. He lifts the canvas and gently sets her down. She smiles up at Him as the snow begins to fall. Hearing a screech she looks up as ascending white clouds cover the sun and pale the winter sky. The shadow of the great eagle falls one last time over her upturned face.

"Remember, Purity," says Master Potter, caressing her cheek, "You were not made for this world."

CHAPTER SIXTEEN

THE FORMIDABLES

As the twenty heavily laden pottery wagons creak slowly down the snow covered path, a myriad of unseen guardian angels surround them. Master Potter watches His precious entourage turn into the narrow trail leading to the Formidable Mountain Range.

The snowflurries and northern winds have died down, and the late morning sun creates sparkling ice crystals, carpeting the newly fallen snow. The vessels speak softly amongst themselves so they don't alarm everyone in the wagon. They all look to Beloved for encouragement and leadership.

Sweet Adoration speaks up timidly, "Beloved, did he really say thieves will try to capture us? What will we do? How will we protect ourselves?"

Harvester brags, "Like I told you guys before, Master Potter made me for dangerous exploits! Don't worry; I'll protect you," he says patting one of the smaller vessels on its head.

Beloved confidently tells her mugs, "Holy Spirit took me back in time last night to the fireside room where we first saw our beautiful wedding gowns. He reminded me of His invitation for us to become warrior Brides. We're on a difficult prophetic journey and need to stay focused on Him."

Sweet Adoration agrees, "I'll admit I am nervous without Master Potter."

"Let's worship and pray; we'll all feel better," adds Golden Incense.

Joyful tells her, "Don't be afraid; He sent Watchman along as our special guide."

"Let's not forget that we've got to keep our armor on. By the way," Comrade blushes, "has anyone seen my sword?"

Long Suffering chides, "I would have thought from the stories you told about your battle in the fireside room that your sword would be far too large to misplace."

Comrade looks chagrined, and the rest of the vessels all laugh. Harvester punches him in the shoulder. "Maybe Master Potter put it on a wagon all by itself."

"Maybe it's so big that even Master Potter couldn't load it on the wagon," laughs Fearless. "It's probably still back at the house."

"You can ask Beloved, she'll tell you…." Comrade's guardian angel, Courageous, chuckles to himself and touches Comrade on the shoulder. "Oh, forget it," Comrade says as he drops his defensiveness and laughs heartily with his friends. "But it really did grow."

WORSHIP AND INTERCESSION

Beloved's throaty, nightingale like voice fills the atmosphere with soft worship, activating faith in the hearts of all the vessels. She raises her hands and is soon lost in adoration. Worship and intercession spread throughout the wagon, igniting hearts as the vessels all sing and pray in the Spirit.

Watching from a distance, Master Potter smiles approvingly as the perfumed incense of their prayers rises through the old, weathered tarps. Gusts of glory swirl around them and intermingle with glittering snow crystals creating a sparkling cloud.

OFF TO PRECARIOUS PASS

After several hours the wagons stop and Elder and Watchman check on the vessels. The little group hears the concern in Elder's voice as he tells Watchman, "The weather's closing in. We need to get to Precarious Pass before dark."

The wagon rocks side to side as the two men climb aboard. Horses strain against their harnesses, neighing and pawing the ground. Suddenly, the snap of reins signals the eager steeds. The wagons move slowly up the mountainous trail to an intersection where an old sign indicates three different trails.

One sign points down the mountain to Comfort Cove. The next sign points in the opposite direction to the treacherous mountains ahead and reads, Precarious Pass.

Beloved peeks out from under the tarp and shutters as she reads the last weathered sign pointing to Deeper Life Commune. Flashbacks of Death sweep over her. Pushing back fear, she draws a blanket tightly around her shoulders and shudders.

Her arms long to hold her daughter so intensely that they ache, as does her heart. Sadly, she stares out at the snow covered trail and hums the old hymn, *It is Well with My Soul*.

Chapter Seventeen

Spiritual Warfare

The winter sun drops behind the mountains like an clouded orange ball as the wagons move slowly up the increasingly steep and narrow trail. Thick snow blankets the passage with heavy drifts from the previous day's storm. The horses' muscles ripple and strain against their harnesses as they pull their heavy loads.

Wet snow and ice coats the branches of the dense forest at either side of the trail. Elder orders the drivers to light the brass oil lanterns attached to tall wooden posts on the lead wagon.

Shivering in the icy wind that blows through the tarps, the fragile vessels huddle together uncomfortably on the wooden shelves. Hungry and cold, Long Suffering blurts out, "Well, if you ask me this makes the desert look like a day in the park. At least it wasn't cold there." Others join in and start to grumble bitterly.

"I'm starving."

"When are we going to stop to rest?"

Harvester yells, "You guys are sure thin skinned. Stop the belly aching; it only makes it worst!"

Disgusted, Steadfast agrees and tries to quiet the ranks, "We've just started this journey, so why all the complaining?"

"Right," whines Long Suffering, "I'm freezing! But I guess we'll get a fire soon enough."

Comrade moves closer to Sweet Adoration telling her, "Stay close to me, and I'll keep you warm. Would you like to wear my coat and scarf?"

Beloved looks on approvingly, "Comrade, you're a good friend. Thanks for looking out for us all."

Base Camp

Hours later, the trail widens as they approach base camp at a high mountain meadow. Strategically located at the foot of Precarious Pass, it's the last place for the horses to rest before launching their hazardous trek in the morning. The full moon peeks out from behind gathering clouds. Its reflection casts liquid light on the clear mountain stream running through the meadow and into the sea below.

Elder pulls his cold, weary team into camp beside the half-frozen stream and orders the men to take care of the horses. The vessels rejoice, expecting to be taken inside a warm shelter and fed.

The last wagons pull into camp. The drivers wipe down the horse's thick sorrel coats and throw woolen blankets over their backs. Then they water and feed them before bedding them down in a makeshift stable. Finally they untie the supplies hitched to the wagons in preparation for the crew's evening meal. Cooking fires dot the campground as Master Potter's crew works together and talks over the day's events.

Praying and Fasting

The snowflurries fall gently as Watchman explains that the vessels will be staying aboard the wagons for the night praying and fasting before they continue through the dangerous pass in the morning. "Fasting is spiritual violence against the enemy's kingdom. It moves the heart of God and releases protection. It will strengthen your spirits for the warfare ahead. We need everyone's prayers."

A groan of disappointment escapes from the wagons as the smell the food cooking over the campfire drifts through the camp.

"As if we haven't been miserable enough in these cold wagons, now they're not going to feed us? I should have known it was coming," complains Long Suffering.

"This is what I call a forced fast," grumbles Harvester.

"You're the expert on fasting aren't you?" chides Comrade.

"Hey, five days out of forty isn't bad for a beginning effort," Harvester pipes up.

"If I remember correctly," says Long Suffering, "you were the tavern's best customer for fish 'n chips during that time."

"At least I tried, which was more than the rest of you," says Harvester, and the tension is broken as they laugh over this fond memory.

After the workers eat, they bring out their guitars and tambourines. The vessels join with them in praise and worship. Watchman brings refreshing to the weary travelers as He moves from wagon to wagon praying for the vessels and giving words of encouragement. Remember, even though you don't like fasting, it tenderizes and awakens your heart to hear His revelation and wisdom. We all must be vigilant. We're a team and a family."

Comrade exhorts every vessel to get out their sword—the Word of God. "Let your hearts be awakened to His love and protection for you. His life is released in His Word."

After Bible study, Beloved leads them in the familiar revival hymn, *The Old Rugged Cross*, which activates a glorious pillar of fire in the spirit realm. Some of the vessels have visions of the Cross and receive a revelation of how they are loved.

Gentle tears of adoration flow down Beloved's cheeks as she is caught up in spontaneous praise. Other vessels move into prophetic songs and music. The windows of Heaven open and gusts of glory sweep through the camp. Valiant, Exhorter, Courageous, and the other guardian angels join in the celebration.

All the while, tucked between two blankets in the last wagon, Purity is sound asleep, exhausted from the long, bumpy ride.

SATANIC BATTLE PLANS

Glorious worship rises through the second heavens on its way to the throne of God. The holy fragrance of adoration violently assaults the demonic realm, causing dark spirits to swarm together in a malevolent cloud of vengeance, frantic to destroy the source of the hated worship. Its abandoned resonance sends waves of torment throughout the demonic realm.

High above in the rugged Formidables the glorious worship awakens a dark Dragon that rules over the geographical region. Superimposed over the rugged peaks of the Formidables, his monstrous mouth opens in a cavernous snarl. His deadly coiled tail wraps around his coveted treasure, the sleepy little village of Comfort Cove. Eyes burning with defiance, he jealously guards his stronghold over it, ravenous to consume the lives of its inhabitants.

In this eerie glacial fortress, Satan angrily spews sulfuric vapor into the atmosphere. Beloved's mellow, yet spiritually powerful, voice wafting through the Dragon's lair throws Satan into a diabolical rage.

"I hate that voice! She should still be singing for Madame False Destiny at the Inn, as she did before she met Master Potter. I must silence her or use her voice to bring thousands to me!" he snarls with intense agitation as he paces on his webbed, gnarled feet.

"I should have won this challenge with the Godhead for her affections long ago. Why am I surrounded by incompetents?" he bellows as he kicks a little demon who thuds high on the wall and slides down to the floor unconscious. A horde of other slimy minions scatter in terror.

"Send a message to Death to round up all the troops and prepare to annihilate that wagon train—and bring Forsaken to me!"

DISCERNMENT

Sensing danger, Watchman motions for Elder. They kneel in prayer and see an open vision of the Dragon manifested over the Formidable Mountain Range and the demonic army assigned against them. Asking Master Potter for battle strategies, they stir the camp to pray with new vigor. Enormous warring angels with flaming swords appear in the darkness at the borders of the camp, ancient sentinels sent to guard the camp and await orders from the Father.

CHAPTER EIGHTEEN

MASTER CRAFTSMAN

Suddenly the moon disappears behind dark ominous clouds, and icy winds blast down from Precarious Pass. Bitter cold penetrates the drivers' winter coats and whips the wagon tarps loose. They rush to tie them down. Elder yells to Watchman, "I've seen lots of winter storms but this one approaching now looks like the worst in years."

"Yes," Watchman agrees, "I'm sensing there's heavy demonic activity in this storm. I'll keep the vessels praying, or we'll suffer casualties for sure."

The furious wind drives sleet from the mountain peak into the pass. Elder yells orders to the men. Watchman tends to the vessels, encouraging them to pray. "Don't give up! The enemy has unleashed an attack that's headed this way." Beloved's team grows increasingly uneasy as the storm gains strength.

In the distance, a low rumble reverberates from the direction of the pass. Peering through the blinding snow, Elder makes out the hazy glow of lanterns.

Pounding hooves advancing over the mountainous trail and the loud cracking of whips signal to all that another wagon train approaches. The praying abruptly stops as the vessels peek out from under the tarps as eight magnificent black horses pull a shiny lead coach into camp.

Ordered to halt, the horses paw the ground impatiently, anxious to continue their flight from the storm. The light from the campfires reflects off their silvery manes as ice crystals quickly form over their sweating bodies. Steam rises from their nostrils in an eerie mist, giving them an unearthly appearance.

Other horses pull black lacquered coaches trimmed in red with the words: "Master Craftsman" hand-lettered in gold calligraphy on each side. Beneath the ornate words are large glass windows protecting and displaying beautiful vessels. Barrels of gourmet food are attached to the sides of the coaches. Each wagon is equipped with two brass lanterns illuminating their way.

Suddenly the storm stops, and Devotion yells to the others, "Look! They can see where they're going! I wish Master Potter would give us lanterns like that!"

The lead wagon stops alongside Beloved's, and a strikingly handsome man leaps to the ground. Brushing snow off his long fur coat, he strides toward Elder. His black snakeskin boots hardly leave an imprint in the packed snow.

LET ME INTRODUCE MYSELF

"My name is Master Craftsman. Perhaps you've heard of me? I see you're a potter too."

"Oh no, these vessels belong to Master Potter. I just work for Him. My name is Elder."

"Master Potter and I are old friends. I thought I recognized those rickety old wagons. One of these days He'll get up-to-date ones like I have. Actually, I was hoping to run into Him on this trip. But, I guess He stayed behind. He doesn't like to get out in this weather and suffer with His poor, cold, hungry pots, does He?"

The vessels are relieved to have company on this dangerous night and glad that an old acquaintance of Master Potter's is there to help. Curious, as usual, Beloved's team moves in closer, straining to hear every word.

When she catches a glimpse of Master Craftsman, Beloved is startled and turns to her widemouth mugs and whispers, "I know him. He's the potter from Comfort Cove. He had a large pottery shop in the village square. I saw many of his vessels thrown away and broken on the Potter's Field."

Comrade confidentially adds, "He was an intimate friend of Madam False Destiny. He sat with us at Mayor Lecherous' table many times."

Memories flood Beloved in a torrent of emotion, "When I sang at the inn, Master Craftsman brought servants to her to mentor for the dark side."

Turning red with anger, Comrade agrees, "That's right! They fooled a lot of us! We thought they were so nice, but all they wanted was to keep us under their thumb and get us to do their dirty work for them. We should know! We were victims of their schemes, weren't we Beloved?"

She nods, "I think this is serious. We need to get in groups and pray. Things aren't what they seem."

Comrade yells, "Get your armor on!"

Harvester calls out to his canisters, "All my team, quick, quick, let's get praying."

Fearless shouts, "Wine goblets, over here. Meet in this corner."

There's a sudden stampede in the wagon as vessels run to get in their groups. Fervent prayer arises from the wagon.

NEW FIRING TECHNIQUE

But not everyone joins in. Confidence and Self Assurance stand off to the side, captivated by the elaborate coaches, and begin to compare themselves to Master Craftsman's vessels. "Just look at them. Who do they think they are, riding in such comfort and ease? They're even sitting on velvet cushions."

"Yeah! While we sit on old wooden boards! Their master takes better care of them!"

Eyeing the luxurious lap blankets covering his vessels, others chime in. "It's not fair! Why should they be warm and cozy while we practically freeze to death?"

Confidence complains, "They even have springhinged axles to soften their ride. They don't have to worry about getting chipped and broken."

Contention spreads throughout the wagons as dark, demonic spirits stir jealousy and division among the vessels.

Gesturing toward his team Master Craftsman tells Elder, "You know, of course, it's no longer necessary to go through the Mountain of Fire to make these vessels beautiful. I've come up with a revolutionary process to omit the second firing completely. It's called Cold Fire. I very much wanted to share my process with Master Potter so these precious vessels would not have to suffer any more. Where is He anyway?"

"He's put me in charge of this wagon train and ordered me to take the vessels through the pass to the Mountain of Fire," Elder answers.

The vessels begin to debate the wisdom of Master Potter and whether it might not be a good idea to go with Master Craftsman.

"A new process? We don't need to be fired?" questions Confidence.

"Maybe Master Potter is old fashioned. Maybe there are better techniques now," replies Self Assurance."

WE COULD DIE!

Elder ignores the complaining vessels. "We're planning to leave at first light, but you're welcome to bed down with us for the night."

"It's too dangerous! We barely escaped with our lives! An avalanche almost wiped us out! We're trying to outrun the storm and get our vessels back to the safety of the village. That pass will be closed all winter, and you'll be trapped. You need to get out of here while you can!"

Elder's voice takes on an uncharacteristic steely quality as he retorts, "Master Potter told us to go through Precarious Pass. Until further orders from Him, we don't turn back."

Meanwhile, demons of fear terrorize the vessels. Speaking to each other through chattering teeth, the cups and pots, goblets, and vases exclaim, "Trapped?"

"Avalanche?"

"We could die!"

Golden Incense tells her cups and saucers, "We need to pray for wisdom and discernment for our leaders. We can't let the enemy take any grounds here tonight."

Drawn by their fervent prayers and obvious anointing, Comrade wanders from his group and joins theirs. After a few minutes, he becomes aware of a shy little saucer standing to one side. No one notices as he introduces himself and tries to encourage her.

"Don't be afraid. What's your name?"

"Tenderhearted"

"Well, Tenderhearted, I've been through lots of warfare before. I'll stay with you through this. We can pray together."

CHECK OUT THE PASS

The spiritual warfare increases in momentum and swirls around the wagons. Beloved tries to rally her team to intercession, but few stop complaining long enough to hear her.

Meanwhile, Master Craftsman's oily voice cuts through the night, "Well Elder, perhaps you should check the pass out for yourself! Go ahead if you must. I'll keep an eye on these vessels for you."

Without answering him, Elder signals Watchman for a private talk. "I have to know for sure before I risk the lives of the vessels. I'll stay here while you and some of the drivers check the pass."

Watchman looks intensely and shakes his head. "I sense real danger here. We need to stay together. Remember, the enemy always wants to divide and separate."

"I'm not sure this is the enemy. He says he's a friend of Master Potter's. We'll be fine! Just be back by daylight," says Elder reassuringly.

"It's not a good idea for me to be outside the camp," Watchman reasons.

"I insist! I have to know what's going on out there, and you're the only one I can trust."

Watchman sighs in resignation, "I still don't think it's wise, but stay alert and keep the vessels praying and fasting until I return."

Elder walks back to the wagons as Watchman and several drivers quietly disappear into the stormy night.

CHAPTER NINETEEN

FUR LINED BLANKETS AND GOURMET FOOD

Snuggled together in the drafty wagon Beloved's team talks among themselves. Soon they hear approaching footsteps as Master Craftsman tells Elder, "I'd like to see an example of Master Potter's workmanship."

Elder opens the tarp proudly, "Here is a excellent example of His work. These vessels are ready to go into the high fire. Even at this stage, you can see how beautiful they'll be."

Master Craftsman looks sympathetically at the little pots. "They'll never be beautiful if they freeze to death out here. Why did Master Potter abandon them to these dangers? They're so valuable, but as clay vessels they can be broken so easily."

Speaking directly to Beloved's group, he adds, "I would never put you in such a hazardous situation. Why doesn't Master Potter take better care of you?" The unexpected question releases a renewed uneasiness in the wagon, and many of the vessels anxiously look to Elder for reassurance.

Alarmed by Master Craftsman, he doesn't give them an answer and quickly closes the tarp. They hear him angrily reply, "You're upsetting them for no reason. We both know this journey is not about comfort. Master Potter knows what's best for His vessels."

"Best for them? You've got to be joking. Sitting here in this dark, cold wagon? This is what you call 'best for them!'"

"Just move away from the wagon. Since you're so anxious to get to Comfort Cove, maybe you should leave now. The quicker you go the better." Elder protectively stands beside the wagon until Master Craftsman moves away. *Why did I send Watchman away? I need His discernment in this situation.*

Taking off his hat, Elder runs his hands through his hair in deep thought before telling the vessels, "Watchman has taken a few of the men to check out the pass. We need to see if this guy knows what he's talking about. Everything is going to be fine, but keep praying. I'm going to check on the other wagons."

SEEDS OF DECEPTION

Undetected, Master Craftsman assigns spirits of Unbelief and Deception to infiltrate each wagon. Many start to doubt Master Potter's love for them. Others just fall asleep, oblivious to the battle over their destinies. The enemy's force increases, bringing a heavily oppressive atmosphere to blanket the camp. The vessels pray fervently, but as quickly as their prayers are released the icy breath of the demonic realm snuffs them out.

Trembling, the little saucer Tenderhearted reaches out to Comrade. He takes her hand and comforts her, "Don't worry, I'm here. I'll protect you."

The intercessors pray in the Spirit, frantically groping for the right intercessory keys to unlock the heavens. The challenge is on as mighty warriors in the unseen realm battle for souls in Precarious Pass.

Making sure Elder is out of sight, Master Craftsman stealthily approaches the lead wagon and throws open the tarp. "Elder doesn't want me speaking to you because he's afraid you'll find out the truth. I'll bet he didn't tell you about the thieves that raid pottery wagons in this pass, did he? They destroy unprotected vessels just like you. Have you thought about what could happen in this isolated place?"

Confidence loudly tells Self Assurance, "A blizzard and now thieves! Let's get out of here!"

"Even Watchman has left you. He obviously doesn't value your lives," Master Craftsman goads.

Self Assurance agrees, "That's right! He was supposed to protect us! He probably hightailed it to safety!"

Spurred on, Master Craftsman asks, "But think for a moment. Not only does Watchman abandon you, but where is *Master Potter*?"

Beloved shouts, "Don't listen to him! Master Potter has not left us here to die. He said He'd meet us at the Mountain of Fire, and He will!"

Stopping in front of Beloved, Master Craftsman challenges, "What if you're wrong about Master Potter? Are you willing to risk the lives of your team?"

Moving in closer, he glares at her as he continues to address the vessels. "Didn't you hear me? It isn't necessary to go to the Mountain of Fire. It's archaic to fire vessels. What can you gain by more suffering?"

"Master Potter has always been faithful to us. He won't forget us now," says Comrade.

Generosity whispers to his friend Champion, "What he's saying sounds so good! What do you think? Should we go with Master Craftsman and get out of this cold?"

MUTINY

Smiling warmly once again, Master Craftsman continues, "Just look at my vessels! They're warm and snug in the best wagons money can buy. And I'm right here to protect them. Since the pass is closed, the most sensible thing for you is to come with us to Comfort Cove. Master Potter will probably be there when you arrive—all toasty and warm wondering what took you so long. I've had to help Him out like this before."

Self Assurance begins to waver, "If I could really be sure that Master Potter would be waiting for us, I'd go. Maybe our entire team should."

Hearing that, Master Craftsman smiles widely, "I have a lovely house there. I'll send ahead and have my assistants prepare for your arrival. They'll have a cozy fire, sumptuous food, and warm beds waiting for you."

Confidence's eyes light up in anticipation of the comfort that awaits them in the village. "This sounds like a promotion to me, and without the fire! After all, we're entitled! Like he said, we've gone through enough already!"

Beloved calls her team together. She desperately wants to combat the negative influence that Confidence and Self Assurance are having on them. After telling them what she and Comrade saw Master Craftsman do in Comfort Cove, she pleads for them to listen to her.

"You must not go with him. Master Craftsman is a liar. I don't believe for a minute that he'll take care of us. There is always something wrong with his vessels. They look beautiful on the outside, but can't hold any substance. He's evil. He and Madam False Destiny are partners in crime."

Confidence retorts, "Beloved, you were once damaged too. What makes you so sure he hasn't changed? After all, he's a friend of Master Potter, just as we are."

Self Assurance adds, "Look at him; he's obviously successful and wealthy. It seems to me he takes better care of his vessels than Elder does. For instance, see how Watchman left us, and who knows when he'll come back?"

Others agree, "Have you seen the barrels of gourmet food tied to their coaches? They're even protected behind weatherproof glass, snuggled under fur lined blankets."

Self Assurance whispers to Generosity and Champion, "Confidence and I are seriously thinking about going. If everyone came, we could remain a complete set."

"That's right!" says Confidence, "We can always find another pitcher to take Beloved's place."

CHAPTER TWENTY

THE CHOICE IS YOURS!

Undeterred by Master Craftsman and the complaining vessels, Beloved tries to rally her troops. "These circumstances are bad, but I learned in the wilderness that trying to find comfort and ease outside of Master Potter's will only brings disaster. He has given us a destiny, and we must meet Him at the Mountain of Fire. We have to go on!"

Confidence yells, "You can stay here in these drafty old wagons if you want, but Self Assurance and I are going to travel in the warmth and safety of those coaches. Who's coming with us? Beloved is putting us all at risk!"

"Don't forget, this is avalanche country. We could die out here," says Self Assurance.

"What about the thieves and robbers?" asks Confidence, his eyes wide with fear.

Tenderhearted looks up to Comrade, "I just don't know what to think. Maybe Beloved doesn't know what she's doing."

Comrade's eyes soften as he returns her gaze, "I'm Beloved's second in command, and I can tell you from firsthand knowledge that she's right. We both knew Master Craftsman in Comfort Cove. He's not a nice man, and his friends aren't either."

Long Suffering has been listening to their conversation for some time and decides to speak up, "Tenderhearted, you need to ask your own leader, Golden Incense. That faithful teapot has known Beloved for years. And Comrade, you need to rejoin your team; it's where Master Potter placed you."

Blushing, Tenderhearted quickly lets go of Comrade's hand as Long Suffering shakes her finger at them. Running to her team, she looks back to see Comrade speaking angrily to Long Suffering.

A SERIOUS WARNING

Beloved motions for Comrade. Taking him aside she tells him, "I need you to stay and help me with the others. I see you've been hanging around one of Golden Incense's saucers. She's not for you, Comrade."

He blurts out defensively, "We were just praying together. She was upset and just needed someone to encourage her. There was nothing wrong in what we did."

"I'm sure that's true, but remember, she's already spoken for and is going to be paired with a teacup. So don't get too intimate. It will only lead to problems for both of you."

"Every cup needs a saucer. Why didn't Master Potter give me one? We could fit!"

"Comrade, you're not a cup. You're a mug, made to be a part of my team. Mugs are not made to have saucers. So I don't want you to see her anymore. The enemy would love to use something like this to take you out."

"Beloved, I could never fall for that old trap. But if you insist, I'll stay away from her. Now, what do you need me to do?"

"Join us in prayer for those who are weak in faith. Talk to every team member, and make sure they're standing with Master Potter. Confidence and Self Assurance are causing a lot of hearts to waver."

Relieved to see Comrade come to his senses, she goes to Golden Incense and asks her to continue to pray, "This is not just a storm. We're up against strong demonic forces. Ask Master Potter to uncover the enemy and expose his plans so that none will be destroyed."

THE BATTLE RAGES

Master Craftsman's evil influence increases even as the fiery swords of prayer pierce the atmosphere. The fearful complaints of the compromised vessels give renewed vigor to the demonic forces. They double their assaults on them with lies and half-truths and succeed in weakening the vessels resolve, convincing others to join Confidence and Self Assurance in mutiny.

Swirling clouds of perfumed incense enter the Throne Room as petitions for friends and loved ones are offered. Master Potter looks painfully into His Father's eyes, each silently acknowledging the vessels choices as He continues to intercede.

With one glance from Master Potter, the warring angels cross over from a realm of indescribably beauty and eternal harmony to join their comrades in the chaos raging below. Glistening wings and celestial armor clash with the foul demonic horde disguised as a churning winter storm.

Beloved yells, "Comrade, some of the team has taken off their armor. Encourage them to fight. We need everyone's help."

Valiant cheers as Beloved holds up her shield and challenges Master Craftsman. "Since you're such a good friend of Master Potter, would you and your vessels join us in prayer?"

His rage explodes, "My vessels don't need to pray to someone they can't even see! That's ridiculous! Why would they need to do that when I'm right here? Master Potter is not their protector. I am. When they need help they simply call out. I'm right here to rescue them and you, if that's what you decide."

In the churning dark clouds, thunder rumbles as demons unsheathe their swords and spew out blasphemous curses. Lightning flashes as they clash against the radiant glory of the angelic warriors.

Unable to contain their fears any longer, Confidence and Self Assurance break under the pressure. "Master Craftsman, help us! We don't want to die in this storm! Can we go with you?"

CHEESECAKE ANYONE?

Smiling warmly, Master Craftsman picks them up, "At last, I hear the voice of reason! Anyone else want to come? There's always room for one more." He carefully places them in one of his wagons, making a show of covering them with the blankets and offering them gourmet food. Many vessels watch with undeniable longing as deception creeps over them and finally overtakes them. Like a dam suddenly bursting they make a rush for safety and comfort.

"I want to go too!"

"Can I have a piece of that cheesecake?"

"Just let me snuggle into that fur lined blanket!"

"Can I sit next to that famous worship leader?"

The angels stand by helplessly, grieving for the vessels who gave permission to be taken away.

To Beloved's horror, two more of her little mugs, Generosity and Champion, elbow their way to the front of line. She hears the oily sweet voice of Master Craftsman tell them, "No need to push and shove. I've brought plenty for everyone, for my desire is that you all be warm and safe."

Frantically, Beloved tries to stop them. "Please don't go! It's a terrible mistake! Master Potter designed you to be a part of this team. You'll never find your destiny and calling with Master Craftsman. We need to stay together!"

Master Craftsman's drivers move quickly to pick up the vessels that decide to go with him. They place each one on soft cushions and throw warm blankets over them.

CHAPTER TWENTY-ONE

CRACKED POTS

Unwilling for the vessels to be taken without a fight, Elder follows Master Craftsman to his coaches. Stalling for time until Watchmen and the other drivers return, he prays in the Spirit, knowing they're on the verge of an explosive battle. In the midst of the deteriorating situation, he ponders how to rescue the duped vessels. Looking closely at the finished pots so beautifully displayed behind the glass windows, he finds his answer.

Forcefully he tells Confidence and Self Assurance, "It's not too late to come back. You must understand what you're doing! If you look closely you'll see Master Craftsman's vessels are marred and cracked."

Master Craftsman retorts, "That's ridiculous! Look at this quality," he says pointing to an emerald green pitcher. "He's a well-known prophetic voice. I've given him influence and wealth. He'll be the next mayor of Comfort Cove!"

"You must be kidding. He clearly has a hairline defect! What kind of mayor would he make? Words just dribble out of his cracked lip," chides Elder.

Opening the glass door, Master Craftsman picks up another vessel, a blue platter this time. Some of the vessels gasp as they recognize the renowned minister. "His evangelistic ministry brings many vessels into the warmth of my coaches."

Elder moves quickly to further expose his poor workmanship, "This vessel has a structural crack carefully hidden in his design. He will never last through the heat of ministry, so don't be fooled by his fancy words. You need to go to the Mountain of Fire where Master Potter is waiting."

Pointing to a purple wine goblet, Elder barks, "Hold that one up!"

"I'm glad you insist. You've all heard this famous worship leader. How could you even imagine there's anything wrong with him? He's been through my new process or he couldn't possibly have such a beautiful finish!"

Before Elder has a chance to point out the goblet's off-centered stem, Master Craftsman shouts angrily, "I give comfort and protection from life's storms, but you can choose to be vulnerable to whatever comes your way. The choice is yours! Wisdom or pain and discomfort! You choose! But you must decide quickly if you're to get safely back to Comfort Cove!"

Convinced by Elder's speech, Generosity and Champion change their minds at the last minute and are brought back to Master Potter's wagons, literally snatched from the enemy's hands. Sadly, many others are swayed by the subtle deception of promised ease and comfort.

WAR IN THE CAMP

Insidious spirits swarm over the wagons, challenging faith and obedience. War rages in the camp as the angelic and the demonic hosts fight over each vessel's destiny.

Elder sounds the alarm for his drivers to secure the wagons. They begin tying down the tarps to protect the vessels from the demonic onslaught as they continue to pray fervently.

The fiendish screeching of demons can be heard in the maelstrom of winter winds and snow. "Only Master Craftsman can save you. You must come quickly before it's too late!" The deep, soothing voice cries through the driving wind and blowing snow.

Elder and his men earnestly shout their own warnings as the storm intensifies. "Don't be deceived! Stay with Master Potter! It's a trick. You must go to the Mountain of Fire."

Choices are made and destinies decided amidst desperate pleas from families and friends. Master Craftsman's men collect dozens of vessels, placing them in his coaches. The grieving vessels left behind in Master Potter's wagons offer fervent prayers for captured friends.

"Oh Lord, open their eyes to deception."

"Please, don't let them miss their destinies."

CHAPTER TWENTY-TWO

A MOTHER'S LOVE

Meanwhile, Master Craftsman focuses all of his attention on Beloved. You might as well come along and bring the rest of your mugs with you; I have most of your team already. I believe that Master Potter would want you to stay together. Aren't you their leader? I'll put you in my personal coach. Only very important vessels are allowed to ride there."

Comrade looks at Master Craftsman and says, "You're the thief Master Potter warned us about!"

Beloved shouts angrily, "I'll never go with you!"

"Let's see about that," sneers Master Craftsman as he turns on his heels and marches toward the end of the wagon train. When he returns he is clutching Purity. "My, what a beautiful little mug!" he sneers, leaning toward Beloved. "She looks a lot like you. Could this be your daughter?"

Purity is paralyzed with fear, too scared to speak or move.

Beloved reels, feeling as though she's in a bad dream. "How... where?" She chokes, unable to speak or even comprehend from where Purity came.

Bringing the frightened little mug up to his dark gaze he whispers, "Promiscuous, isn't it? I know your brother. He belongs to me. If you come with me, I'll reunite you two. Your mother will follow wherever you go. She doesn't want to lose you again."

Struggling to get free from his awful grasp, Purity shouts as loud as she can, "You're a liar! I don't believe my brother is your friend!"

Hearing Purity's cries for help jolts Beloved into action. "Give her to me now. She belongs to Master Potter. The enemy has robbed our family for years, and I will not let it happen again. In the authority of Master Potter, I demand that you release her now."

"You have no power Forsaken," he says sneering at her.

Turning her tear-streaked face toward her mother, Purity calls out, "Mom, help me!"

A violent mother's love rages in Beloved as she watches her struggling daughter. She declares, "By Master Potter's shed blood you were defeated at the Cross. I break your demonic hold over my family. I bind you in His name."

As Beloved fights for her, Purity feels the fiery coal growing larger in her heart, filling her with warm feelings of her mother. Awesome revelation of Beloved's love for her explodes as a torrent of raw emotion overwhelms her.

Seeing in the Spirit, Purity watches two enormous guardian angels fighting along side her mom. Beloved shouts, "You have no authority to take her without her permission. Purity, fight! Declare your allegiance to Master Potter."

"Master Potter, please help me!" Turning toward Master Craftsman she screams, "By the power of His blood, let me go!" Doubling her fist, she smacks him in the eye. He cries out in pain and flings her toward the ground.

Beloved cries out, "No...Purity."

Always alert, her guardian angel catches her before she hits the snow covered ground.

Without a second's hesitation, Purity responds to Beloved's outstretched arms and the angel gently places her in Beloved's embrace.

A Failed Mission

Master Craftsman climbs on his wagon, cursing. At the crack of his whip, the horses snort and he heads out of camp. *No matter how many vessels I get, I'm in trouble for returning without Forsaken.*

Heavy deception covers the eyes of Self Assurance, Confidence, and other disillusioned vessels traveling with Master Craftsman.

Elder cringes as the coaches head down the mountain trail. The howling wind taunts his inability to protect the vessels. Some vessels left behind still question if they made the right decision as the departing coaches disappear into the blowing snow.

Joyful Reconciliation

In Beloved's wagon, Comrade and the remainder of the vessels huddle together praying and watching the reconciliation that is taking place. Beloved, clutching Purity tightly, rocks her crying daughter, "I'm so sorry; I'm so sorry," she wails. "Please, can you ever forgive me for leaving..."

"No Mom, I'm the one who's sorry..."

"Oh, Purity, you have nothing to apologize for. I'm the one who left. Please forgive me. I'm sorry you and Crusader had..."

"MOM," interrupts Purity, backing up to arm's length to look straight in her mother's eyes, "Amazing Grace told me how you wanted to come back, but

He wouldn't let you. It wasn't God's timing yet. I forgive you, and I'm sorry I hurt you when I screamed at you."

For a moment Beloved is motionless, trying to understand what Purity just said. Then a wave of relief sweeps over her, washing away years of anxiety. Unable to contain herself, she collapses into Purity's arms and sobs, "My baby, my baby…I'll never let you go again. You don't know how much I love you."

Deep in her heart, Purity can feel the coal burning again as her affection for Beloved continues to grow. "Mom, you fought for me, you protected me."

Comrade shouts praise to Master Potter for the miracle his best friend has just received. All the other vessels pray, praise, whoop, and holler, sharing in the joy. Beloved and Purity are oblivious to the commotion as they hold each other and weep.

COMRADE'S SECRET

For a split second Comrade stops rejoicing and watches Purity. He chokes back the emotions accompanying old memories churning inside him. Hidden secrets of his past erupt, the painful thoughts of his own daughter whom he didn't get to raise. Unlike Beloved who has shared her story, his shameful sin remains concealed.

Turning to the others, he clears the knot in his throat and yells, "Praise God for answered prayers!"

CHAPTER TWENTY-THREE

CAVERNS
OF ANCIENT MYSTERIES

꧁꧂

S nuggled under their fur lined blankets in Master Craftsman's wagon, Confidence and Self Assurance are filled with excitement at the thought of leaving the freezing mountain and going to the seashore at Comfort Cove. They
can't help but wonder at the foolish decision of the vessels who chose to stay
behind.

"Can you believe they didn't come with us, even after hearing that Master
Potter would be waiting for us in the village? It can't be His will for us to stay
in the midst of a storm when we're offered a way out. If this was a test they sure
blew it!"

The vessels discuss their prophetic destinies and recite to each other the
wonderful words they've received in the past. Some get notes out and read their
powerful promises, "For lo, the winter has passed and spring has begun."

Jumping up and down with excitement they squeal, "I can hardly wait!
Have you got your bathing suit and towel?"

Excitedly, Confidence shares his word, "Wait till you hear this... 'Your season of suffering is over. Now is the time for your destiny to come forth.'"

"That's an accurate word," Self Assurance says, "but I like mine better!
'He's taking you out of the fire; this is a time of promotion.'"

"Wow! Whoever gave you that word must really be a prophet!"

Self Assurance blushes. "Actually, I was concerned when I first got it. I
always thought the prophets said things about how we would suffer more. ...you
know, that dying to self stuff."

"Times are changing. Just as we don't have to go to the Mountain of Fire
and suffer, we no longer have to listen to gloom and doom prophets. Those old
guys are outdated. The latest trend in prophecy is to tell people what makes
them feel really good. It's a new time. I call these guys 'New Age prophets.'"

Brass lanterns illuminate the path ahead with an eerie yellow glow. It reflects off snowladen trees, casting long, tall shadows against the snow. When the wagons pass the wooden trail marker pointing to Comfort Cove, Self Assurance and Confidence exchange looks of surprise. They realize they just took an unexpected turn in the opposite direction.

Self Assurance decides to ask one of Master Craftsman's vessels, "Why are we turning here? This isn't the way to Comfort Cove. I thought he was in a hurry to get us to his house in the village?

HE HAS GREAT PLANS FOR YOU

Confidence squeals with excitement, "I'm really looking forward to those sandy beaches."

The emerald green pitcher looks down at them, "There's no need for concern! He has great plans for you! Didn't I just hear you telling each other your prophetic destinies?"

Hours pass as they climb higher into the rugged mountain range, leaving the tree line far below. The demonically driven storm catches up with the coaches. Master Craftsman relishes the fellowship of his unseen companions disguised in the negatively charged atmosphere of the storm.

Glancing at the captured pots behind him, ghoulish delight gushes from deep within as he thinks back on the havoc they just wreaked at the campsite. His joy is cut short by one black thought. He has failed to get Forsaken. He spits out a vile curse under his breath.

DON'T BE AFRAID

The vessels become quiet and pensive as the storm engulfs the string of coaches. Sensing their uneasiness, Master Craftsman calls out, "Don't be afraid. We're headed for my winter fortress just ahead. You'll be out of this storm before you know it."

A huge cavern cut into the side of the mountain looms ever larger in the distance. An enormous granite obelisk, hundreds of feet tall, stands as a silent sentinel before the entrance. The peaks of the rugged mountain rise to such lofty heights that they diminish its overpowering size. Etched in ice over the threshold of the entrance are the words, "Cavern of Ancient Mysteries."

Confidence points, "Self Assurance, we really have arrived! Look at those words! We're going into the deeper things of the Spirit. I knew we made the right decision to follow Master Craftsman."

As they enter the gaping mouth of the Dragon's fortress, Self Assurance excitedly yells, "Look at that! They're actually pulling the coaches right inside!"

CHAPTER TWENTY-FOUR

ENTRAPMENT

Four priests dressed in black hooded robes and wearing white aprons hurriedly light torches set into the center of eight granite columns bordering the dark room. Master Craftsman descends from his coach, but before his feet touch the ground the priests quickly grovel on their faces, careful to keep their heads lower than his.

Pompously marching toward an ornate throne adorned with double-headed eagles, Master Craftsman nods, signaling the priests to rise. The first priest, whose huge girth makes it impossible to get up without assistance, pushes himself up to his knees and flails his arms to signal for help. The other priests, after much pulling and groaning manage to lift him to his feet. Master Craftsman clenches his fists exposing white knuckles.

Looking up, the vessels try to make out the mysterious designs and celestial deities elaborately painted on the high ceiling. Huge winged gargoyles guard the passageways leading off from the main room.

The priests swarm around the wagons and carefully separate the vessels. The men are taken to one room and the women to another.

"Where are the ladies going?"

Master Craftsman reassures them, "Brothers, our sisters are going to a different sanctuary for purification purposes. You, on the other hand, are here to join the Brotherhood. Our society has survived the most diverse political, military, and religious conflicts through the ages. We do, however, have one woman in the Brotherhood. She is the Grande Dame. You will meet her very soon. But, now is the time for your initiation."

INITIATION RITUAL

Removing the vessel's old garments, the priests replace them with new black linen robes. Cords are tied around their necks symbolizing that they're being joined to the Great Architect of the Universe. Then they are blindfolded, and a knife is pressed against their hearts as they swear never to reveal the secrets of the Brotherhood.

After the short ceremony, they are placed into elaborate coffins made from acacia wood, inlaid with silver and gold, and decorated with a skull and crossbones.

Master Craftsman assures them, "Don't be afraid. This is just a symbolic drama of passing from death into life. It's part of the initiation all must go through in order to be brought into greater enlightenment.

"My priests will carry you down hidden passageways into my sanctuary. Your blindfolds will be removed when you reach your destination. Later when you have attained spiritual maturity, you will mentor others through these same channels."

Eight priests, acting as pallbearers, carry the heavy coffins on their shoulders, each filled with dozens of vessels. Traveling into the bowels of the mountain they enter into a silent, secret darkness.

The winding labyrinth of this impenetrable fortress leads them into a beautiful, subterranean cathedral. Removing their blindfolds, Master Craftsman points high on the icy wall directly above them to a huge eye framed inside the top point of a pyramid.

NEW WORLD ORDER

Pointing to the All-Seeing Eye he explains, "It penetrates into the unseen realms, giving you revelation and new insight. This is a universal symbol of my New World Order, where men of all religions come together based on their belief in one god."

Confidence tells the vessels next to him, "Master Potter told us He was the only way to salvation. This is awesome! It means no one has to be left out. Everyone can be saved!"

The priests place the vessels on granite pews lined with velvet cushions. The seats are in rows on either side of the room facing a black and gold marble altar decorated with bronze serpents.

Facing east, it sits in the center of an encircled five-pointed star, a pentagram. Directly behind the altar stands an 80-foot ice sculpture of Master Craftsman with his arms opened wide to welcome all that come.

Two pillars, only slightly lower, stand on either side of the towering ice sculpture. The pillar on the left is topped with a terrestrial globe. The pillar on the right supports a celestial globe containing the signs of the zodiac.

"Usually it takes long seasons of discipline and study to come to this very special place. You men have showed great courage and maturity at Precarious

Pass when you chose to go against your deceived friends and associates. With that in mind, I have decided to allow you to take part in this ceremony and be initiated into the Brotherhood."

THE GRAND DAME

The vessels watch as a bulky woman, whose face is obscured behind an elaborate feathered half-mask, makes a slow, dramatic entrance. She scans the room greedily, making sure that all eyes are appropriately adoring her. Wearing a black satin dress with a draped neckline, she cradles a jeweled scepter in her arms as if she's holding a baby. A flowing purple robe with a multicolored satin lining is draped ceremoniously over her shoulders.

The four priests quickly scurry toward her and bow. She releases them with a nod of her head, and they rise. "So good to see you Madame False ...er...a...hum...Grand Dame, I mean," blurts the bulbous priest as he breaks out in a drenching sweat from his bright red face as he attempts to bow low over his rotund body.

"You idiot," she hisses through yellow teeth. She takes a swing at him with her scepter hitting him squarely on the shoulder, which causes her to slip off her high heeled shoe and teeter off-balance. Catching herself, she regains her composure, smoothes down her black dress over her ample bosom, and nods toward Master Craftsman. The four priests flank her, two on each side and they step together in formation approaching Master Craftsman.

Several priests gather around Master Craftsman and slip off his long fur coat. Another priest replaces it with an exquisite white hooded garment. Gold framed mirrors run down the front of this ceremonial robe and refract the torch-light throughout the cavern. Gold embroidered symbols are sewn into the hem and sleeves.

"Wow, he almost glows like Master Potter. He's magnificent," gushes Confidence.

"Maybe God had two sons," says Self Assurance.

The last priest hands Master Craftsman what appears to be a large, leather-bound book.

"Look at that huge old Bible they gave him."

"I wonder why he's placing it on the altar? When Master Potter told us we should live by the Word, I didn't know He meant this."

Master Craftsman meticulously opens the bible, revealing beautifully engraved illustrations on each page. Turning to face the vessels, he extends his hands to the Grande Dame and she hurriedly rummages through the inner pockets of her purple robe. "Just a minute...just a second. I know they're here," she says producing worn Tarot cards, a crumpled grocery list, a package of ciga-rettes, and three long mother-of-pearl cigarette holders. "Here, take this for a minute," she says shoving the items into Master Craftsman's hands.

"I put them in here this morning." She continues pulling items, a crystal, a candle, several silver flasks of alcohol, and a set of keys. "Ah, here they are!" she croaks in a deep, throaty voice finally producing a compass and a square. She exchanges them for her other items and stuffs everything back inside her pockets, oblivious to Master Craftsman's clenched teeth and white knuckles sig-naling his deep irritation.

A HIGHER SPIRITUAL PLANE

Reverently he holds them up. "These are ancient symbols of your right of passage out of the physical realm into the higher spiritual plane. The square rep-resents our duties to our brothers. The compass gives enlightenment in the duty we owe ourselves."

He places the square on top of the open bible and sets the compass on top of them both. "Each one of you must come forward and seal this initiation by kissing the compass and square cradled in the open pages of the ancient scrip-tures."

Master Craftsman describes the great honor awaiting them when their names are added to many others on the great obelisk. The privilege of being chosen to join the Brotherhood is deeply felt by each vessel as he eagerly wait his turn.

Confidence is the first to go. As he is ceremoniously escorted to the altar, he reverently bows to deliver his kiss. Master Craftsman thrusts his face into the hard cold metal of the compass.

As he rises, he crinkles his nose and coughs because of a slight sulfuric odor, but shrugs it off as he is handed a pen and told to sign his name in the an-cient book the priest is holding. His signature becomes a witness to his ever-lasting covenant with Master Craftsman.

BLINDED TO THE TRUTH

He's no longer able to grasp the truth as demons of deception and witch-craft wind their evil shrouds around him. His heart becomes veiled and his eyes so dim the light of life can barely be seen within them.

The elaborate ceremony continues and long white aprons are put on over the men's black robes. They are told the aprons are designed to cover their loins and symbolize the fact that the covenant blessing and curses will be passed on to their future generations.

Confidence is given a gold ring with the compass and square etched into it as a sign of the alliance. Gasps of delight fill the room as each of the vessels follow his lead in bowing to a different god.

When all are back on their cushions, Master Craftsman directs their attention to the area behind them. "These walls were specially designed with a mirror like quality to reveal your true image. Just look at your reflection. You've truly become beautiful through this sacred rite."

Fiery torches arranged around the room create dancing rainbows of color on the cavern's icy walls, a shimmering lightshow of muted blues, reds, and oranges. Enthralled by their own reflection, they view themselves as lovely glazed vessels instead of the awful reality of their distorted images.

The deceived vessels look at themselves and each other cheering wildly at their good fortune to be the chosen of Master Craftsman. He tells them proudly, "You're experiencing my new revolutionary kiln. How do you like it? I call it, Cold Fire! It brings the same wonderful results, but without the pain of Master Potter's antiquated firing process."

Unable to see their ugly, dull finish, the vessels believe the lie that one firing is enough. They congratulate themselves on their decision of not going to the Mountain of Fire. After all, their true colors are coming forth in shining glory.

Master Craftsman looks around the room and sees the Grande Dame posturing in front of the mirrored wall, strutting and turning like a model, enjoying the slim, young image she sees. "God I love this room," she says. "I haven't looked this good since I was 18!"

UNHOLY COMMUNION

Shaking his head in disgust, he announces to the vessels, "I've planned a sumptuous meal in honor of this very special occasion. But first let us take communion." At the sound of his hands clapping, servants enter carrying silver platters with crystal goblets filled with red wine and piles of hot bread.

The euphoric vessels eagerly raise their glasses in salute to the day they were rescued from a freezing death on the way to Precarious Pass. "To Master Craftsman! He saved us! Hurrah!"

Hours later, the vessels are gorged with gourmet food and too much wine. Some of the sleepy vessels doze. Confidence looks at Self Assurance through bloodshot eyes. Putting his arm around Confidence's neck, Self Assurance slurs, "Whadya think? Is this the life or not?"

"Yep!" replies Confidence. "To the Brotherhood! Burrrrp!"

CHAPTER TWENTY-FIVE

THE PRIESTS UNVEILED

In a backroom, the priests pull off their hoods and hang up their robes. "It was a moving ceremony today," says Pastor Compromise.

Pastor Beguiler adds, "My son, Enchanter, couldn't make it this time, but sends his regrets. He missed a good ceremony."

"Yes, it was very moving," says the Chief of Police.

As the fourth priest pulls off his hood, the smell of stale cigar smoke and gin wafts from him. The huge hulk of Mayor Lecherous is revealed as he takes off his robe. Running his fingers across the few strands left on his mostly bald, greasy head, he adds, "Our numbers are growing."

"Don't be so quick to congratulate yourselves boys. It doesn't matter how many vessels we get if we don't get Forsaken! Our master wants to win that challenge with the Godhead," says Madame False Destiny rummaging through her pockets for a smoke.

"At the next meeting, Master Craftsman has OK'd the dedication of my adopted granddaughter to be a priestess. The baby that was left at my door is almost five. I'm anxious for you to start mentoring her, Madame. Maybe some day she'll be a Grande Dame like you."

Striking a match and taking a draw on her mother-of-pearl cigarette holder, Madame snips condescendingly, "Very few make it to my level boys."

CHAPTER TWENTY-SIX

DEATH IS SUMMONED

S atan prepares to hold court with his generals high above the Cavern of Ancient Mysteries. His strategic leaders from Comfort Cove are ushered forward and given front row seats—Pastor Compromise, the Chief of Police, Mayor Lecherous, and Madame False Destiny join Pastor Beguiler, who retired to the seashore from Deeper Life Commune.

Farther back in the ranks, Fear of Man, Religious Ritual, and Law n' Order exchange blows, fighting each other for better seats. Each one is grateful they aren't the one being summoned to trial.

Master Craftsman appears out of a yellow green sulfur smoke and waits for Satan to appear. An ominous black portal opens from the second heavens, and Satan's thunderous voice shatters the atmosphere. Horrifying stench precedes this vile being's descent to earth. The mountain quakes under the force of his fury, and Master Craftsman braces himself to keep from falling. Chills run up his back striking terror in his heart. Struggling to maintain his composure, he quickly changes into vapor and takes on his true form: Death.

Terrifying anticipation electrifies the atmosphere as Death bows low before the Prince of Darkness.

Satan coldly smiles, "Well brother, what have you been up to?"

DEATH'S DEFENSE

"I've just initiated hundreds of new converts. They've bowed low to your image, Most Worshipful Master. I'm so pleased I'm here to give you the good news in person. We should have the final count soon."

Sadistic laughter breaks out in the court as the demonic jury snickers over the anguish this must have inflicted in the heart of Master Potter. Satan is not amused and continues to stare at Death through evil, piercing eyes.

Erupting in murderous contempt, he bellows, "Do you really believe you can fool me? Are you so stupid to think I don't know what you're up to? Tell me again whose image they worshiped."

Nervously groveling, Death stammers, "Oh Most Worshipful Master, may I explain? This was only the beginning. These weak and sniveling vessels are not sufficiently initiated into the deeper mysteries. We must wait before we reveal your magnificent splendor. Even my image was a disguise as Master Craftsman. We must take them slowly, step-by-step, or they may run back to Master Potter."

Hearing the name of his archenemy, Satan vomits a fiery blast of sulfur and brimstone. "That sculpture of you is blasphemous! I am the only one worthy of worship! Get rid of it!"

Law 'n Order nudges Religious Ritual next to him as they try to anticipate what Death will say next, "He's got him now!"

"Oh, Great Architect of the Universe, builder and designer of all that exists, we could get rid of the sculpture but hear me—this is only the initial stage of their spiritual demise. Soon they will be ready to journey into the deeper caverns to the Inner Sanctum. There you will be revealed in your true image, and they will adore and worship you forever.

You Failed

Satan thunders. "Not only do you erect images of yourself and steal my worship, but you failed in your assignment to capture Forsaken's heart. She still gives herself to Him freely, and now she has her daughter back!"

Beloved's face materializes before Death reminding him of his failure to enslave her for his master. Slamming Him against the wall, Satan growls, "You remember the wager I made with the Godhead for Forsaken's affections? You have one more chance to persuade her to be my prophetic voice. She could bring thousands into my kingdom."

Death tries to conceal his fear, "If she will not serve you then I'll just drag her bloody carcass here as your eternal trophy."

"No. I don't want to take her out. I want to win her affections. I want the Godhead to see this precious Bride betray Them. I want to thrust the knife in the Trinity's heart."

Morbid excitement pulses through Satan's blood as he formulates his next diabolical plans for her capture. "I don't want Forsaken dead, but Promiscuous is a different story. Forsaken would renounce Master Potter, she would become His enemy, if she loses her precious daughter," he bursts into maniacal laughter, "again!"

A dark prophetic vision of the earthly realm appears showing the pottery wagons at the base camp. "They're tired, cold and vulnerable. Now is the time to attack. Remember, the daughter is the key the Forsaken's heart."

CHAPTER TWENTY-SEVEN

THE LONG NIGHT

The shrieking cries of demons fuel the howling winds blowing down from Precarious Pass. The strange resonance issues a fierce warning to anyone trying to advance that way. Snow drifts into steep banks against the wagons leaving the mournful little vessels even more uncomfortable.

Elder moves from wagon to wagon. "We've got a dangerous day ahead of us. Finish your prayers, and then I want you all to get some sleep—all except you two," he says winking at Purity and Beloved. "I think you've got some catching up to do."

The vessels join together in little groups grieving for their loved ones and petitioning Master Potter to save them. With great passion the intercessors travail for those captured by the lies of Master Craftsman. After shedding many tears the rest of the vessels fall into a fitful sleep.

THE LOST YEARS

Purity and Beloved are huddled together under the itchy burlap blankets in the corner of the wagon. The hours pass quickly and emotions come tumbling out healing the pain of their long separation.

Stroking her hair and holding her close, Beloved covers Purity with kisses. "Now that we've found each other, we'll never be apart!" Taking Purity's tear-streaked face into her hands, she gazes into her eyes, "Oh how I love you!"

"Mom, I've missed you so much. They told me you didn't love me and didn't want to see me again. Sometimes I believed them, and it would be so hard... I'd sneak out to the edge of the commune and plead for you to come back to me."

"Oh Purity, I've been so afraid you'd never want to see me again. I was afraid you didn't understand what happened. Please forgive me for not being there for you."

"I always knew it wasn't your fault. You protected me that day they drove you out of camp. I've searched for you for such a long time. I'd all but given up finding you. One day in town I was standing on the docks just watching the tide and I got invited to come to the Potter's House. Then I got put in this set. When I saw you I was so afraid you wouldn't want me in your life, and I guess I thought I'd hurt you before you could hurt me again."

"Not want you! My child, if you only knew how I've longed for this day and the day I'll see your brother again."

"Oh Mom, I don't know where Crusader is. They sent me away when I was 13 years old, and I'm glad they did."

SUPERNATURAL PROTECTION

"Grandpa began sneaking into my room at night and staring at me. I'd pretend to be asleep and pray he would just go away, but one night he began touching me. Mom, I was so afraid! All I could do was call for Master Potter to help me."

Beloved clenches her fists, "I knew he was an evil man. It makes me sick just thinking of it."

A new excitement enters Purity's voice, "Calm down, Mom, wait till I tell you what happened! When I called out, Master Potter's name, and it was as if some invisible force lifted Grandpa up and threw him across the room. You should have seen his face. He was really scared! He started to back move toward me and was thrown against the wall a second time. He was too afraid to touch me again. He left the room, and they sent me away that night."

"Oh Purity, I'm so sorry for you. You couldn't have known it, but I was abused as a little girl."

"Mom, I'm sorry."

"Thank you, sweetheart. But let me tell you the rest of the story! I had a terrible nightmare one night. First I saw myself as a little girl being abused by my father, and then suddenly it changed to you and Grandpa Beguiler. I woke up terrified, and Holy Spirit urged me to pray. I went into a deep travail and stayed there until I knew you were OK. I've never forgotten that night."

Beloved looks sadly into her daughter's eyes, "I'm certain it was the same night, and those were guardian angels protecting you. I'm so sorry I wasn't there to protect you. Can you ever forgive me?"

"But you did protect me with your prayers. Oh, Mom, I've waited so long to find you, and I was so afraid you had died out there in the desert. All I've wanted was to see you again. Of course I forgive you."

Beloved embraces her tenderly, telling her, "I'll do all I can to make up for those lost years. If I could, I'd go back there and tell that evil man a thing or two!"

"Grandfather's no longer there. After Grandma died, I heard he retired to the seashore at Comfort Cove.

"Oh Purity, what can I ever say or do to make up for all you've been through?"

"Mom, please don't worry. Master Potter has made up for all I will ever go through. You did the best thing a mom can do. You told me about Him."

A huge wave of love sweeps over Beloved as she hears the promise Master Potter made to her so many years ago come true. He has been faithful to heal her daughter and to reunite them. She fingers the necklace again and offers a quick prayer of thanksgiving.

The bitter, howling wind pours in under the tarps and causes the two women to snuggle closer together. "Here sweetheart, take more of this blanket," says Beloved, tucking it around her daughter.

"What's that noise?" asks Purity. "It sounds like an injured animal, and it's very close by."

"Oh Purity," laughs Beloved. "That's Comrade snoring."

CRUSADER

"What about Crusader? Does he hate me? He was so little. When I close my eyes I can still see that last forlorn look on his face. I was sure he didn't understand, and I knew they'd lie to him."

"It was pretty bad after you left. He hated father and grandfather for what they did to you and never forgave them for making me a servant. I would tell him what really happened whenever we were alone. When he got a little older he saw right through them, and he despised their religious rules and refused to follow them."

"Your father, Enchanter, was always a charmer. He could convince anyone of anything. I guess I'm proof of that," Beloved admits with a shrug. "He destroyed many people's lives. He and his father hid behind their titles as pastors and led Deeper Life commune into great deception. I'm so glad you helped Crusader see the truth."

"We talked about you all the time Mom, and I know he loves you. I tried to stay and protect him, but that wasn't possible. As bad as it was there, I begged to stay, but Grandma would have none of it and sent me to her relatives in Comfort Cove."

ENCHANTER'S NEW FAMILY

Sighing, Purity continues, "Almost immediately after you left, Dad married again and had twins, a boy named Charmer, and a girl named Bewitched. I guess he's raising his son Charmer to take over for him one day.

"Eventually they branded Crusader with the name Rebellious and forbade the other kids to have anything to do with him. I heard he ran away as soon as he was old enough. I looked for him, but could never find him. Someone told me he took a job as a crew member on a merchant ship and sailed for the Land of Lost Promises.

"I wish I could say I didn't love Dad after the way he treated me, but something in me always yearned for him to accept me. It was so hard watching him hug his other daughter, Bewitched, while he treated me as if I didn't exist."

FAMILY SECRET

"I'm so sorry Purity. To have your family abuse you so horribly!" Fresh anger surges through Beloved's heart. "I don't know how you survived." Sorrowfully, Beloved tells her, "There's something else I want you to know now that you're old enough. Remember that terrible day I was driven out of the commune?"

"How could I forget?"

"I'd like you to know the truth about that day."

Purity nods solemnly.

"Your father had a history of unfaithfulness, and I caught him with one of the young people from the church. When I tried to expose him, he and your grandfather had me kicked out. I tried to take you and Crusader with me, but they wouldn't let me. Just when I thought I was going to die in the wilderness, Amazing Grace rescued me and brought me to the Tent of the Lord where I was reunited with Master Potter. If only I could have been there to protect you."

"Mom, you told us about Master Potter when I was a little girl. When you left we talked to Him. Sometimes it didn't seem that He was listening, but He's always been there in those darkest hours. At times I thought I didn't want to live, and He would come to me and bring such comfort and peace." Purity drops her head and stares at the floor. "I did have a season that was really difficult. I got into trouble…but I've always loved Him."

Beloved is overwhelmed as she hears of Master Potter's faithfulness to her daughter. The deep anguish of their lost years is released, and huge sobs rise up from the depths of their hearts. Beloved buries her face in Purity's shoulder. Laughing and crying together they look again and again into each other's eyes wondering if there will ever be enough time to make up for the lost years.

Chapter Twenty-Eight

WATCHMAN RETURNS

After several hours the vessels are awakened by the sounds of horses entering camp. Fearful it might be Master Craftsman, Beloved quickly covers Purity with the blankets and whispers for her to lie still.

Harvester goes to the back of the wagon to see who has arrived. Smiling widely, he comes back to announce, "Watchman and the men have returned. Our prayers have been answered." Beloved lets out a deep sigh.

The howling wind and driving snow continues down the mountain pass leaving behind drifts and icy snow packs. The returning men jump down from their horses and hurriedly report to Elder.

"We tried to get back sooner but had to hole up for the night because of the heavy snowfall. But just as we thought, there was no avalanche. It's going to be slow going, but if we travel quietly we should be able to make it before the next big one hits."

Elder extends a cup of hot coffee to Watchman. "You were right about Master Craftsman. He convinced some of the vessels to go with him. We had quite a war on our hands. I'll never forgive myself for sending you away. We could have saved more if only you'd been here."

Walking to the wagons they rouse the sleepy vessels to tell them they must leave immediately. Approaching Beloved's team, Elder declares, "Master Potter is waiting for you at the Mountain of Fire. None of what happened last night escaped Him. Just remember, He's aware of your pain, and Watchman and I will bring you to Him safely."

DAMAGE ASSESSMENT

Elder turns to Beloved, "We need a head count. Do you think you could organize one for your wagon?"

"Comrade, you're good at getting things done; would you take care of it?"

"You bet Beloved, I'll get right on it."

"Long Suffering! Are you there?"

"Where do you think I'd be? I knew that guy was up to no good, but no one ever listens to me."

"Harvester?"

The deep booming voice comes back, "Yeah, I'm right here."

"Golden Incense?"

"I'm here! Any chance for a cup of tea?"

"Who else is missing?"

Fearless calls out, "I'm missing one of my wine goblets, but the rest are here with Joyful and me."

Comrade tells her, "Two of our mugs are gone."

Numb with the loss of her friends Beloved announces, "We almost lost Champion and Generosity. I'm so glad they're still with us."

Names of missing loved ones are shouted throughout the wagon as the vessels renew their efforts to bring order out of the dark night's chaos. Elder directs the drivers to harness the horses and ready the wagons for the hazardous journey ahead.

Watchman tells the vessels, "Last night's snowfall has built up on the slopes above us making the pass extremely dangerous. In addition to that, we have powerful enemies who would like to see us destroyed before we reach the other side. We must be very silent as we traverse the pass and remember to pray. The slightest noise could cause an avalanche."

I CAN'T LEAVE

Beloved raises her tearstained face to Watchman's loving gaze. "I can't leave without my team. You have to rescue them! Master Potter wouldn't want me to leave without them!"

"There's no time to go back. They've made their decision to follow Master Craftsman. They wouldn't come with us, even if we tried to convince them to. They doubt Master Potter's love for them and refuse to believe He knows best. Bottom line is, when things got difficult they loved comfort more than Him."

Golden Incense agrees wholeheartedly, "That's right! I've seen plenty of vessels like that. So selfcentered they always take the easy way out and then blame someone else for their bad fortune."

Watchmen smiles sadly, "They didn't take the easy way out; they just think they did." A tear trickles down his weathered face.

Beloved remembers her battle in the wilderness with the same issue and how hard it was to hear the voice of Holy Spirit after she gave into her old ways. She looks at Watchman sadly; compassion floods her heart for all the lost vessels.

Watchman takes her hand and tells her, "Everyone must go through the high fire! The choices they made will have awful consequences and may take years to undo. But, when they finally call out to Master Potter, He will rescue them. You know that from experience."

Beloved smiles and blushes.

"And," continues Watchman, "even in the midst of great loss, this is a wonderful time of reunion with your daughter. It's the answer to many of your prayers. You can't go after those vessels; they're Master Potter's responsibility. Your responsibility is to spend more time with your daughter."

SHARING STORIES

"I won't argue about that assignment," she replies with a smile. Turning to Purity she says, "When I was wandering in the desert Amazing Grace was such a wonderful guide. He was such a faithful…"

"Oh, Mom, He was so faithful to me too."

"I couldn't have made it without Him."

"Sometimes it was hard to understand the things that He required. Once He actually had me jump across a deep ravine cut in the mountainside…"

"Did you have to do that too? I had to jump there. I thought I would die."

"I was sure I would die!"

"I threw a little fit there because He wouldn't come help me. The only reason I jumped was because I knew I couldn't get back to the Potter's House."

"Me too. Did you try to return?" asks Purity.

"Yes. I tried to march right back down that tree lined path toward the Potter's House. I didn't like the desert or Amazing Grace in the beginning…"

"But," interrupts Purity laughing, "You can't get out the way you got in!"

"I know that to be a fact!" says Beloved overcome by laughter. "You can bet I tried. When I finally jumped my guardian angel, Valiant, caught me in midair as I was falling toward the rocks below."

"Your guardian angel is Valiant? That's so funny; mine's Gallant."

"Maybe they're brothers?" Beloved giggles.

"Did you go to the Tent of the Lord?"

"Yes!"

"Did you follow a star?"

"Yes!"

"Oh, Purity, we've walked the same path."

"Look, Mom! You're twisting your hair around your finger. I do that too!" The two women delight in their similarities and bond as they share more of their journeys with each other until the sun comes up the next morning.

MOVING OUT!

Everything that makes noise is tied down or discarded. Burlap is bound around the horses' hoofs to silence their steps. The wagons begin to move slowly out of camp toward the Mountain of Fire.

The vessels huddle together in the cold wagons to comfort each other and find warmth. Spirits of Depression swirl around the grieving vessels in an effort to block any encouragement the vessels are feeling.

Purity takes her mother's face between her hands. Lifting it up she softly tells her, "I love you Mom. You look so tired; I want you to rest for a while. Will you do that?"

Beloved nods her head and lies down. Purity pulls the cover up around her neck. Looking around she spies Long Suffering not far away and asks her to keep an eye on her mother as she goes to find Comrade.

Chapter Twenty-Nine

Precarious Pass

Sitting atop his pinnacle in the Formidable Mountain Range, Death territorially governs the vast expanse before him. From his lofty heights he watches the activity below as the wagons move out. His evil cohorts gather round him waiting for their orders. Not wanting to provoke his awful fury, they remain strangely quiet so his fierce rage won't explode on them.

Finally his dark scaly eyes turn to them, "If any one of you fails...he'll answer to me. We will make Forsaken curse the day she met Master Potter! But if you fail, you'll curse this day even more. Get her, get her daughter, and anyone else this pathetic creature loves."

One of his vile spirits breaks the silence, hissing, "I want Comrade, and I know just how to do it!" Sadistic laughter and competition breaks out in the cruel ranks. Each devil boasts how it will be the one to please the master and destroy the most vessels.

Deep, guttural growls escape from Death's gaping wet mouth as he launches in flight. His huge wings move in powerful accelerated surges to join his horde of evil disciples in midair. Dodging the missiles of glory shot from cannons of praise they cloak themselves in the ancient camouflage of a violent storm.

The sky darkens with black ominous clouds, and bloodcurdling shrieks blend with the howling wind as it drives relentlessly toward the base camp.

The pottery wagons slowly creak up the narrow trail toward the Mountain of Fire. As they leave the base camp behind the eerie wind once again howls through Precarious Pass.

Avalanche?

A thick, wet fog hovers over the winter landscape of icecovered trees and boulders creating an unearthly scene on the slopes above. Long dagger-shaped icicles hang from branches of the fir trees causing them to groan in the winter wind.

Suddenly, a gunshot echoes through the pass filling the vessels with terror. Eyes wide with fear, they run to look out from under the tarp.

"Get down; someone's shooting at us."

"No, no! It's an avalanche!"

Holding up the flap, Harvester points to the scene above them. Passing by a tall grove of trees, they watch as a frozen limb suddenly snaps off with a loud cracking noise. It hits the snowpacked ground with a heavy thud. A powdery fountain of snow and ice crystals sprays the passing wagon.

Sweet Adoration grips Harvester, "I'm not sure whether to laugh or cry! That was so close. It could have hit us or even caused an avalanche."

Wicked laughter erupts among Death's henchmen, delighted by the apprehension of the vessels. A small force swoops down and lands on the icy boughs lining the trail. Jumping up and down furiously, they gleefully snap off more limbs. Snap! Crack! Each impact creates explosions of snow and ice, sending shudders through the vessels and whipping the demons into an evil frenzy.

"We're going to die!" Generosity cries.

Champion joins in, "I knew we should have gone with Master Craftsman."

"We couldn't go back if we wanted; the trail is too narrow! We need to trust Master Potter." Steadfast exhorts, trying to calm the vessels.

Harvester also realizes they can't go back as he looks down the side of the wagon into a deep chasm below. Shivering at the sight of a sheer cliff just a few feet from the wagon wheels, he quickly closes the tarp. Nudging Beloved, he urgently whispers for her to gather her team and pray.

CHAPTER THIRTY

GARMENT OF PRAISE

The storm intensifies and frozen gusts engulf the wagons. Death's voice screeches amid the thunder, "Attack! Destroy!" Tormenting spirits of Accusation and Shame drop from the churning clouds and slither under the tarps to harass Beloved.

"You could have saved your team if you weren't so distracted with Purity."

"You never should have been a leader anyway!"

"A divorced woman!"

"Who do you think you are?"

Weak and worn out from loss of sleep and the trauma of the previous night, Beloved tries to summon the troops to pray. Demons beat her down at every turn with more poisonous accusations that explode like arrows into her heart and mind.

"If you're such a great leader, why didn't you rescue them? Master Potter will never trust you in leadership after this."

"What good is it for you to pray? It didn't help your team, did it?"

Purity moves close to her and whispers, "I'm really proud of you Mom. It wasn't your fault they made bad decisions." Putting her arm around her mother, Purity rubs the back of her neck affectionately. "You're too hard on yourself. You're not Master Potter."

"You did your best," adds Harvester.

Long Suffering sits by watching. *I wish I knew how to help Beloved. I guess I'll just pray silently.*

"I'm their leader! They could be injured or dead right now." Beloved bows her head in despair, remaining unresponsive to Purity's affection.

All efforts to encourage Beloved fail as the demons gain more ground and she entertains the sinister spirits. Invigorated by their success, they renew their efforts to lure her to Death and his master.

"You should go back, even if the others won't. How can you leave them in his hands?"

"You could become a hero instead of an utter failure. Master Potter made you responsible for them!"

Beloved covers her face with the burlap blanket and turns away.

REPEAT AFTER ME

Long Suffering watches her old enemies of Self-hatred and Despair attack her friend. *Master Potter help Beloved now*, prays Long Suffering.

"You help her Long Suffering. You're the answer to your own prayer," says her guardian angel, Exhorter

"I...I don't understand. What can I do?"

"You're familiar with these tormenting spirits; you've struggled with them all your life. But they can be defeated."

"Should I use my sword?"

"Yes, use the Word, but I'm going to give you another weapon," he says holding up an embroidered multicolored robe.

"It's beautiful; what is it?"

"Slip it on, and you'll see," he says holding it open. "It's the garment of praise for the spirit of heaviness."

Boldness comes over Long Suffering that she's never before felt. "This can't be happening to me!"

Exhorter rolls his eyes at her and touches her head.

Faith immediately floods into her, "I mean, praise the Lord. Master Potter will provide a way of escape!"

She kneels by Beloved and begins to sing over her, "Let God arise and your enemies be scattered."

"I'm such a failure; I lost two of my mugs!" moans Beloved.

Long Suffering looks discouraged and turns back to her guardian angel. "I can't help her."

"Don't give up; your friend needs you."

Self Pity and Despair wrap their tentacles tightly around Beloved's chest making her voice dull and lifeless. "Go away Long Suffering! I just want to be left alone!"

"No Beloved, your team needs you. Help, help! Get it off me!" Long Suffering screams as a tentacle of Self Pity grabs her too.

Exhorter comes alongside her and whispers, "Just stay calm. You can prevail over these spirits. I'll teach you. Lay your hands on Beloved." Long Suffering leans over Beloved, and another tentacle coils tightly around her. "Help. I can't do this! We're both going to die!"

"You have power you don't understand," says Exhorter. "Repeat after me: I break the familiar spirits…"

Whimpering, Long Suffering repeats, "I break the familiar spirits…"

"…of self-hatred and pity…"

"…of self-hatred and pity…"

"…and I command them to leave now."

"…and I command them to leave now."

A NEW BOLDNESS

"Now sing," commands Exhorter.

Hesitantly at first, then clearer and clearer she sings, "Let God arise, and let His enemies be scattered."

Long Suffering watches in amazement as the garment of praise begins to glow. Her warfare songs activate angelic swords to slice through the demonic realm holding her and Beloved. Whimpering, the evil spirits exit the wagon.

Freed, Beloved cries out, "Thank you Long Suffering! I'm going to be all right now."

A new boldness comes over Long Suffering. "Everybody listen," she says excitedly. "We need to break the enemy's back with praise. Really, it works. Sing with me!"

Exhorter laughs, "She's getting it."

Beloved begins to sing in her prayer language, and warm tears gently flow down her cheeks as her rich alto voice activates the heavenly realm.

Turing to her guardian angel, Long Suffering asks, "I really like this coat. Can I keep it?"

He laughs and says, "It was made just for you."

CHAPTER THIRTY-ONE

FALLEN WARRIOR

Watchman rides to them and encourages the little group in their worship and adoration. Before leaving to go to the next wagon, he informs them they are about to enter the treacherous pass. "Last night's storm added another heavy layer of snow to already dangerous conditions. At this time of year, there's always a possibility of an avalanche. You must be very quiet until we reach the other side. The slightest noise could bring it down on us."

Golden Incense gathers her delicate cups and saucers, "Hush everyone. Now is the time to silently pray in the Spirit. It may not be loud in the natural realm, but it shouts in the spiritual realm!"

COMRADE'S DEMISE

Huge angelic warriors position themselves strategically along Precarious Pass, fully armed and ready for battle. Their fiery eyes search out the landscape infuriating the demonic horde. Ministering angels move among the vessels giving comfort and imparting faith that Master Potter has not deserted them.

Nonetheless, tension builds as they progress along the narrow trail. The vessels are not used to being quiet for very long. Looking for Comrade, Purity calls out softly, "Comrade, it's Purity. Where are you?"

Listening carefully, all she hears is the crunch of ice under the wagon wheels and the howling wind outside. About to give up, she makes one last effort, looking in the dark shadows under the shelves. Gasping in surprise to see Comrade with his arms around Tenderhearted, she hurriedly returns to her mother.

LUST ATTACKS

The winged serpent, Lust, coiled in the recess of the wagon watches the couple. He waits for just the right moment to deliver his poisonous venom. As soon as Purity leaves, he quickly intrudes into Comrade's thoughts with powerful fantasies and delusions, awakening deep, sensual urges.

Holding them tightly within his ghastly wings, Lust puffs up into an enormous cobra, striking Comrade with his deadly venom. No longer able to keep his lusty appetites under control, he erupts in desire and passionately pulls Tenderhearted to himself.

Beloved comes running to the scene just as Comrade jumps on the fragile china saucer. A loud clanking precedes a sharp crack as his heavy weight falls on her. Tenderhearted cries out in pain as she breaks in half.

The sexual sin of Comrade provides the open gate for which Death is waiting. Signaling his troops to launch fiery missiles into the mountainside, they set off tons of snow and ice.

A thunderous roar and terrible shaking of the earth vibrates through Precarious Pass.

Before the vessels have time to react, the snow violently tears through the tarps, smashing the fragile pots against one another.

Watching from above, the devils delight as the avalanche's powder cloud rolls down the slope, taking out Beloved's wagon and six others. Tumbling over and over in the horrific onslaught, the wagons finally come to rest in the bottom of a steep ravine, crushed by the enormous weight of snow and ice. Morbid excitement gushes over Death, and he orders a new assault on the hurt and dying vessels.

Out of the powdery catastrophe below the huge winged serpent, Lust, arises, screeching his victory over Comrade.

CHAPTER THIRTY-TWO

SEARCH AND RESCUE

A fter the deafening roar of the avalanche, all is still, and for a moment there's a strange silence. As Elder listens, all he can hear is the wind howling down the pass. Looking down the incline, he and Watchman see only splintered pieces of wood and pottery shards strewn across the slope.

Faintly at first, and then more clearly, the cries of snowbound vessels begin to be heard. Elder turns around and shouts orders to the drivers of the unscathed wagons, "You men come with me! We're forming rescue teams. The rest of you get warm clothing and food prepared! And pray with all you've got! We need Master Potter to help us." When he turns back around he sees Watchman already at the bottom of the ravine starting to dig. Several drivers grab shovels and start the climb down the steep ravine.

Death ruthlessly leads his demonic invasion into the depths of the snowbound wagons, attacking the helpless vessels. Chaos and confusion reign over the devastation.

Watchman takes out his shotgun and fires off a supernatural blast of glory opening heavenly portals into the realm of eternity. Two celestial gates swing open, allowing explosions of light to burst into earth's atmosphere as angelic reinforcements thunder through the portals.

THE BATTLE INTENSIFIES

The righteous anger of the Father roars through Heaven for the victims of Death and his henchmen. The battle intensifies, and fiery angelic warriors release surges of resurrection power.

Glistening swords slice through the demonic shroud over Precarious Pass giving entrance to divine light and burning off the heavy fog. This heavenly invasion brings new strength to the rescue teams as they courageously fight to release the vessels from their snowbound tombs.

Caught offguard by the sudden explosion of heaven's power erupting in their territory, the demons regroup and rush once again to the battle. Vile black wings emitting demonic energy come into contact with the glory and radiance of the angelic warriors.

Soon terror fills the bloodshot, hooded eyes of the diabolical horde, as yet another demon is pierced. Screams spew from their blasphemous mouths as judgment from the throne is visited upon them.

The dark spirits realize they're overwhelmed by the determined fierceness of the surprise attack. The battle intensifies, and confusion hits their ranks, causing some to flee as their evil cohorts are flung into outer darkness off the tips of fiery swords of light.

BURIED ALIVE

Encased in an airpocket of debris, Beloved opens her eyes and sees a soft, golden canopy around her. Tears well up in her eyes, and she prays, "Oh please let Purity be OK!"

Unseen by Beloved, her guardian angel, Valiant, is holding up the siderails of the wagon, preventing them from destroying her. The golden light from his celestial body shimmers brightly as she prays. Still she is pinned down, and she panics as the reality of her situation presses in upon her. "Oh, God, we're buried alive! Where's Purity? Get us out of here! Master Potter, where are you? I need you!"

In the midst of this snowy grave, a powerful surge of peace flows into Beloved and quickly changes her panic into faith. Through the wooden shelves, she can hear the faint cries of other vessels. She waits for her rescuers to come and prays fervently for her daughter.

Radiating hotspots of prayer rise through the snow pack covering the wagons. The ministering angels see fiery flames shooting forth from the icy prisons alerting them where to dig. As the men reach the wagons and begin to shovel they partner with the angelic receiving supernatural strength.

The first one to be uncovered is Fearless. Watchman gently wipes the snow from the wine carafe, and clutching him tightly asks, "Are you okay?"

"Yes, I'm fine. What happened? It feels as if the entire mountain came down on us!"

"It did! We got hit by an avalanche."

"Is everyone okay?"

CASUALTIES

"No, Fearless, there are many lost and injured. We're setting up a firstaid wagon in the back for the chipped and cracked ones. Will you help transfer the injured ones to the firstaid wagon?"

SEARCH AND RESUE 151

Angels draw the rescue workers to the hotspots of prayer. Unseen hands guide the men to each vessel. Shouts of joy reverberate throughout the camp as trapped vessels are uncovered.

But some are crushed beyond repair and do not survive. They find a heavy wagonwheel lying on top of Steadfast. The crushed platter lies still and lifeless. His guardian angel carries his spirit to the Father. Grieved at the tremendous loss, the exhausted crews work even harder to locate survivors.

The sounds of shoveling and the voices of excited drivers send hope to Beloved. Strong hands enter the little airpocket, grasping, yet unable to reach her. Suddenly she feels unseen hands and sees a glimpse of golden wings as she is lifted to the top.

After wrapping her in a warm blanket, the angels return to pull Comrade out. Just as he is starting to regain consciousness, they bring up the broken pieces of Tenderhearted. Clutching the side of her stretcher, he begs to go with her.

"Sorry, but she didn't make it. You're obviously not part of her set, so you can't go with her. Where's the cup she belongs to? Who's her teapot?"

Comrade is in shock, but manages to stammer, "Golden Incense is her leader, but she's still in the wagon with the rest of her team."

HAVE YOU SEEN PURITY?

Hurrying to a group of rescued vessels, Beloved scans their faces. "Purity? Have you seen my daughter? She's just a little mug!"

"I don't think they've found her yet."

"No, we don't have any mugs here; you might try over behind those wagons."

Frantic, Beloved runs through the snow. "I can't lose you again. I just got you back. You've got to be okay!"

THE OPEN DOOR

Deep groans divert her attention back to the rescue site as Fearless helps Harvester to the surface. Limping up to Comrade, he angrily confronts him, "Comrade! What were you thinking? She wasn't your saucer," shouts Harvester. "You endangered everyone just so you could get what you wanted."

Weeping, Comrade grieves, "We were made for each other. You don't understand. I really loved her. She understood me; we prayed and worshiped together. We had so much in common. We should have been put on the same team."

"You were not made for each other! It was wrong!" Gesturing to the rescue efforts, Harvester tells him, "When you jumped on that little saucer, it gave the enemy an open door to bring the avalanche. Your sin gave the enemy the right to attack all of us."

"How can you say that? It may have been wrong, but it was just between the two of us. I feel awful about her, but don't try to blame me for all of this."

Fearless angrily pushes in, "Grow up! What one person does affects everyone! Your sin opened the door for this demonic attack whether you want to admit it or not. You were Beloved's second in command, and you used your influence to seduce Tenderhearted. Just look around at the devastation and pain." Fearless continues his journey to take Harvester to the firstaid wagon.

Unable to locate Purity and wild with pain, Beloved returns to the splintered wagon and begins to dig. It seems like hours to Beloved, but finally Elder runs to the exhausted Beloved and yells, "We've found her over here. She was thrown from the wagon. She's been under the snow a long time. We need to get her out of here as soon as possible."

RESCUED

Running after Elder, she rounds the corner. What she sees causes her to stop abruptly. Purity is wrapped in a wool blanket, unconscious, and being cradled in Watchman's arms. Rocking her gently, he sings quietly over her.

Beloved's mind suddenly flashes back to the wilderness when Amazing Grace held her in her despair. Revelation dawns on Beloved—in a flash of insight she realizes that Watchman is Holy Spirit. Throwing herself down, she weeps with joy. "Holy Spirit, you saved my daughter. Oh, Purity, I thought I'd lost you again."

Barely breathing, her lips blue from the awful cold, Purity is racked with pain from her wounds. Elder gently reaches down and removes Beloved so Watchman can start the hazardous climb.

"Where are you taking her? Most of the wagons have been destroyed!"

Watchman responds, "Master Potter has sent new ones Beloved. Purity and the others injured vessels will leave immediately on the first wagon. Of course you can ride along. Follow me."

Beloved and Watchman, who's carrying Purity in his arms, start the treacherous climb to the road. Unseen by Beloved, Gallant and Valiant follow closely behind.

Purity and dozens of other injured vessels are loaded. Casualties are high, and many are still buried below. Watchman tells the driver, "Night is quickly approaching, and we must get these vessels to the Mountain of Fire. Master Potter is waiting for them."

Cries of desperation escape the loaded vessels. "We can't leave our friends behind again! We just can't lose any more vessels!"

"There are plenty of helpers still digging. We'll keep searching as long as there's hope for any survivors."

The loaded wagon moves out of Precarious Pass. Unable to sit up from exhaustion and pain, Purity rests her head on her mother's chest. Wrapped in her arms, she falls asleep as her mother sings their special lullaby. A mournful, tender song fills the wagon with love and hope.

Imposing guardian angels keep watch over the wagon as it slowly makes its way toward the Mountain of Fire. Despite the wind and cold, their expansive wings cast long shadows against the wagons.

PART THREE

THE DARK NIGHT
OF THE SOUL

CHAPTER THIRTY-THREE

MOUNTAIN OF FIRE

Traveling through the night, the wagon moves laboriously out of the Formidables, climbing to higher altitudes. A regiment of guardian angels surrounds it with a canopy of glory.

Numbing frostbite afflicts many of the injured as they shiver in the drafty wagons. The vessels cry out as their bruised and aching bodies are jarred by the rough roads.

Little Purity's breathing is shallow and her temperature rises. Soon her blanket is soaked with sweat. "Mom…I…hurt," she wails as the wagon wheel jerks into another rut.

Stroking her brow, Beloved brushes the hair back from Purity's face. "We'll be there soon sweetheart. It's not much further, and Master Potter will be waiting."

Long Suffering makes her way from one injured vessel to another. "Be brave in the Lord. You can do it! Don't give up! This setback is just temporary."

Turning to her friend, Beloved sighs, "I can't wait to get there! Just one look from His fiery eyes, and I know she'll be healed. I just wish He were here now. I know Purity was snatched out of Master Craftsman's grasp, but I'll feel better when I see Him."

Putting her arms around Beloved, Long Suffering reassures her, "He'll take care of her. She's going to be just fine."

Comrade has been quietly sitting by himself, but scoots over to them. He looks hopefully at his best friend. "You look tired Beloved. Would you like me to hold her and give you a rest?"

BROKEN FRIENDSHIP

"Don't touch her! It's your fault she's like this."

"I'm truly sorry. I didn't mean for anyone to get hurt, especially Purity. I'll do anything to make it up to you."

"Comrade, you can never make up for all the pain you've caused. I don't even want you around her. Go away and leave us alone!"

Comrade stumbles to the back of the wagon and drops down in the shadows. Long Suffering puts her arm around his shoulder. "Stay away from those two for a while. She has enough to deal with right now. It's too soon for you to expect her forgiveness. It will take time, but we both know Beloved will eventually come around."

Holding his head in his hands, he cries forlornly, "How could I be so stupid? I hurt so many people. Master Potter will never forgive me. I can't bear to face Him."

A FOREBODING MOUNTAIN

Finally the frigid winter wind dies down and early morning light glints through the old tarps. Lifting the flaps, the vessels see snowladen fir trees dotting the landscape. A foreboding mountain towers over them. Other snowcapped peaks gleam in the morning sun, but this one is scorched and covered with soot. Barren trees blanket the side of it like enormous dark skeletons in the morning mist.

The vessels have heard much about the Mountain of Fire, but nothing has prepared them for this dark devastation. Too weak and injured or disheartened to talk, each silently wonders if he or she can make it through the next season.

The horses quicken their speed, roughly jostling the weary vessels. Just ahead is a massive cavern carved out of the blackened mountainside! Huge doors stand open, and before they know what's happened, the drivers spur the horses through the entrance.

CHAPTER THIRTY-FOUR

WELCOME HOME

Watchman quickly dismounts and removes the tarp.

When their eyes adjust to the darkness of the mountain's tomb, the vessels are astonished to see the familiar ancient cedar beams inside the Potter's House. Hundreds of other vessels sit on the old wooden shelves eagerly awaiting the next process in their journey. Looking at Beloved's ragged group, they wonder what calamity these new arrivals have endured.

The weary and injured travelers are too exhausted to move.

At the sight of Master Potter, some of the traumatized vessels begin to weep while others talk over each other telling their stories.

"Master Craftsman stole our team members…"

"Comrade jumped on Tenderheart…"

"The mountain came down on us…"

"Tenderhearted and Steadfast died."

"I was trapped in the snow for…"

"I have a large crack. Master Potter help me."

Motioning for help, the guardian angels crowd around. Master Potter reaches into the wagon. "Welcome home," He says warmly, His sparkling brown eyes are filled with compassion. He touches and greets each vessel.

Each vessel is tenderly inspected by the calloused hands of this ancient Potter and handed to his or her guardian angel. A sick bay area is set up on the shelves nearest the fireplace in the fireside room for the wounded vessels. The atmosphere is alive with Holy Spirit's presence swirling and resting upon them.

The crackling fire in the old stone hearth feels so warm and comfortable, just like it was before they left. The aroma of freshly brewed tea drifts through the cozy room.

CAN YOU TRUST ME?

With the wagon nearly unloaded, Purity is still resting in Beloved's lap. Master Potter holds out His arms. "Beloved, will you let Me have her?"

She draws back. "I don't think I can. I can't give her up again."

"Can you trust Me with her?"

"Just heal her! That's all I ask. I'm her mom, and she needs me. She's had too many years without me. I can't let her go, not again! Besides, she doesn't want to leave me."

Looking down at her daughter she sees Purity gazing at Him with lovesick eyes. Sighing with resignation, Beloved tells Him, "If You promise to heal her I'll give her to You...only then."

Master Potter remains silent as He watches Beloved rock Purity back and forth. "I'm so afraid. Why can't You just heal her in my arms?"

Purity softly asks, "Master Potter, can we spend some time together?"

"Of course, little one."

"No! Stay with me. Please don't go."

Long Suffering tenderly tells Beloved, "She needs Him, and, besides, He's the only one who can heal her."

Her mother's heart can't refuse the longing in Purity's eyes. She hugs her tightly and tells her how much she loves her. "Purity, I'll be waiting anxiously for your return." Tears trickle down her cheeks as she nods to Master Potter. He carefully gathers Purity into His warm embrace.

Ministering angels light brass lanterns throughout the room as Master Potter settles in His big comfortable chair with Purity. Holding the fragile mug in His arms, He strokes her hair, pulls a blanket around her shoulders, and sings softly over her.

His song transports her into a realm of worship and adoration. The fireside room slowly fades away as the beauty realm becomes Purity's only reality. Her aching body and the sickness afflicting her are lost in His great love. Gallant stands protectively behind them.

Hours later, with Purity still cradled in His arms, Beloved drifts off to sleep hearing her daughter softly murmur, "You're so beautiful," over and over again.

MORNING

Harvester's big booming laugh awakens Beloved as the other wagons arrive with the rest of the survivors from Precarious Pass. Everyone's spirits are lifted as they rush to welcome him and hear the news. "No more casualties, and no more serious injures. Everyone on these wagons is in pretty good shape."

Deliriously happy to see Master Potter again, they wonder how it can be possible that they're back in His house.

Smiling affectionately, He explains, "Remember the hallway of mysterious doors? Your prophetic journey has taken you all through different seasons and trials, but always you will come home to Me."

WE NEED ANSWERS

Master Potter walks around the room talking to all the vessels. Mourning the loss of their friends, they need answers.

"I know you've been under quite an attack, and you've all lost friends in Precarious Pass. Some have chosen to leave for the illusion of comfort and ease. But realize that, even though they've left Me, I have not left them. My eyes are upon each one. Holy Spirit will orchestrate their circumstances as I wait longingly to hear them call My name."

"What about Tenderhearted and Steadfast, the ones who died in the avalanche?"

"No situation, no enemy, no sin can separate my vessels from Me. Steadfast, Tenderhearted, and several others are rejoicing around My Father's throne right now.

"Some of your friends were wounded by the sin of others," He says pointing to the shelves. You must understand that what you do affects the entire wagontrain."

"But why should the innocent be put in jeopardy?"

With compassion flowing from His eyes, He softly tells them, "In this life war, sickness, and tragedy is a fact of life. Trouble comes to everyone, even the innocent. But that is why it's so important that they all know Me. Vessels are not isolated unto themselves. Every vessel's choice affects many others. The test is, when there's great loss, especially to innocent lives, can you forgive the offender, and can you trust Me, even when there are casualties, even in matters of life and death?

"Before you point your finger at the guilty party, remember, no one is without sin. It's easy to be offended when you or someone you know is unjustly treated. How easy it is to pick up their offense, but it's a test of the heart. You can forgive or use the excuse of being hurt unjustly to sanction your bitterness."

He looks lovingly at His little pots. "Ultimately your contention is with My leadership over your life."

He walks to the sick bay shelf where Beloved sits holding her daughter. Long Suffering and Golden Incense have already gathered the other intercessors. He pauses for a moment to enjoy the sweet fragrance of their prayers.

"Good job ladies." He winks at Long Suffering, "That's a new robe isn't it? If I didn't know better, I'd think it was made for you."

Fits of coughing rack Purity's body, and her breathing seems even more labored. Sweet Adoration leans down putting her head on Purity's chest. Looking up at the intercessors, she says, "After being buried under the snow for so long, her lungs are congested. This could quickly turn into pneumonia. Let's get more blankets and pray in shifts."

VISIT FROM AMAZING GRACE

Amazing Grace visits Purity after all the vessels are asleep. "Hello, little one," he says tenderly.

She rolls over, sees Him and smiles.

"Purity, the days ahead in the Mountain of Fire will challenge you to your core. I want you to be prepared.

"Remember when we were by the arbor, and I told you to read the Word?"

She looks away, "I tried, but it's kind of…um…boring sometimes…."

"Invite Me to your study times. Under my anointing, your heart will flow like a river, awakening joy even in trying circumstances. Your goal in reading the written Word is to meet the living Word, Master Potter.

"When that happens you'll begin to love the things you used to hate and hate the things you used to love. Your earthly perspective will shift to an eternal perspective. Then you will see things clearly for the first time in your life. This is the deep work the Father wants to do in your life."

Jutting out her chin, Purity declares, "From now on when you see me, Amazing Grace, I'll be carrying my Bible!"

CHAPTER THIRTY-FIVE

THE LORD'S BEAUTY PARLOR

Master Potter gestures to the artistic angels to carry any vessel that isn't injured into the glazing room. "Now, we've got to get you cleaned up again. I see nicks and scratches in your glaze." Their old friends, Angelo and Rembrandt welcome them. "Don't worry; we'll have you beautiful again in no time."

Laughter breaks out for the first time in many days as the vessels look at each other and then at themselves. They are glad to be in Master Potter's beauty parlor!

The angel's wings shimmer and glisten in the light as they examine the pots for smudges or chips in their glaze. Dipping their long brushes in colored pigments, they touch up the previously painted designs on each vessel.

Harvester, along with many others, is washed and completely re-glazed using a light tan with purple and blue accents. Angelo and Rembrandt work quickly with other artistic angels preparing them again for the high fire.

INTRODUCING BLESSING

Golden Incense and her matching set of cups and saucers are also washed and set aside to dry. Their white glaze is carefully reapplied, and delicate lavender roses are added as the finishing touch.

Master Potter comes to Golden Incense holding a beautiful little saucer. "This is Blessing! She will take Tenderhearted's place on your team. I want you all to know that she's not second best or just a fill in. I've always planned for you to walk out your destinies together."

Turning to Blessing, she smiles warmly, "I'm so glad you're on our team. We're just getting ready to pray for a friend of ours named Comrade. He's been missing since we left Precarious Pass."

Harvester bellows, "You guys can just wipe him off your list! He's the one who got us in this jam in the first place. The last time I saw him, he denied he was guilty of anything!"

"You should be ashamed of yourself," Golden Incense scolds, "...telling my team to write somebody off. Master Potter can rescue and redeem, no matter what we've done. I suppose you're perfect!"

Harvester's face flushes a deep red as he mumbles an apology and shuffles over to join them. The others are delighted to include him in their prayer for the missing mug. Prayer intermingled with singing in the Spirit rises from grateful hearts. Angelic voices join with the clay vessels in devotion.

Chapter Thirty-Six

I Deserve to Die

Filled with self-disgust, Comrade slouches down in the back corner of a wagon wishing with all his might that he could just disappear. Ashamed, he tells himself again and again, "I can't face them after what I've done. They'll never trust me again! I didn't mean to destroy Tenderhearted and hurt so many others! My life might as well be over."

Hearing an invitation, the grotesque figure of Suicide slithers toward Comrade.

"Well, it's my old friend Comrade."

"Just get out of here. I don't want to see anyone, especially you."

"Poor Comrade. No one understands you. I'm sorry that no one knows the depth of love that you had for Tenderhearted. You seemed made for each other. You really miss her don't you?"

"I miss her so much. I can't believe she's dead. I should have been the one who died not her."

"You would be willing to switch places with her, wouldn't you?"

"Yes."

"Now you're all alone. All your friends have abandoned you. I just over-heard some of the vessels saying that even Master Potter is angry with you."

"He is? Now my life is over for sure. I totally messed it up."

"It does seem to be beyond repair."

"I should do everyone a big favor and jump off this wagon."

"That would certainly put an end to this agonizing state you're in."

Feeling himself eerily drawn to the edge, Comrade agrees, "It would be better for everyone! No one would even miss me, that's for sure!"

Poisonous venom pierces his heart. "You deserve to die! You're perverted! You gave into your lusts, just as you did back at Comfort Cove. You haven't changed, and never will. Murderer! You killed all those people!" Suicide's talons pierce deeply into Comrade's brain.

"I deserve to die!" wails Comrade.

MY SIN IS TOO GREAT

Comrade's agonizing cries bring Watchman. He yanks Suicide off of the despairing vessel and commands him to leave. Seeing their slimy leader in retreat, the other demonic spirits cringe and quickly follow.

"Comrade," says Watchman tenderly, "what are you doing standing on the edge of the wagon?"

"I...um," stammers Comrade before breaking into sobs. "I just want to die. I hurt too badly, and I hurt everyone else. My life is over; I'm going to jump and end it right now."

Watchman says, "How will jumping help you fulfill the great destiny that Master Potter has for you?"

Surprised by Watchman's response, he composes himself for a moment. "Destiny? You've got to be joking. I gave away my great destiny at Precarious Pass," he says, dissolving into tears again. "Master Potter can't love or trust me now. I don't blame Him either. I caused an avalanche. I killed Tenderhearted. My sin, the pain I've caused...it's...it's too great to be forgiven. He could never love me now...."

"Well, why don't you ask Him. He's standing right behind you."

Strong, nail pierced hands reach into the shadows of the wagon and lift Comrade out of the darkness, embracing him. Comrade buries his face in Master Potter's robes and sobs loud, deep, devastated sobs.

"No more hiding, Comrade! It's too dangerous to be separated. The enemy picks off My loved ones when they're isolated. Your life is valuable. I love you and will not let you go."

"You can't love me after what I did. Tenderhearted and the others are dead because of me. I killed them, I killed them...."

"Comrade, I love you."

"Quit saying that. You can't love me. I'm evil. My sin is too dark. It's too deep. Good people died."

"Comrade, I can forgive anything. I died for the most horrific sins—things you've never even thought of. My blood covers it all—I mean all."

"But it can't. My sin was too bad."

"You're saying that your sin is more powerful than My blood that was shed to forgive it?"

"No, not exactly, but what I did was bad, really bad. My friends died. Everyone hates me."

"Was it so bad that My atoning blood, shed on the Cross for every sin of all humanity, can't cleanse it?"

"Your blood is stronger than anything, I think, but..."

"Comrade," He says, gently turning the little mug's face toward His own and wiping the tears with his hands, "Your sin came as a surprise to you, didn't it? You thought you were past that."

Comrade nods yes and breaks down sobbing again.

"It didn't surprise Me."

"It didn't?"

"You're devastated by what you did. You thought you were beyond all that. You're disgusted with yourself, so you assume that I'm disgusted with you."

"Yeah. I'm really disgusted."

"But Comrade, when I chose you before the foundation of the world I knew everything about you. I've already seen every day of your life. I've already seen every sin you'll ever commit. Knowing all that, with My eyes wide open, I chose you to be My very own. Your sin surprises you, but it's no surprise to Me. I didn't choose you then to reject you now."

Tears flow freely down Comrade's face. "But it was so bad. I'm so ashamed."

"All sin has consequences, and this one is no different. It will be a process for the other vessels to forgive you, but I'm not like the other vessels. The enemy wants you to believe that I no longer love you or that I am angry with you so you will run away from Me instead of to Me.

"Learn this lesson now Comrade, my friend: When you are overcome by sin, run to Me. There you will find deliverance when you confess your sins. I can forgive sin. I took care of sin on the Cross. I can't forgive rationalization, but I can always forgive sin."

Comrade's cries out, "Oh Lord, please forgive me. I'm so sorry for everything. Please help me to change."

Holding the little mug close to Him, He says, "I do forgive you and I don't hold it to your account."

I Am the Word or Secret History

"You must develop a secret history with Me, an aggressive plan to study the Word." He hands Comrade an old leather Bible. "I am the living Word, the Word in your heart. Search the Scriptures that testify of Me."

Comrade opens the pages and is stunned when they begin to glow.

Master Potter smiles, "The Word of God is living, for it has supernatural power. It's does not contain merely words on a page. It will transform your emotions and awakens Godly desires. It strengthens your spirit, and your heart will become alive in righteousness.

Comrade runs his fingers across the pages and feels a supernatural living energy and impartation.

"You need to let the Word of God take root in your heart. It will deliver you from negative emotions, but it takes time for the Word to take root. Grow a root system in the garden of your heart Comrade."

Comrade holds the Bible next to his chest, and his heart absorbs the life-giving warmth.

A GIFT OF HEALING

"Comrade, the enemy has tried to use your selfish appetites to destroy life. He will whisper that your sin has disqualified you. But, the only one who can thwart your destiny is you—by giving up on yourself. I'm jealously guarding your destiny. Although the enemy may come against you so you can learn to grow and fight, I will never give him permission to steal your destiny.

"He wants you to believe that the result of great brokenness is only failure. But I can redeem anything. If you will commit your life to Me, Comrade, I can use your brokenness to work humility and a mercy toward others deep into your heart.

"I'm committed to you Comrade; I've called you as an evangelist to bring thousands to salvation. Now, because of your great brokenness, I'm giving you a gift of healing. Satan would say you're a murderer, a taker of life. I'm going to reverse his accusation and make you a releaser of life bringing healing and deliverance."

Master Potter wraps a humble looking brown garment of healing around Comrade's shoulders.

Comrade is stunned, unable to move or speak as torrents of unconditional love touch and heal his heart.

"When you lay hands on the sick many will recover. The secret is to wear this garment with great humility, for many before you have lost their ministries because of pride and sin," Master Potter smiles as He looks tenderly into Comrade's eyes.

"Remember, in the midst of the fiery trials ahead I want you to stand in faith, even when others around you are giving up. You've been through a lot, brave warrior. Let's wash you off and give you a fresh coat of glaze, and you'll feel like a new man."

CHAPTER THIRTY-SEVEN

EXCOMMUNICATE HIM!

Master Potter begins to add new pieces to the sets that suffered loss to Master Craftsman and the avalanche. Looking up, Beloved watches Him approach with a board of freshly glazed and decorated vessels.

"These are the new mugs to complete your team. Their names are Mercy and Kindness." Beloved looks at the two vessels and sighs.

"I don't want a team; I'll just mess up! Why make me a leader? I just want to be a mom!"

"I've called you to be both, Beloved. I know things feel are difficult right now, but that's how I work maturity into My vessels."

Looking down at the mugs, she can't help but be touched by their innocent little faces. She smiles at them, but tells herself, *I'm not giving them my heart.*

At that moment Rembrandt appears next to Master Potter with two mugs. Beloved is distraught to see Purity's fevered head resting on Comrade's freshly glazed shoulder.

Without thinking she explodes, "Give me my daughter this minute! What are you doing with her? Haven't you done enough harm already? I thought I told you to go away!"

FORGIVENESS ON TRIAL!

Master Potter firmly tells her, "Comrade has always been a part of your team, and I want him to remain so. I'm asking you to forgive him and welcome him back."

"Beloved, I'm really sorry. I know I don't deserve it, but please forgive me. Master Potter said I would pray for the sick and many would recover. I believe He's going to use me to heal Purity."

Reaching for her daughter, she yells, "Master Potter would never use you to heal my daughter. You caused this; it's your fault it happened in the first place."

Turning to Master Potter, she angrily tells Him, "I don't want him back. I don't trust him with any of my team!"

Other vessels on the shelves voice their opinions, and court is in session.

"That's right! He's guilty!"

"Yeah! Let's excommunicate him!"

"We can forgive him, but we don't want him back."

Harvester adds his two cents, "Come on you guys … give him a chance."

Comrade is grateful to Harvester but so wounded by the other vessels he wants to give up. Looking to Master Potter, he says, "I told you they'd never accept me, and who can blame them. Please send me to another team! I'll go anywhere! I need to start over someplace else."

Golden Incense cries, "I'm the one who lost Tenderhearted. I loved her more than you all. Comrade, I forgive you, and want you to know that I love you. If Master Potter forgives you, how can we not do the same?"

"Thank you, Golden Incense. I know I don't deserve it but I really didn't mean for anyone to be hurt. You trusted me, and I failed you all miserably."

FORGIVENESS IS A CHOICE

The grumbling quiets down as Master Potter addresses the self-righteous vessels. "Before we go any further, you must settle this issue in your hearts and forgive. This doesn't have to be difficult. It's a decision, an act of your will—then your hearts will eventually follow."

The atmosphere changes, and a soft blanket of love and acceptance is released from Holy Spirit and settles over Comrade. With tears streaming down his face, he lifts his hands in gratitude.

Falling to his knees, he prays, "Oh Father! Thank you for loving me. I've made so many mistakes. I'm so sorry! Please make a way for Beloved and the others to forgive and accept me again. Please heal Purity."

The vessels watch as he humbles himself in genuine repentance. Their hearts are moved, which opens a door for Holy Spirit to powerfully bring conviction and repentance to them as well.

Going to each one, Comrade asks forgiveness for the pain and loss they suffered. After many tears, they embrace him and welcome him back into the fold.

Beloved sits away from the group, brooding. When Comrade approaches, she turns her back to him. Sadly, he shuffles back to the group.

CHAPTER THIRTY-EIGHT

DIVINE MYSTERIES

Holy Spirit ushers in a spirit of praise, and the vessels excitedly unpack their musical instruments. New songs come forth, angels dance, and all celebrate Comrade's return—all except Beloved who sits by herself to the side thinking of ways she can make Comrade pay.

Quickly, the worship deepens into adoration. The atmosphere becomes saturated with glory as portals open into eternity. Visions of their destinies and callings strengthen and renew the vessels.

Many remember the last day they were in the fireside room and Master Potter entered with their wedding gowns over His arm. Light emanated from Him as heavenly swirls of glory invaded the room.

LONG SUFFERING'S VISION

Long Suffering sees herself being escorted into a heavenly garment room by two enormous angels. She recognizes one as Exhorter, her guardian. Fragrant aromas and celestial sounds fill her senses, and she gasps in wonder at beautiful, shimmering gowns being readied for the brides.

One of the angels points to a pearl encrusted gown near her. "This is yours, Long Suffering. Each one of these pearls symbolizes the suffering you will endure in your lifetime. He fashioned it for you, but as you can see it's not yet finished."

"Beloved, can you see my wedding dress? Isn't it beautiful! Look, I wonder if that one is yours. It's so elegant! It looks just like you."

Beloved tries to peer into the glory realm, but her eyes are veiled.

"Everything looks dim. Lord, what's wrong? Why can't I see?"

"Anger is clouding your vision. You have unresolved issues concerning My leadership over your life. You must truly repent and keep your heart soft. Only then will you regain your spiritual sight."

Stirred by jealousy over Long Suffering's vision, she halfheartedly repents. "OK Lord, if you want Comrade to be part of my team then I'll trust you. I'm sorry, please forgive me."

Rembrandt gently sets Comrade and Purity next to Beloved and the other mugs. Taking her daughter into her arms, she discreetly turns her back to Comrade.

Master Potter gestures around the room, reminding them, "You've all come into the Potter's House through different doorways, but all roads lead back to Me. Now I want you to prepare for the journey into the high fire."

The vessels secretly wonder if they will survive.

HOLY COMMUNION

Holding up a simple stoneware goblet, He asks, "Will you take communion with Me? This is the cup of My fellowship, and those who willingly drink from its contents will enter into a revelation of *My Cross*."

Holy fear sweeps over the vessels as He moves through the chamber offering the humble cup. Some hesitate to make the weighty decision that will bring them into a profound revelation of the price behind the anointing. Then, taking their first sip, an impartation of faith sweeps through them bringing strength for the high fires ahead.

Beloved's heart softens as she and Purity take communion together and pray, even though they are unable to comprehend what drinking the cup really means.

CHAPTER THIRTY-NINE

SILENCE FROM HEAVEN

Heavenly energy permeates the room when Angelo, Rembrandt and other artistic angels join the vessels in the fireside room. They bring wooden boards to carry the bisque ware vessels to the door in the hallway leading into the firing chambers.

These angelic beings have marveled throughout the centuries as the mystery of the high fire has unfolded before their eyes. They recall the first time they witnessed the process as their own Master Potter endured a heartless Cross. They waited passionately for the Father's orders to rescue Him. "Just one word," they pleaded, but the orders never came.

Angelo reminisces to the waiting vessels, "All we could do was stand by silent and helpless, desperately longing to release Him from unjust cruelty. Armed and ready for instant flight, the warring angels never took their eyes off the Father. Just one word…but He did the unthinkable and turned His face away from His beloved Son."

Rembrandt pauses in his work, still overcome by emotion. "I was so confused at the awful silence of Heaven. How could it be possible that His glorious, innocent Son would be put through such agony? How was it possible for the Father to turn His back on the Son of His love? All we could do was grieve as He died. We felt that life itself was being sucked out of the world, as if the universe would surely come to an end."

Angelo picks up the last clay vessel placing him on the board, "We were stunned! We just couldn't comprehend anything we were witnessing."

THE SECRET OF SUFFERING

The angels didn't understand that there was a day of resurrection, a glorious day of victory and rejoicing. They could not fathom the secret of suffering and dying in order to bring forth the mystery of unending life. Now, only after the resurrection do they understand the mystery of death. They have repeatedly seen that suffering brings out the hidden beauty of the vessels.

Countless times they've watched the vessels go into the fire, dull and insignificant, only to reemerge on the other side blazing with color and beauty, reflecting the image of Master Potter. Not only do they contain His very essence, but they are able to impart it as well. They become vessels of substance and destiny wrought in the fires of affliction and heartache.

Beloved and her team soberly contemplate what lies ahead for them. The little upturned faces look to her for reassurance as they are placed together on a board and carried out of the rustic room. She tends to her sick daughter, forgetting the others.

"Here we go," says Loyalty, with a waver in his voice. Generosity takes him by the hand to comfort him.

"Mercy, are you all right?" asks Kindness. "You look a little pale."

"Um...I...I...I'm a little scared of what's on the other side of that door."

"Let's all stay together," says Champion.

"We'll look after each other," says Champion bravely.

"Don't forget me," says Devotion, crowding into the group.

Comrade stands off by himself, and Beloved huddles over Purity.

Entering the hallway of intriguing doors, she remembers a day long ago when she asked to see what was hidden behind them. He gave her a momentary view of Rembrandt and Angelo painting in the glazing room.

Even though she caught glimpses, she didn't fully understand what it meant until she entered the process. Now she wonders about this next door and reflects on how little she really understands about it all.

Praying for wisdom, she tells her team, "Don't be afraid. This is just another part of the journey. The high fire is a gift of love planned from the beginning. Remember the visions and words Master Potter has given each of you." She is careful not to look in Comrade's direction.

Kissing her daughter's forehead, she says, "Purity, I love you. It's my heart's desire to see your wonderful destiny come forth."

CHAPTER FORTY

A NEW DOOR

The mysterious door swings open. Immediately the vessels find themselves inside a huge firing chamber hollowed out of the Mountain of Fire. Artistic angels carry thousands of vessels into the vast room.

Towering rock walls, black with soot and carbon, are the first foreboding images they see. Master Potter stands inside the chamber, in the center of activity, orchestrating the placement of vessels according to His sovereign purposes.

In obedience, the angels unload vessels onto shelves according to height and size. Tall, graceful vases and pitchers are placed on the top. Dinner sets are separated according to height, using shorter shelves for the mugs, cups, and saucers. Also, because different glazes melt at various temperatures, the vessels are placed on the shelves accordingly.

Suddenly, Beloved hears Golden Incense cry, "Why are you taking them away? I need to take care of them, especially my new little cup, Blessing."

She grips Purity as she hears Master Potter explain. "I'll take care of Blessing and I'll bring you all together again. Remember, each fire is custom designed so that My character can be imparted to you."

Pointing to her team, He tells Golden Incense, "Your saucers will be placed on a shelf just the right height for them, and your cups will go on another." He picks her up, and she's pleasantly surprised to see her friends Fearless and Harvester waiting to greet her.

"At least I won't be cut off from everyone I love," she says as they throw their arms around her.

"Now I know we'll be all right," says Harvester, "We've got the number one intercessor with us!"

Sitting on a top shelf, Fearless tries to encourage his wine goblets and yells toward the lower shelves, "Hey, Joyful, look at your three new brothers and sisters! You'll get to know them real well in the high fire. It looks as if you'll have to teach them the ropes since I'm up here."

The goblets wave to Fearless. Joyful shouts back, "We'll be fine; we're getting to know each other real well. We can't wait to see how our grapevine designs will come out."

SHE NEEDS ME!

Angelo approaches Beloved's team and takes several of her mugs, Generosity, Devotion, Champion, and Comrade, one-by-one to a lower shelf. He reaches for Purity, but Beloved holds on. "She stays with me! I'm her mother, she's still quite ill, and she needs me."

Pausing, he looks toward Master Potter who is quickly approaching. Gently Master Potter tells her, "I know you're very afraid, but you'll have to trust Me. You don't fit on her shelf, and she doesn't belong on yours. She must go to the shelf with the other mugs next to Comrade."

"No Lord," she blurts out, then quickly drops her voice, "You can't put her next to *him*!"

Comrade tries to reassure her. "Don't worry, Beloved! Joyful and Sweet Adoration are right here with me. Besides, I won't let Purity out of my sight! I'll take good care of her!"

Sure! Like you took care of Tenderhearted? Beloved hates that her thoughts are so dark about him, even now…

"Beloved, please listen, Master Potter told me He was giving me the gift of healing," Comrade hollers from his shelf. "Maybe that's why He's putting her next to me. That way I can make up for all the things I've done to hurt you. I'll stand for her healing, no matter what."

"Why should I believe you after all you've done?" Turning to Master Potter she pleads, "Please let her stay with me. I don't trust him anymore."

"Beloved, where I place my vessels is a critical component of the high fire. Everyone wants to be someplace else or with someone different. It's difficult for you to understand, but this is what's best for you and Purity."

"Mom," Purity says coughing, "I want to stay with you more than anything, but if Master Potter wants me to go with Comrade then I should go."

Beloved sees Master Potter nod His head in approval, and summoning all her resources to fight back tears she finally consents, "I love you so much! It's just hard to let you go especially when you're sick. But, remember, we'll be together after the firing, and then nothing will separate us."

"I love you, Mom. Don't worry; I'll be okay."

Beloved gently surrounds her frail, weak daughter in a long embrace as tears freely flow, and they say good-bye. Deep in Beloved's heart, anger continues to burn against Comrade every time she considers her daughter's suffering.

Angelo picks up Purity and smiles. "I see you have the Word."

"Oh, yes. I don't go anywhere without it these days. I used to find it boring, but now it brings such comfort to my soul." He places Purity on a low shelf and says, "Keep it close by. It won't fail you in your trials ahead."

The minute Angelo sets her down, Comrade reaches for her hand, "Purity, I'm so sorry you're sick. I never meant to hurt you. I made a terrible mistake with Tenderhearted, but I can't change that now. I really want to be your friend if…if you can find it in your heart to forgive me."

Laying her arm on his shoulder, she tells him, "Of course I forgive you, Comrade." He sighs in relief. The other six mugs gather round smiling.

"Let's not waste any time; let's have a Bible study," suggests Comrade. "You know it's important that we all let the Word of God take root in our hearts."

THE TOP SHELF

Coming back for Beloved, Angelo takes her to the top shelf where Harvester, Long Suffering, Golden Incense, and Fearless are waiting. Seated high on her lofty perch, Beloved can see most of the chamber. She watches as hundreds of vessels are placed on shelves.

CHAPTER FORTY-ONE

FIRING CHAMBERS

Master Potter combats their fears by explaining the process ahead. "This mountain kiln has been fired for centuries. I use huge pinelogs to bring the temperature up quickly and melt your glazes. As the kiln gets hotter, the colorful ash from accumulated firings drips from the ceilings, adding additional pigments and luster to your glazes."

Beloved sees artistic angels covering some of the vessels with ceramic containers.

"The colors from pine ash are a wonderful addition for some, but we're putting these vessels in covered containers to protect them. They have been handpainted with a distinct destiny."

Master Potter points across the room to angels placing several large pieces close to the firebox where the wood will be stoked. "This creates artistic effects as the fire flashes across the glazes on My vessels. Even though this process is very painful, many of these strikingly beautiful vessels will end up in palaces and museums."

Beloved comforts herself; *I guess it could be worse. I could be next to the firebox.*

The clay pots nervously wait to see what will happen next as Master Potter inspects the shelves. After carefully examining each vessel, He walks toward the doorway singing a lovesong that echoes throughout the kiln. His soft, melodious voice causes their hearts to become tender and receptive.

Standing guard on the outside of the Mountain of Fire, the angels watch dark storm clouds approach. Thunder rolls across the peaks, reverberating through the firing chambers. Flashes of lightning strike the already scorched and barren terrain.

Golden Incense gathers the other intercessors to earnestly pray. The sound of wood being thrown into the firebox causes others to anxiously join in with the little group. Crying out for an impartation of faith, they fall to their knees in travail as the angels brick up the doorway.

Long Suffering quotes the Word: "I will never leave you nor forsake you." Her guardian angel beams with pride.

"Come Holy Spirit, we can't endure the high fire without You. Please come," says Harvester.

Holy Spirit quickly responds and flows as a rushing wind into the Mountain of Fire. Dry kindling ignites, exploding into long, licking fingers of orange and yellow. The heat becomes suffocating as flames quickly travel up the walls. The force of the intense fire overwhelms the vessels as more heavy pine logs are added.

TRUE CONFESSION

Beloved hears her daughter coughing. Peering through the growing smoke and flames, she sees Comrade waving at her. She ignores him, calling out, "Purity, are you all right?"

A small, weak voice can barely be heard above the roar of the flames, "I'm fine Mom. I just need to sleep for a while. Comrade is taking good care of me. We're studying the Word all the time."

Comrade lovingly looks at Purity. She is a reminder of the dark secret he has kept—a daughter born so many years ago in Comfort Cove. *Did she turn out as lovely as Purity?* Does she know Master Potter? He feels the tug of pain in his heart and quickly tries to push the ache back down.

Trying to make her more comfortable, he lets her head rest on his shoulder. Paternal feelings wash over him, and he asks, "Can I tell you a secret that no one else knows?"

"Sure Comrade," Purity chokes.

"Do you promise not to tell anyone?"

"I do."

Comrade hangs his head in shame. "I once had a little girl. She would be about your age, Purity. I loved her very much."

"Oh, Comrade, what happened to her?"

"Actually, I only had her for a few months, but I still think of her often, and I think about Loveless, which was her mother's name."

"I didn't know you'd been married."

"I wasn't; this was before I knew Master Potter. I wanted to marry Loveless, especially when our baby, Abandoned, was born. I always called her Cherished, though. But my parents were totally against it because Loveless was just a poor little nobody from the docks."

"What happened?"

"My folks paid her off, and gave her a one-way ticket out of town. She left taking Cherished with her. She didn't even say good-bye or tell me she was leaving. For years I thought it was because she didn't love me. It wasn't until my mother died that I learned the truth. She and Dad felt no one was good enough for me, and the irony is that now I have no one."

"I'm so sorry, Comrade. Have you tried to find them?"

"Going through my mother's things, I found an old address, but it all happened so long ago. I'm sure they've moved by now. Anyway, my daughter probably doesn't know I exist."

Kissing her softly on the forehead, he whispers somewhat embarrassed, "When I see you I sometimes think of you as my daughter."

"Oh, Comrade, I'm so flattered. You'd be a great dad. Maybe after this last firing you can really try to find your daughter."

UNFORGIVENESS

Impatiently Beloved calls again, "Comrade, how is she?"

"I'm sure she is going to be okay. Joyful, Sweet Adoration, and I are taking good care of her, but…" his voice drops off, "I think her temperature starting to rise!"

Suffocating flames move through the lower shelves with increased swiftness. Comrade looks on the frail, suffering little mug and is moved deeply as he watches Purity racked with another coughing fit. He earnestly prays for her healing, and others join him.

Beloved agonizes as she listens to the coughing fit, realizing she is helpless to rescue her daughter. "What am I going to do Long Suffering? Purity's so sick, and I can't do a thing about it! I'm glad someone is with her, only I wish it wasn't him."

"Comrade has been your best friend for years, Beloved. He never meant to harm her or anyone else. Deep in your heart you know that."

"But he was selfish; he was only thinking about his own desires. And there are things you don't know. This isn't the first time he betrayed me. I forgave him once before for what he did to me back in Comfort Cove. I made him like one of my family."

"Beloved, wait just a minute. He helped you reconcile with Purity, and he fought for you when you were going to take your own life. You need to forgive him."

"I'll never trust him again! Not only was he my best friend, but I made him second in command."

"Master Potter made you the leader. Maybe you promoted Comrade before he was ready for it."

"Listen, Long Suffering, I knew he was immature in some areas, but I never imagined he would do what he did. I thought he would grow into the position."

"Obviously he didn't. Besides, did Master Potter ever tell you to make him your assistant? Ultimately the responsibility for the team is yours. Isn't it?"

"What are you trying to do to me? Don't you realize my daughter could die? Or hasn't that occurred to you? I can't believe you're blaming me for everything! I thought you were my friend." Fists clenched, she turns her back toward Long Suffering.

Beloved's anger opens the way for harassing spirits of Self-Pity and Depression. Walking to the back of the shelf by herself, she broods silently. *Maybe Long Suffering is right. Perhaps everything is my fault. Am I responsible again for Purity's pain?* The awful heat permeates her vessel but has only just begun to soften the glass particles in her glaze.

Her guardian, Valiant, stands quietly beside her. More wood is heaped onto the already intense fire. The temperature takes another leap as her anger fuels the raging emotional fire inside of her. Through the waves of burning, she thinks she sees Holy Spirit manifesting Himself as purifying flames in the fiery tempest.

The vessels' hearts continue to undergo the test.

THE FIRE RAGES

Worship and fervent prayers soar throughout the chambers releasing bursts of faith and courage. Holy Spirit reminds them to hold fast to their destinies and promises.

"Remember, there are mysteries yet to be revealed on your journey through the high fires. Master Potter loves you and is preparing you to be His Bride."

Not all heed His words; some allow bitterness and contention to fuel the flames around them into seething clouds of sulfuric fumes, which greatly adds to their pain. As these tortured vessels look into the raging fire, grotesque, demon faces appear in the flames mocking them in sadistic glee.

"Where is Master Potter now? He threw you into this mountain and left you to die! You're fools to have followed Him; you are losing everything you've worked so hard for."

Master Potter patiently removes a brick from the doorway and peers inside. He gives the orders to throw larger logs into the fire.

Angels effortlessly heave huge pine logs into the fireboxes. They shout with joy, "For the Father, the Son, and the Holy Spirit—that the Bride may come forth!" They have seen the mystery of purification through suffering before and are eager to see it again.

A spiritual battle rages in the mountain kiln. The intercessors assault the vile demonic horde. Many put on their armor and fight, while others shrink back in fear. Exhausted, they struggle with doubt and unbelief. Some question Master Potter's ability to lead them. Others read the Word, their flashing swords overcoming the many demonic assaults.

"It needs to be much hotter," says Master Potter. "And shut those dampers down even more. We need to smoke the kiln."

The angels quickly close the dampers at the top of the mountain to prevent the incoming air from exiting the chimney. This pushes the raging fire back into the chamber, exerting incredible heat and pressure on the vessels. The fire greedily consumes the oxygen, spewing billowing black smoke into every crack and crevice of this living inferno of suffering.

The kiln is alive with noise. The wood splinters in hundreds of ear splitting explosions. The roar of fiery flames makes it difficult for the vessels to hear. Unable to communicate, they feel even more alone. The kiln shakes and rumbles as the insatiable fire devours the pine logs, shooting brilliant yellow and orange flames into the atmosphere.

In the bowels of the earth, the immense heat and pressure produces precious gems such as diamonds, emeralds, sapphires and rubies. In the same way, the heavy, black reduction fire forces the vibrant hidden colors out of the glazes and changes the chemistry of the clay forever.

CHAPTER FORTY-TWO

FAITH FOR HEALING

Deep in the mountain the dense smoke and consuming fire makes it difficult for Beloved to see Long Suffering standing next to her. The warfare has been brought to another level as the unrelenting pressure of the fire and suffocating heat overwhelms them. The cruel onslaught of the enemy ceaselessly torments her as she fights to hold her place in the Spirit.

DISOWNED

Holy Spirit comes to Long Suffering, unearthing a long repressed memory—that of being left by her mother at an orphanage when she was four-years-old. She wails loudly as Holy Spirit holds her close. The years of feeling rejected and unloved surface violently. "I was too old for the potential parents who came, and no one wanted to adopt me. I stayed there until I was eighteen, and then *they* asked me to leave."

After much loving encouragement, Holy Spirit asks the question, "Can you forgive your mother?"

With tears still rolling down her cheeks, Long Suffering shakes her head no. "She never wanted me. She never came back for me. It hurts too bad."

Holy Spirit gently tells her, "Long Suffering, you need to forgive. Unforgiveness and bitterness opens a door to the enemy.

"I want to, but I can't. Not yet."

SICKNESS AND DISEASE

In gleeful camaraderie, Sickness and Disease open putrid black bags, releasing an evil swarm of paralyzing and crippling diseases. Their arsenal of weapons includes insanity, heart disease, and many other varieties of wretched illness and debilitating pain.

Crawling out, the foul spirits quickly advance to their intended victims. A malignant spirit of Cancer boasts, "I've got an open invitation," and attaches itself to Long Suffering. Unseen, it invades her body and enters her blood stream.

A loathsome spirit of Pneumonia drops to the lower shelves. He stretches his long tentacles around Purity's chest causing her to cry out in pain.

"Mom," she gasps, "Can't….b…br…breathe."

Beloved's heart is breaking, and she decides she must go to her, no matter what the consequences. "Oh, Purity, hold on! I'm coming! I'm coming!"

Strong hands take hold of her. Angrily, she shouts, "Let go of me, Fearless! She needs me! I told her that if she called, I'd come. I can't let her down this time."

"You can't go to her. Master Potter knows what's best. Take courage and pray, and don't let fear steal your faith. We are all with you in this." Holding her tightly, he allows her to cry out her frustration and pain before releasing her into Long Suffering's outstretched arms.

Long Suffering pleads, "Beloved, if you jumped off this shelf you would just shatter into a million pieces. That's what the enemy wants you to do. How would that help either of you?"

Shoving her friends away, she yells down to Comrade, "Is Purity OK? What's happening down there? I demand that you tell me now!"

The roar of the fire swallows her cries in its deafening swirl. No longer able to see Purity and barely able to hear, she refuses to give up, "Comrade what's going on? Tell me now. I mean it. Talk to me!"

Through the chaos of tormented voices and the awful consuming fire she can only make out snatches of Comrade's reply.

"Worse … fever … pray!"

Distraught, Beloved cries, "What if I lose her? I couldn't bear life without her." Turning to Long Suffering for comfort, she collapses into her arms. "I'm sorry for getting mad at you. I'm just so scared. What if she dies?"

Rubbing her back, Long Suffering gently tells her, "It'll be OK. Master Potter loves her. We need to fight for Purity. Now is not the time to fall apart."

HEART ATTACK

Harvester smiles warmly at the two friends, and he and Fearless start to walk over to them when suddenly he clutches his chest as a fiery spear enters his heart.

His legs give out and he crumbles to the ground. Long Suffering and Beloved run to his side, and all three begin to pray. Kneeling beside him they cry for Master Potter. Holy Spirit opens Beloved's spiritual eyes to see Death holding the spear and twisting it cruelly into Harvester.

Mocking her with malicious lies, he spews, "Beloved, I'm going to take out each one of your friends until you renounce Master Potter. I've already taken most of your team. When I get through with Harvester, then I'll visit Purity."

Holy Spirit floods them with fiery faith and these instructions, "Beloved, it's not time for Harvester to die! Death was defeated at the Cross. Take authority and command him to leave!"

Beloved fiercely screams at the foul spirit, commanding Death to leave and prophetically proclaiming, "Life! I call forth life over Harvester. Death, by His blood you were defeated. Leave now!" Others join the battle, "Yes, we call forth resurrection life!"

A bolt of white-hot lightning pierces the black smoke sending a jolt through Death. A victory cheer in the heavens can be heard as he's hurled backwards. Exploding with rage, he curses Holy Spirit and threatens Beloved, "You're going to pay for this!"

Valiant and the other guardian angels raise their shields and swords to Death's threats. Fearless and Long Suffering pull the bloody spear out of Harvester. As they quickly lay their hands on his chest, a healing anointing is released. Electricity flows through them, and golden oil from the heavenly throne flows over his body healing the wound.

Helping the astonished canister to his wobbly feet, Fearless tells him, "That was a close call. For a minute there I thought you were a goner!"

Harvester gratefully gushes, "I've never been so scared in all my life! If you hadn't been there, I wouldn't have made it. I guess I'm not as big and tough as I thought. Beloved, when you spoke those words I felt Death let go of me."

After seeing Harvester healed so quickly, hope fills their hearts for the other suffering vessels. They quickly report the miracle, encouraging others to lay hands on the sick and believe they'll recover.

Beloved's faith rises. "Now I know we'll see Purity healed."

Fearless and Long Suffering join in, "We'll stand with you Beloved. After what we've seen today, nothing can stand in our way!"

CHAPTER FORTY-THREE

FIERY ORDEAL

The vessel's fervent prayers empower angelic warriors to launch a battle against the snarling, demonic horde as it rushes in to take more captives. Sickness and Disease urge their malevolent troops on with renewed vengeance. In this high fire, shouts of triumph and the cries of agony echo together throughout the chamber.

The battle rages as angelic swords clash against the vitriolic enemy. Many vessels demand to be taken out of the high fire, blinded to the fact that their glazes would only be partially melted. They would be ugly, unfinished, and unable to fulfill their destinies.

Mercifully, their angry petitions go unheeded, and unbeknownst to them, Master Potter signals for more wood.

The raging fire and unmerciful heat continues to mount, amplifying its continual pressure and tension on the clay vessels. Comrade's deep brokenness and contrite heart enables him to pray with great compassion and mercy, and he witnesses astounding miracles.

Beloved's group of mugs and Fearless's goblets gather around him, and before long he has many young disciples. He has a deep longing to see others healed and starts holding tent meetings. He advertises, "Revival Fires Tonight," and draws capacity crowds.

Each day the line grows longer as his fame spreads. Multitudes bring their loved ones to him, begging him to cure them. Many are healed, and all can feel the power surges of God moving through him. Yet, Purity continues to decline to attend.

Praying to Master Potter, Comrade agonizes, "Why? Why isn't she getting better, since so many others have received miracles? Why not her?" He receives no answer.

Sweet Adoration becomes frantic as the vicious spirit of Pneumonia tightens his grip on Purity, and her frail body grows weaker. She calls out, "Comrade! Quick come over here!"

Running to Purity, he grabs hold of the foul demon, wrestling for her freedom. "Spirit of Pneumonia, I break your hold and command you to leave! I call forth her healing and declare she will live and not die! By His stripes you are healed."

Purity manages to open her Bible; an aromatic fragrance wafts out of its pages. "Yes, it says here, 'by Your stripes I am healed.'"

Life flows into Purity, as the power of the Word strikes the demon, flinging him off. In a moment, color starts returning to her ashen face. She begins to talk easier, free from the chronic, labored breathing.

"I'm feeling better now," Purity announces as she sits up for the first time in days.

"Way to go, Comrade," shouts Kindness.

"You did it!" says Devotion excitedly. The other mugs and goblets gather around cheering.

Comrade declares, "You're healed. I know it for sure. Master Potter healed you."

Reports spread quickly from shelf to shelf, informing everyone of Purity's miracle. Relieved, Beloved lets out a shout, "Thank You! Oh, thank You, Master Potter."

Fearless and Harvester laugh and celebrate while praising Master Potter. Long Suffering joins in for a while but becomes so tired she decides to rest. Undetected, cancer settles into her bone marrow.

RENEWED VENGEANCE

Angered by their retreat, Sickness and Disease rebuke their evil subordinates.

"Watch! We'll show you how to do it!"

Aggressively advancing, they clamp Purity in a vise-like grip. They squeeze her chest and press their long talons into her flesh, inflicting a new level of misery. Calling upon a spirit of Abandonment to torment her mind with lies about Master Potter, they complete their heartless performance.

Purity's face pales and her lips take on a bluish tinge. She looks at all the little mugs and goblets standing around and weakly moans, "I ... can't ... br...breathe! H...he...help...me!"

Her pleas pierce Comrade's heart like arrows. He becomes secretly worried, but refuses to exhibit any doubt, "Get in the Word. You're healed! We just prayed, and you got better. We both saw it! You felt it! Where's your faith?"

Sickness and Disease call in spirits of Condemnation and Shame. Tears run down her cheeks, and she softly replies, "I'm sorry Comrade, but I just don't have any faith right now."

He takes her into his arms, "Don't be afraid, Purity. Remember what Master Potter told us? This high fire is not going to last forever, and soon you'll be reunited with your mom. You're an important part of our team. We need you. I'll stand and fight for you."

Silently he prays, "Lord, please help her. I love her so much, and Beloved would never forgive me if she dies."

Word of Purity's relapse travels through the kiln, and the vessels all recommit to a renewed prayer battle.

Sickness and Disease order the spirit of Pneumonia back into the battle. Coming with a renewed vengeance, he encases her chest. Sharp pain radiates into her back as her lungs fill with fluid. She looks helplessly at Comrade, and laboriously pleads, "I need…my…m…mom."

He gently lays her down. Unseen, Gallant, Purity's guardian angel, steps out of the shadows and imparts strength to her frail body until she falls asleep. He whispers gently, "Master Potter loves you so much, little one."

Meanwhile, the raging fire swirls around Purity's clay vessel, parching her throat and drenching her with sweat. Her life seems to be slipping away before their watchful gaze.

ENCOURAGING VISION

Golden Incense and her group of intercessors storm the gates of heaven on her behalf. Praying fiery petitions, they remind Master Potter of His promises.

"Lord you taught us that healing is the children's bread. You said You conquered death and sickness on the Cross. We call upon your shed blood and proclaim that by the stripes afflicted on Your body, Purity is healed."

Rising from the intense heat of the dark, fiery kiln, the vessels hear Beloved's sorrowful sobs. "Master Potter, I thought she was healed. What happened? Why isn't she getting better? Please heal my daughter. I can't go on without her. She's everything to me."

Golden Incense agonizes in prayer for her friend, "Why isn't she healed? We've been fasting for days. What are we up against? Show us Your strategies so we can pray in agreement with You."

Through the flames, Golden Incense sees an open-eyed vision of a graceful couple dancing on a sapphire sea. Laughing together, their eyes are totally engaged with each other's, and they are lost in each other's presence as a whirlwind of celestial colors engulfs them.

With her lid rattling in excitement, she yells to Beloved, "Oh my goodness, I think I'm getting some results from all our fasting. I just saw a vision of Purity wearing her wedding gown dancing with the Bridegroom King. I think it means she'll be healed for sure."

The team cheers and prays even more fervently.

CHAPTER FORTY-FOUR

CRISIS OF FAITH

The sound of more wood being thrown on the fire echoes through the mountain kiln, and the deafening roar of the raging fire increases. Death erupts out of the flames. His cruel, hooded eyes pierce souls as vessels struggle to escape from him. Terror buffets the shelves as he unleashes his venom of hate and contempt.

Appearing as a triumphant commander strutting back and forth, he emits a deep, guttural growl, barking out orders to his fiendish troops. He stands arrogantly with gnarled hands on his hips, his huge wings fanning the blistering flames. His ugly mouth gapes open in a malevolent grimace as he surveys the fiery chamber of death with fiendish delight.

He thunders out his evil invitation, "I'll put an end to your suffering. I'm not cruel like Master Potter. He tells you that you must endure the pain, but I assure you I can end it for you."

PERSONAL GETHSEMANE

In the kiln, the pendulum of emotions swings wildly back and forth from times of powerful intercession to times of profound despair and back again. The wicked horde bombards the vessels ruthlessly, wearing down their defenses, while the angelic host fights for the lives of the clay pots. Each intercessory prayer spurs them on with renewed power.

Desperate cries fill the chamber. Those without their armor are buffeted and even destroyed. Distraught voices wail out in agony. Some lose their loved ones to Death's pitiless grip. Other vessels groan from the bad choices they've made, as these hairline cracks widen, rendering them useless.

In the smoky black flames, other voices cry out in faith, pleading for miracles, "You forgive all my iniquities, and heal all my diseases." Filled with compassion, and responding to their faith, Master Potter, the living Word, walks among the vessels as a consuming fire, healing many of the sick. Those who are healed rejoice and glorify God.

"Master Potter just healed my brother."

"Strength just returned to my leg. I can walk again!"

In this horrific black inferno, many lose everything they've built and trusted in for years. Homes, finances, ministry, or health! Master Potter's consuming fire purges everything that's not of Him. Each one is brought into a custom-designed death—a personal Gethsemane—a dark night of the soul where each is challenged with the question: "Am I enough?"

In the midst of the fiery turbulence, Beloved can make out the faint voice of Golden Incense. "Beloved! We're fasting and praying. Don't give up! We've asked Master Potter to strengthen you."

"Did you hear that, Long Suffering? They're really doing warfare for her life. My daughter's going to live!" Her heart is encouraged and swells with love and gratitude for the intercessors and Master Potter.

"Of course!" Harvester booms, "If Master Potter would heal an old sea dog like me, I'm sure He'll heal that pretty little thing."

WINNING THE CHALLENGE

Gruesome excitement runs through Death's dark being as he contemplates Purity's final breath. Even more thrilling is the thought of watching Beloved suffer the anguish of her daughter's death, along with it the possibility that he could witness her renouncing of Master Potter. "Yes," he hisses, "my plans are working."

Now he's certain his evil strategy will win the challenge between his master and the Godhead. In fact, he's already planning his triumphal procession into Hell dragging Promiscuous's limp body behind him. What a mockery it will make of Master Potter's handiwork.

Expanding his huge webbed wings, Death quickly rises to the top shelf and watches approvingly as spirits of Unbelief cast their shadowy nets over Beloved.

Without warning, Death's terrifying voice rumbles through the dense smoke and flames, and a sickly sweet odor permeates the atmosphere as he materializes before her, spewing his hot sulfuric breath in her face.

"Forsaken! We meet again. Why aren't you with your daughter? She's ill and needs you now, if she hasn't died already. It seems that everything you touch is cursed. Your life, your children, your friends, your ministry! Why don't you just give up and come into my open arms!"

"Never!"

Death hoarsely whispers, "Why doesn't Master Potter heal Purity? Everyone's been fasting and praying, obviously that doesn't work. She's in such pain!

If He really loved you, He'd let you be with her instead of Comrade. After all, you saw Harvester healed, and Comrade's prayers aren't working!"

Even though Beloved has walked with Master Potter for many years now and understands His mercy and unwavering commitment to her, still doubt tags along like a nipping dog at her heels. She silently cries out to Master Potter, *My little girl has suffered so much of her life. Why are you allowing it to continue? You healed Harvester immediately. Why not her?*

Her head throbs in the awful heat, and his evil presence sends chills down her back, but she manages to shout, "You're a liar! Master Potter gave me promises for my children and our future!"

"Future? Promiscuous has no future! How does it feel to know she'll be with me soon?"

"She won't! And her name is Purity. She belongs to Him—not you! In the name of Master Potter I command you to leave!"

But instead of departing, he lunges for her, "Your words have no affect on me. I'm on assignment to take your daughter's life. Master Potter has given her to me." Reaching out, he grabs Beloved with his huge gnarled talons.

Nauseated by his gross appearance and horrible stench, she struggles to free herself from his grasp. "That's a lie. Master Potter will save her."

"Are you really that stupid? Do you think I can be here without His permission?"

THE WAR IS ON

Beloved's vessel begins to glow in the intensifying fire, and her glaze starts to melt as Holy Spirit releases new heights of faith. In a torrent of righteous anger, she declares, "You put me down! Purity will live and not die!"

The powerful release of faith stuns Death momentarily, and he backs away. Regaining his composure, he snarls, "You don't even know what's going on do you? I told you if you didn't come with me, I'd take her! Today's the day."

"Never! Master Potter would never give you my child. She has a great destiny!"

"A false destiny! She never should have been born. She was a mistake in the first place, conceived only by your unbridled lust."

"No, she wasn't! Even in my womb Master Potter called her into being. She has a long life ahead of her."

"Maybe she did until you put Comrade in charge. He couldn't keep his lust under control, either! He didn't cause the avalanche! Your poor judgment did! Those mistakes short-circuited her life. Now she's mine—unless you renounce Master Potter."

"I'll die first!"

"Remember, I know where your son is, and he'll be next. He's been flirting with me for years, and he's damned to Hell! Another one of your little mistakes I believe!"

Refusing to back down, she glares at him, "I was run out of the commune. I did not abandon my children! Besides, the mercy and forgiveness of Master Potter covers anything I've done."

"Mercy? I'll show you His mercy."

DIABOLICAL VISION

Death's mesmerizing eyes begin to change before her. The sickly yellow iris diminishes, and the black pupils expand into mirror-like screens opening a dark portal into the supernatural, revealing his diabolical plans.

She can clearly see Purity racked with fever, delirious, and unable to get free from the brutal attack. As she watches, Comrade stands by helplessly as Sickness and Disease tightly attach themselves to her. His prayers and the prayers of the other little mugs and goblets are consumed in the raging fire.

Shivering and coughing, Purity painfully cries out, "Mom, please help me. I can't breathe!"

"Purity, Purity, I have to go to her! Please don't take her."

"Renounce Master Potter, and I'll be merciful and take her quickly."

"I will never renounce Master Potter."

"Have it your way then," Sickness and Disease laugh scornfully as Death swoops down to the lower shelf and approaches helpless little Purity.

Clutching her heart, a frantic Beloved wails, "Master Potter, where are you? You have to save her! I can't live without her. Help us!"

As the heat escalates, a torrent of dense black smoke swirls around the upper shelves blocking her view. Death releases an invasion of demonic spirits to infiltrate the chamber. The battle becomes so intense each cruel lie feels like a physical scourging as she struggles in a crisis of faith.

Terrifying voices screech amid the roaring flames, "She's suffering an agonizing death! You can't save her, and Master Potter won't! You're a fool. He's taking the one person you love the most! And you still love Him?"

"I love Him. He's my life and breath."

CHAPTER FORTY-FIVE

THE CUP OF SUFFERING

Slumped helplessly on the shelf weeping, Beloved feels strong, tender arms pick her up and embrace her. Entering into a sphere of Master Potter's glorious presence, she's shielded momentarily from the fierce battle. His appearance pushes back the gross darkness, and suddenly the cruel voices stop.

She finds herself sitting beside Him and is shocked to see that He's covered with bloody wounds. He looks at her and softly says, "Hello, My friend." His words pierce her heart with revelation of His suffering and death.

"I understand the pain you're feeling in this terrible fire. You're entering into the fellowship of My suffering.

Desperately, she cries out, "The fire isn't the worst part. The worst part is that my daughter is dying. Are you going to heal her or not?"

"That's not the issue Beloved. Will you love Me whether she lives or dies? Is your love conditional, based on My dealings with Purity?"

Lord You know I love You, but I just can't lose her again. Why have You healed others, but not her?"

"Beloved, you have endured much pain in your life, some from your choices and some for My sake. I want your destiny, your hopes and dreams, everything. I want your whole heart. I want you to release your daughter to My purposes, not yours. I'm calling you into a deeper, unconditional love relationship with Me."

"Will you fellowship with Me in My sufferings?"

WILL YOU PARTNER WITH ME?

Reacting to the thought of more pain and loss, Beloved draws back shuttering, "There must be another way. What are You saying? You're not really intending to take Purity? Please, anything but that. I can't live without her."

"No Beloved. You can't live without Me. Will you be betrothed to Me, not only in celebration and victory, but also in suffering. Will you be my suffering Bride?"

Looking through her tears at His tender face, she follows His gaze to an approaching angel holding a stoneware goblet. Master Potter takes it and offers the simple cup to her. "Will you marry Me in affliction? By drinking this cup of betrothal, you enter into the mystery of My suffering."

Staring at the cup, the revelation that she can't control Purity's destiny chokes her with grief. Weeping, she stammers, "I...I can't drink it. I can't bear to it."

"Don't despise this precious gift of fellowshipping with Me in My suffering."

"There must be another way. This is too hard."

"But, this is Holy Communion; this is partaking of My flesh and blood.

"No, I just can't," Beloved breaks down sobbing.

Master Potter asks, "Beloved, do you trust Me whether Purity lives or dies? Will you love Me?"

"I do love You, but it's not fair. I can't lose her again. I just can't. Please heal her."

When Beloved stops shaking her head no, she looks around and sees she is alone again in the raging, black fires.

Chapter Forty-Six

Fear Not!

Joyful, Comrade, and Sweet Adoration stand by helplessly watching Purity grow weaker and weaker. Her body systems are shutting down causing her to shiver in the blazing heat. The black, billowing smoke makes it nearly impossible for her to breathe. Her breaths grow increasingly shallow and labored.

In the depths of the inferno, Purity can hear the tender voice of Holy Spirit, "Even in the darkest night you are not hidden from Master Potter. He has numbered the days of your life, and none can be stolen."

Holy Spirit signals His glorious presence to the discouraged intercessors rallying them to war. The vessels begin praying again and fight valiantly for her healing.

"Let's pray the Word," shouts Comrade. "It's living and has power in it."

Joyful takes the lead. She opens her tattered Bible and light radiates from it as she reads aloud, "He took our infirmities and bore our sicknesses."

A bone chilling laugh echoes through the chambers as Death ridicules their futile attempt to cut the binding cords of his henchmen. "You think you can stop me by reading from that ancient, outdated book? How foolish! Some day you will all be mine."

Mighty angelic warriors draw their fiery swords preparing to do battle on Purity's behalf. Peering through the smoky fire into the Throne Room, they eagerly await orders.

Silence echoes down the corridors of time as they stand, ready at a moment's notice. Holy Spirit nods approvingly at their submission, knowing the Father's will is perfect and that hidden mysteries are yet to be revealed.

IN FOR THE KILL

Death suddenly becomes very real to Purity as he throws his dark mantle over her. Bending over her, just inches away from her face, he looks deep into her eyes. As her fragile body weakens, he speaks tenderly, stroking her hair. "Can you feel me taking over your body, Purity? This is what dying feels like.

Just relax and let it happen. Death is nothing more than my passionate embrace."

Fear washes over her mind as she feels her body becoming numb and unable to respond to her wishes. *He's right. I'm dying.*

Death torments her further, "I'm all you have left. Master Potter has given you to me for all eternity. Rebellious is lost, and, of course, your mother's not here for you, as usual."

She unsuccessfully tries to lift her head out of the murky pool of lies, but it only brings on a painful coughing fit. Horrifying glimpses of tormented souls appear in Death's gruesome eyes as he hypnotically pulls her down into a swirling vortex of oblivion. Terror fills her being, and she silently screams, "Master Potter, save me."

Beloved watches helplessly as Death slides his arms under Purity, clutching her in his gruesome embrace. She watches in agonizing terror as he slowly lowers his head to touch her parched lips with his own, sucking the life from her ravaged body.

Beloved falls to her knees sobbing hysterically, "No! No! Not my daughter! Not Purity!"

HOLY BOUNDARIES

Unseen by the clay vessels, Master Potter thunders through the dark veil in a holy vengeance for Purity. Clothed in regal authority and sovereignty, He severs the gruesome embrace. The same burning eyes of flaming love that allured the hearts of the vessels are now turned in vengeance on Death, reminding him of his end in the Lake of Fire.

Death and his horde cannot refrain from committing wickedness because they are driven by hatred and rage. Swarming with everything evil and foreign to the heavenly kingdom, Death stutters, "But, but … you gave her to me! She's mine!"

The voice of holiness resounds, "Silence! She belongs to Me."

As Master Potter's words resonate through the kiln, the attacking demons pause, secretly delighting in Death's predicament. Driven by their evil malevolence they find their amusement steeped only in suffering and pain, even when it's a fellow fiend on the receiving end. Yet, they too tremble, knowing their fate is soon to come.

Death recoils instantly at the rebuke of Master Potter. The words pierce his evil being and inflict violence on his hideous form. He is filled with terror at the reminder of the divine retribution that is coming and the destiny that has been appointed for him.

The glory radiating off Master Potter's being permeates Death. In the unbearable agony, he pleads for release, "Yes, I know she's Yours."

Releasing the vile creature, Master Potter returns through the dark veil once again, but not before lovingly watching Holy Spirit breathe life into Purity. Her countenance begins to change.

"It's working," says Loyalty.

"Keep praying," shouts Kindness.

"Color is returning to her face," says Mercy. The other mugs continue to fervently pray.

Comrade and the other vessels watch a heavenly glow of peace radiate from her face.

Peace floods Purity's soul as Holy Spirit penetrates her trembling spirit and powerfully forces fear of Death away, replacing it with His powerful love. He whispers gently, "Fear not little one. Master Potter is the giver of life. You will never be separated from Him. He is with you even now." Full of new energy, Purity sits up.

CHAPTER FORTY-SEVEN

A MIRACLE

"I always knew Master Potter would answer our prayers," shouts Joyful.

Comrade jumps up and down waving his arms. He yells to Beloved, "It worked; she's healed. We just kept praying and praying, and Master Potter just healed her."

Beloved collapses onto the shelf in relief, "Thank you Master Potter, thank you. You do love me. I knew you wouldn't take Purity."

Harvester's voice booms out, "Great balls of fire. It's a true miracle."

Fearless, Harvester, and Long Suffering hear the good news and all run to Beloved.

"It's all worth it now," shouts Long Suffering. "All the pain of the high fires is worth it just to see dear, sweet Purity healed."

The good news spreads, and Golden Incense and her intercessors shout their congratulations from their different shelves. "Beloved, I'm so glad for you. Praise the Lord. Master Potter is the great healer." She turns to her intercessors and says, "OK, our job is done for now. Who wants to get something to eat?"

Still sobbing in joy, Beloved manages to choke out, "Thank you all for your prayers. It took everyone pulling together.

"Mom, mom," yells Purity. I feel so much better. My lungs are clearing up. I can breathe."

Shouting to the lower shelf, she says, "Soon the firing will be over and we'll be together forever."

"Oh, Mom, I can't wait. I miss you so much. Comrade took such good care of me and he prayed so hard."

Gratefully, Beloved says, "Thanks Comrade. You really are a true friend. You kept praying for Purity, even when I was mad at you."

As the news spreads through the fiery chamber, the vessels celebrate one more victory for Master Potter. Faith soars to new levels as they continue to pray for others who are still stricken.

LATER THAT NIGHT...

Night falls, and most of the vessels are dozing happily, but Comrade awakens to the sound of Purity's muffled coughing. Making his way to her, he lays his hand on her forehead. *It's burning with fever! Master Potter, this can't be. I thought she was healed?*

Comrade sits down beside Purity, holds her close, and wipes her fevered brow.

"Purity, what happened," he asks horrified.

"I...I don't know. It came back," she whispers.

"Don't look at the circumstances. Purity, you need to stand on your healing. Let's stay in agreement. This is not the time for us to yield to unbelief."

"But I can hardly...breathe."

"It doesn't matter what it feels like or looks like, you're healed."

"I don't know, Comrade. I really....hurt."

Motioning Joyful and Sweet Adoration to come aside, Comrade says, "Don't wake the others, but we need to pray for Purity. She's relapsed."

"How dreadful; what do we do?" asks Sweet Adoration.

"When I received this gift of healing, I knew Master Potter meant for me to stand for Purity's life. I've seen others much closer to death than she is. Let's stand on our faith."

For the next hour the three vessels labor in prayer—confessing, rebuking, quoting scriptures, singing, praising, worshipping, and exhorting poor little sick Purity to "claim her healing, and walk in faith."

"But she's getting worse," says Joyful. "She's as sick as she was before. I don't think she's going to make it."

"If you're not going to stand with me in faith, then I just need you to leave. I don't need your unbelief."

"But what does Master Potter say about Purity?" asks Sweet Adoration. "What if He wants to take her home?" They begin to argue over faith doctrines as Purity's condition continues to deteriorate.

Their angry voices echo through the billowing flames and smoke, and one by one the other vessels awaken and learn of Purity's relapse.

Meanwhile, the raging fire swirls around Purity's clay vessel, parching her throat and drenching her with sweat. Her life seems to be slipping away right before Comrade's watchful gaze.

CHAPTER FORTY-EIGHT

PURITY'S SECRET

Haltingly, Purity whispers to Comrade, "Listen…"

Comrade interrupts, "Shush, don't talk. Save your strength. Please don't give up! Master Potter is going to heal you. I just know it."

"Listen…I had a baby almost five years ago. I left her on the Mayor's doorstep. I named her Grace…but he calls her Disgrace."

"Does Beloved know?"

"No I was waiting … for the right time. Tell her…for me."

Stunned with the news that Purity's daughter is in the hands of such an evil man, Comrade struggles to remain quiet.

"I wanted her to have good things … I couldn't…I couldn't give her. Promise… to find her … Mom and you raise her to love…Master…Potter."

He encourages her, "Purity, fight to live, and we'll find her together. Master Potter wants to heal you. Now I'm convinced more than ever that you must live."

"Tell Mom… being together was wonderful...I…love her. Give her this." She grimaces as she pushes herself up and pulls a golden locket over her head. "I met Mom's dad, my grandfather, at Comfort Cove. He's an alcoholic…gave me a box of family heirlooms…they brought him bad memories."

Comrade looks at the back of the locket. "What's this inscription? I can't make it out."

"It's Hebrew; it says, 'Hear, O Israel, the Lord our God is one Lord'…. His parents were Jewish, they were …taken away. He never saw them again. There's a menorah, a prayer shawl, an old ring, and photo album. I can't remember other things…kept the locket because of pictures of my…great grandparents…hid the album, and gave everything else to Mayor Lecherous for Grace when she's older." Purity chokes and coughs deeply.

A burst of adrenaline rises from deep within Comrade to zealously fight for Purity and her five-year-old daughter. His father's heart throbs wildly within him, and he boldly proclaims her healing as the fiery inferno builds to an excruciating level.

On the top shelf, Golden Incense leads the other vessels into a warfare cadence of instruments and music as they join into the heat of the battle. Faith and confidence rise in the fiery kiln as they call upon Master Potter. Surely, He will heal her!

CHAPTER FORTY-NINE

NOT MADE FOR THIS WORLD

Holy Spirit opens the heavenly realm for Joyful so that she can see Master Potter at the end of an emerging tunnel of glorious light. Stunned by the revelation, she cries, "Look Comrade! He's coming for her! Can you see His blazing eyes of love?"

Comrade protests, "What are you talking about? Master Potter told me He would heal her and restore me. I'm not changing my mind in the middle of the battle."

Joyful tries to convince Comrade again. "I know He heals, but He also ushers us into His presence. That's what He's doing with Purity! I just saw it!"

Looking down at her, Comrade desperately cries, "I refuse to believe God would allow her to die! I stand against Death and his evil plans. They will not prevail! I'm not going to give up until she takes her last breath."

Suddenly the hideous form of Death is present, and Comrade hears Purity's labored breathing change into a death rattle. Still, he refuses to give up and shouts, "Death, I command you to let her go! Purity don't give up! Fight for your child and your life. Please don't leave us!"

AMAZING GRACE

A shaft of pure liquid light pierces through the billows of black fire and smoke to welcome her home. The Father nods to Gallant, releasing His heavenly orders, "She was not made for this world. Take her to My Son. He's waiting for her."

Walking through the flaming inferno, Amazing Grace makes His way to Purity's side. Opening her eyes, she slowly focuses on His compassionate face. "Amazing Grace, oh, Holy Spirit, You're here."

Reaching out to her, He gently strokes her head. "I told you I'd never leave you."

Looking deeply into His eyes, Purity sees into the realm of eternity. With renewed energy she explains "Look! It's Master Potter coming for me."

"Yes, He's coming for you."

"He's so beautiful."

"Do you feel the incredible love He has for you?"

Her already radiant face now lights up with excitement and joy as she peers into the glory of His presence. The unquenchable fire of His love enlarges and flames the coal burning in her heart, consuming all desires for this life."

"Oh, Amazing Grace. I want to go with Him. I love Him." She cries out, "I'm coming Master Potter."

Smiling, Amazing Grace whispers tenderly to her, "Purity, I told you that you were made for eternity."

Joyful, Sweet Adoration, and the other little vessels drop to their knees beside them. Joyful softly tells Purity, "We release you to go with Him, Purity. We want you to be free."

Amazing Grace orchestrates Purity's death, even to her last breath, as He nods, giving permission for Death to approach.

Death put his arm under her head, delivering his final smothering kiss and claims her lifeless clay vessel for his own. The spark of life fades from her blue eyes.

Intercession and travail rise to a fever pitch as the vessels contend for a miracle to happen. Comrade demands, "I command you to come back into your body! Purity don't go! Please come back!"

Unseen by the vessels, Amazing Grace tenderly gathers her spirit into His protective arms. By clothing her spirit in a mantle of glorious light, He prepares her for her majestic Bridegroom. Then, He gives her spirit to her waiting guardian angel.

Clutching her body tightly to his chest, Comrade's voice erupts in anguish, "Lord take me instead! Please take me and let her live. Raise her from the dead, Lord! Augh!"

CHAPTER FIFTY

HEAVEN'S GATE

Having left her diseased vessel behind, Purity suddenly finds herself being carried in Gallant's strong arms into an incredibly brilliant beam of pure white light. It seems to be emanating from a circular opening far above her. She feels like a speck of dust being drawn at incredible speed into the immense opening.

Entering, she finds herself inside a long narrow passageway of translucent light. At the far end of the tunnel she can see the source as it draws her. It's so incomprehensibly glorious that she thinks it must be the center of the universe.

She watches a wave of dazzling light break off from the source and move toward her. As it touches her, it gives off the living emotion of warmth and comfort as healing floods her spirit. It passes on through her into the darkness far behind her.

She welcomes another wave of light as it breaks off and comes toward her. With greater intensity than the first, it passes through her entire being and feels like liquid peace flowing through and remaining in her.

She looks at her right arm expecting to see a human appendage, but instead she sees a nearly transparent arm of light, her spirit form. She tries to feel her face with her fingers, but her hand moves right through her head. She is amazed, but not fearful. No one could be fearful in such a glorious place.

The opening gets bigger as she's drawn toward the fiery, brilliant light. It looks like a mountain of the most spectacular diamonds in the world. Radiating from all its facets is this splendorous light.

In the distance, another wave of light breaks off and rushes toward her. This time she has the sensation of pure joy and incredible excitement wells up within her. Every part of her has the expectation that what she's about to see will be the most awesome thing any human being could ever see.

Moving out of the tunnel she has an unrestricted view. Radiant light and incredible beauty emanate to the right, to the left, and above her. *I must have come from earth, through the galaxies and into to the hub of the entire universe.* The focal point of all life and light and power is suddenly before her.

As she stands in the center, it seems brighter and more glorious than the outer extremity. *The constellations in the universe must find their energy source from this focal point,* she whispers.

THE GLORIOUS SON

A magnificent person stands in the center of this blazing light surrounded by dazzling brightness. Life itself pulsates from this radiance, and an incredible loving voice comes out of the center. His speech becomes as thoughts to her. "I've been waiting for you."

She feels His penetrating light search the inner secrets of her heart. Waves of His fiery love wash over her spirit, cleansing her of all shame and fear. This overwhelming love heals her broken heart and touches her deep within! She finds herself weeping uncontrollably in His presence. It's so amazing that He has totally forgiven her and accepted her as she is.

Stepping forward, she finds herself disappearing–immersed in brilliant light. Right in the center, as it opens up, she sees a man's bare feet with dazzling white garments around His ankles. Her eyes travel up to see His chest and His arms outstretched welcoming her.

Then she looks up to see His beautiful face, but the most radiant and powerful light seems to be emanating from the pores of His skin. The light coming from His face is so much brighter and more intense that it makes all the other light around Him dim.

His face shines ten times brighter than the sun, and He has garments of light and His radiance fills the universe. His white hair is blowing as if in a breeze, but His face is shrouded in brilliance. Such purity! Such holiness! Such beauty!

"You're so beautiful—beyond what I ever felt or dreamed. If You had revealed this pure beauty, I wouldn't have been able to tolerate it. All of earth would be consumed by Your majesty. No wonder you didn't show me in the natural realm who You are in the fullness of Your glory."

A NEW HEAVEN AND A NEW EARTH

Purity moves closer to the radiance that surrounds His face. He moves to one side, and now she can see a brand new world, a new heaven, and a new earth hanging in space behind Him. A vibrant green pasture with a crystal clear stream and rolling hills comes into focus.

Tall, magnificent mountains rise in the distance under a sapphire blue expanse. Birds of all shapes and sizes—in colors she's never before seen—soar in the heights of this majestic place. She realizes she can understand their songs, and they are all singing praises to God!

Abounding with life, the unearthly flowers and trees vibrate in a celestial symphony, everything alive and resonating with praise and worship. As she looks at the grass in front of her, she sees the same glory that was emanating from Master Potter radiating throughout His entire creation.

Heavenly fragrances and sounds—a glorious orchestration of beauty and harmony fills her new being, empowering and exhilarating her. This new world is totally unstained by sin, a perfect creation. Master Potter has created her to live here. Heart bursting with joy, she whispers, "I'm finally home."

Do You Want to Return?

Eager to explore, Purity is suddenly back in Master Potter's presence. He steps in front of her shielding her view, "After what you've seen, do you wish to return?"

Purity stands on the threshold of eternity where there is no more death, no more tears, no more suffering. Looking behind her is the tunnel of darkness, and she knows sickness and loneliness are there. She can hear the voices of Comrade and her mother pleading, "Purity, please come back!"

"By the power of Master Potter's blood, I command your spirit back in your body. I speak life to this earthen vessel."

"What about my family? How can I leave them so brokenhearted? My mom! My daughter! Would it be selfish if I stayed? And what about my destiny?"

"Your purpose in serving Me is not short-circuited by death, but has its ultimate fulfillment in eternity. Your prophetic journey continues here, it doesn't stop with the confines of time. You remain a part of their lives and will intercede for them along with the cloud of witnesses that have come before you until the day they join you."

His fiery eyes gaze lovingly upon her, "The choice is yours, Purity."

"How could I ever leave You? I love You so."

Glorious garments of intercession are placed upon her as He escorts her into realms of glory. Her worship is like perfumed adoration as they dance to the celestial symphony entering Heaven's Gate.

Chapter Fifty-One

Almost Defeated

In this black crucible of suffering, heavy flames envelop and penetrate the vessels' glaze. It bubbles into molten glass and fuses onto the glowing vessels in the tremendous heat. In the midst of the intense pressure, Beloved doubles over in grief as the shocking news hits her that Purity is gone.

She screams into the billowing black smoke, "Master Potter, why didn't You heal her?" She hears her voice echo throughout the chamber.

"Comrade, I hate you. She never would have been sick if it wasn't for your sin. You did this to her. You killed Purity."

Flinging herself down on the shelf, she curls into a fetal position and wails. "How will I live without her? We were just becoming a family, and now I've lost her again forever."

On the lower self, Comrade sobs inconsolably. "I killed her, and Beloved hates me. I deserve to die." Sweet Adoration and the other vessels weep with Comrade.

"It's not your fault Comrade. She wanted to be with Master Potter," says Joyful.

"We prayed in Master Potter's name. Why wasn't she healed?"

"Comrade, God's ways are sovereign. We don't know why, but we must chose to trust Him now more than ever," says Sweet Adoration.

"You did all you could do, Comrade," says Generosity. The other little mugs solemnly agree.

"It's a mystery, and we only see in part," adds Champion.

Comrade dissolves into tears, "But I loved her. She was like my own little girl."

On the Top Shelf

A distraught Long Suffering embraces Beloved saying, "I don't understand why this happened. We believed! We prayed! Why does He allow His people to suffer and die?"

Fearless and Harvester are shocked. Not used to handling emotions in front of others, they find it hard to express their own grief. Tears roll down the cheeks of the two big vessels as they attempt to comfort Beloved.

"I'm so sorry Beloved, and I know I can't understand the loss you're going through. But I'm going to stand and proclaim His goodness and faithfulness with you," says Harvester.

Fearless chimes in, "We're the ones hurting. We will see her in eternity. You know, I'll bet she's with Him right now."

Thanks for all the pat answers, thinks Beloved, still curled on the floor. *How could any of you understand what it's like to lose my daughter—twice!*

Soon a blanket of heaviness settles over them as a mass of tormenting spirits attack, "He could have saved her, but He chose not to!"

"She was too young to die!"

"You should have prayed harder."

"If you really had faith she would have lived."

After awhile Fearless begins to process his own doubts about Master Potter. "He could have saved her. I don't know why He didn't. Where was He when the avalanche happened? Sometimes I wonder if He really cares as He says He does."

Weeping softly, Harvester tells him, "Fearless, I can feel His love and protection right now. I don't understand all this either, but I have to trust Master Potter even in this.

The vessels assure Beloved of how much they love her, and each one vows to be there for her. They say a prayer and go back to their spots on the shelf to grieve alone.

MORE DEVASTATION

The report comes back confirming Long Suffering's greatest fear: Inoperable cancer! Long Suffering is overwhelmed by Purity's death, her body is tired, and her heart is pierced.

For the first time Harvester notices how terribly tired she looks. "Are you all right?"

"I'm fine. The heavy fires have taken their toll."

Although she hasn't complained, she doesn't fool Fearless and Harvester and they insist that she rest. Relieved to no longer have to hide her pain around her friends, she shares the report.

Fearless tries to comfort Long Suffering by assuring her that he will get the intercessors fasting and praying for her.

Harvester says, "I'm glad you haven't told Beloved. She couldn't stand another blow right now."

Oppressive spirits of Hopelessness have already caught the scent of Long Suffering's fear. They moved in quickly to abolish her faith and sap her already weakened frame.

"Now that Purity's gone, you're next on our list!"

"Master Potter won't heal you."

"You're old and useless."

"You'll never fulfill your destiny!"

"Just give up!"

Holy Spirit's presence sweeps around Long Suffering, sending the attacking demonic forces fleeing in fear. "Can you forgive your mother for abandoning you so many long years ago, Long Suffering?"

Sadly shaking her head, she says, "She remarried a wealthy man, left Comfort Cove and never came back for me. How can I forgive that?"

SHAKEN FAITH

Purity's death and the tragic news of Long Suffering's cancer shake the intercessors to the core. In the midst of Master Potter's fire, another strong demonic wave is released. Deaf and Dumb spirits pounce on their grief, bringing condemnation and accusations in an attempt to wreck the vessel's faith and silence their voices forever.

Frustrated, they wonder if their prayers work. Some begin to question why more aren't healed. Discouraged, Harvester asks, "Why did He save me and not Purity?"

Fearless compassionately tells him, "Master Potter wanted you to live Harvester. Obviously you have an assignment on this side of Heaven He wants you to fulfill. There are mysteries we can't understand and Purity's death is one of them."

Spirits of Doubt and Unbelief plant more lies in the vessel's minds. "It's not a mystery, healing just doesn't work."

"I think," says one of the other canisters, "That healing was just to get the early church started. It's not for today."

"Look how many people we've prayed for who have died," says a vase forlornly. "We're probably all next."

"Long Suffering is not healed either," says the spirit of Doubt. "It's just too painful to be disappointed again and again."

"You should definitely quit praying for healing," says the demon spirit of Unbelief.

"Harvester got healed," says Golden Incense. "It worked for him."

Unbelief continues to whisper, "Oh sure, you have that rare miracle from time to time, but that can really be attributed to positive thinking."

Golden Incense discerns the enemy strategies and asks the Lord how to strengthen the weary troops. After putting on her armor, she digs into her arsenal of weapons and takes out golden keys that unlock the heavens with worship and adoration. "We can't give up now. Long Suffering and others need a miracle. If we quit praying, they could die. Everyone, get your armor on."

In the raging fire, so thick and black they can no longer see or feel Holy Spirit, the doubting vessels offer a sacrifice of praise by faith. Praying and singing in the Spirit, they enter into unity. Soul travail rises up amidst their prayers as they refuse to believe the lies of the enemy and purpose in their hearts to trust in Master Potter's goodness.

"Don't forget," says Fearless's voice in the darkness, "By His stripes you are healed."

"That's right," says Golden Incense, "He purchased our healing and deliverance on the Cross. He didn't suffer for nothing."

The firebox is stoked hotter. Black, carbon dioxide smoke fills the kiln, isolating them from friends and loved ones and adding to their pain.

Huge pillars of smoke and fire savagely swirl through this erupting, blazing inferno. The strong become weak and the wise become foolish as they struggle in the raging war for their faith.

BURNING OUT THE DROSS

Sulfuric fumes fill the chamber as the dross is burned out of each vessel, plunging them into their own personal hell.

Beloved angrily hides on the back of the shelf. She steadfastly refuses to join the group. When they each try to comfort her, she runs them off with her fury. Then she rages about how her friends really don't care about her.

A deep vacuum of loneliness overwhelms Beloved as the suffocating heat and dense flames scorch her sides. She ponders in her heart how hard life's journey always has been for her. Flooded with a kaleidoscope of events and seasons of her life, she looks through a dark lens and finds only loss and pain. *Why did Master Potter let this happen?*

Sitting alone on the shelf, she wonders where her friends have gone. *They said they would stay beside me and help me get through the grief. Where are they? Why do friends always abandon me? Long Suffering hasn't even been back to see me. Why am I always forsaken?*

The terrible heat has weakened her clay vessel, and she longs for sleep, but the pain of her grief will not allow it. Instead her mind is filled with flashbacks of Purity as a little girl. She holds each memory before her as a precious possession and savors every morsel until it drifts away into the smoky kiln. Sleeplessness and fatigue take her deeper into the spiral of grief.

She sees ten-year-old Purity on the outskirts of Deeper Life, begging her to come back. She sees herself running toward her daughter crying, "I'm coming! I'm coming!" Then it dissolves—just wishful thinking—a mirage in the fiery flames.

She feels again the love that throbbed within her as she looked into the soft blue eyes of Purity for the first time. The aching love for that helpless little bundle she held to her breast brings her into endless tears of sorrow. *I had no way of knowing how painful it would turn out to be.*

The searing flames storm the outside of her vessel and travel inside. She is consumed, immersed in liquid fire. Pain and swirling darkness are her only reality as she lies in the black-hot flames of Master Potter's love. A bitterness rages in her as she struggles with losing all that is precious to her.

She is unaware that in the midst of this most horrendous pressure brilliant colors of her glazes are beginning to emerge.

CHAPTER FIFTY-TWO

WILL YOU DRINK THIS CUP?

As the weeks pass, grief remains always by her side, ready to embrace her at a moments notice. Beloved agonizes over the memory of the humble cup of suffering she refused to drink with Master Potter. She still sees the sad look in His soft brown eyes when she refused.

If only she could make her mind stop spinning around, perhaps her spirit could break free. Wave after wave of the endless fire assaults her vessel. With each wave she sinks deeper into the abyss of despair.

Distorted images of the future make her heart faint with dread. Loneliness is her only companion, and she silently wonders why her good friend Long Suffering never comes around. *She's rejected me in my time of greatest need.*

Fearless comes to Beloved to tell her of Long Suffering's cancer and her declining health. The sad news sends her spinning into even more self-pity. "All those I love have either betrayed me or been taken from me. I can't bear anymore."

Fearless encourages Beloved to join the prayer group and lay hands on Long Suffering. He tells her, "She stood with you, and now she needs your help. She's asking for you, Beloved!"

"I just don't have the strength. I'm sorry … please tell her I love her and I'm praying, but I just can't bear to see someone else I love so sick. What if she dies too?"

"Beloved, remember Harvester? You prayed and he was healed! Everyone is hurting; everyone's in pain! She needs you."

"Just leave me alone! You can't begin to understand my pain."

THE CRUCIFIED SAVIOR

Master Potter appears to the grieving Beloved as the crucified Savior, broken and bleeding. Patches of His beard have been ripped out, His face is covered in dried blood. "I know how deep your wounds are. I, too, have suffered great loss."

Grief and pain are etched in His features. Beloved looks on His nail-pierced feet and hands.

"I know your pain. My heart breaks for you. Only I can comfort you at the depth of your great loss. Will you come to Me? Will you let Me comfort you?"

The crown of thorns pierces His scalp, and streams of blood and sweat flow into His eyes. Blood and water flow from a deep gash in His side.

Seeing His pain and His torn body in the midst of the raging black fire, she cries out, "Oh, you do understand my pain, only You can know my great suffering and loss."

"I've suffered greatly to be able to love deeply. Will you allow Me to love you through your devastating loss?" He gazes deeply into her tear-filled eyes. Unconditional love begins to soften her deeply wounded mother's heart.

Beloved responds to His overwhelming sacrifice for her. Flinging herself into His arms, she cries out, "Oh, Lord, I love you."

Once again the angel appears with the cup. As the fire rages, still in His embrace, Master Potter asks, "Now that Purity is with Me, will you drink the cup of suffering? Will you still love Me no matter what?

She knows He's asking her to endure more pain, and for a moment she hesitates in her answer.

Holy Spirit appears, "He deserves an equal companion. Will you join Him in His sorrows? Will you marry His weakness and love His affliction? Only then will you truly know the power of His unrelenting love."

She weeps softly as she feels her heart come into agreement with His. "Yes, Lord, I have nothing left except my great love for You. I give You everything." Taking the humble cup from Him, she holds it firmly in both hands and drinks it down to the dregs.

Overwhelming peace and grace flood her inner being, and an assurance that whatever happens Master Potter is sovereign. All her life belongs to Him.

"Beloved, this life is truly the womb of eternity. Purity was not created for this world. Death was My vehicle to bring her home to Me."

Now Master Potter takes the crown of thorns off His head and places it on hers. Beloved weeps as she feels the glory and the pain. He has crowned her life with suffering, and she feels the profound dignity and honor of it.

The visitation continues as she looks at His back. It is ripped open from the lashes of the relentless scourging He suffered before the Cross. His flesh is bloodied and torn.

Suddenly, she's lifted up and can see both of them from behind. She sees her own back cut and bleeding, just like His.

She hears angelic voices saying, "Look! She bears His marks!"

"She's wearing His wounds!"

"She looks like Him, doesn't she?"

CHAPTER FIFTY-THREE

COUNTER ATTACK

Wasting no time the enemy comes in to attack what Beloved gained in the Spirit. He quickly releases the familiar spirits of Discouragement and Rejection to wear her down. Using Purity's death as a doorway, they quickly win access to her heart and mind once again. Depression floods her with dark thoughts and delusions. Staring into the flames, she sees a dark vision of Purity's dead body lying across Death's huge arms. Malevolent laughter erupts from his vile, gaping mouth as he approaches her. The lifeless form of her daughter hypnotically holds her gaze. Her mind reels.

"Where's His mercy now, Forsaken? I told you she's mine! She's a beautiful trophy for all eternity, don't you think?"

She reaches out to touch her daughter and the image disappears into the smoky flames. Beloved collapses again.

LONG SUFFERING'S GIFT

Long Suffering's face is pale and drawn, and the knuckles on her hands are white as she grips her sword of the Spirit. By the time she locates Beloved she is physically exhausted. She sits on the floor next to her old friend and sings over her quivering form. Stroking her gently, she says, "Beloved I know you're grieving, and I so want to break the power of it off of you. I want to give you a very special gift."

Humming to herself, she takes off her beautiful, multicolored garment of praise. "Beloved, I'm old. I've got cancer....I'm sure it will fit you."

"No, no, you keep it. You need it. Especially now."

"I was going to give it to Purity anyway, because she has been gifted with your beautiful voice, but...well... I know she would want you to have it."

She helps Beloved on with the beautiful robe. "Now the way this works," she says, her voice growing in excitement, "is, as you praise Him and sing, it starts to glow. I don't have much of a voice, but the garment is powerful anyway. Beloved, with your voice you could really put the enemy to flight. I know a good song that really works. Watch this…"

In her weak and somewhat crackly voice, Long Suffering sings out, "Let God arise and His enemies be scattered. Now sing, Beloved."

As Beloved's beautiful voice harmonizes with Long Suffering's, the robe shines and glows. The last clinging spirits of Discouragement and Rejection release their tentacles and flee. Beloved feels grace flowing into her tired, battered vessel.

Another layer of her grief is removed as she realizes the sacrificial love her old friend has for her. *I'm really not abandoned or forsaken. What a great love Long Suffering has for me.*

Encourager and Valiant, the guardian angels, proudly watch their vessels and sing along.

VICTORIOUS

As Beloved sings, Death visits again. Drooling from between his large, yellow fangs, his grisly voice continues, "Forsaken, there's something you really should know. Before Promiscuous died she renounced Master Potter. Now there's only one way you can be with her." Pointing his grisly finger he motions, "Come with me Forsaken."

She gathers her last bit of strength, and cries, "I'm not Forsaken. I am His Beloved. I belong to Master Potter. Even if I die, even if everyone I love dies, I will never, never renounce Him. I will love Him forever! And I will praise His goodness."

Beloved's quivering voice begins to softly sing as her garment of praise starts to shimmer and glow. "You are my Bridegroom King. I am Your delight. You will carry me through the darkness of the night."

Death screams, "Stop it…stop it. It's burning me."

Slowly she draws strength she didn't know she possessed, and her pure, clear voice grows steadier. She closes her eyes and lifts her hands, "I am Your lovesick Bride; You are my delight. You will comfort me and protect me with Your might."

With tears streaming down her cheeks, she continues singing praises lost in her love for Master Potter, her Bridegroom King.

One by one the other vessels stand and join the worship. Soon a loud chorus of a thousand voices of praise is reverberating through the kiln, bouncing off the walls and shaking the foundations of Hell."

Nearly insane from the growing worship, Death writhes and curses as he retreats to the back of the kiln, regrouping with his evil cohorts.

The vessels' pure, heartfelt worship ascends to the heavenly throne piercing the heart of the Father as He gazes intently at the scene below. He sighs in satisfaction as the dross is burned away from His precious vessels.

CHAPTER FIFTY-FOUR

HIGH GLORY FIRE

Master Potter's thunderous voice shatters the demonic stronghold, shaking the foundation of the mountain. The vessels grab each other as the shelves quake. His fierce passion invades the kiln with the holy fury of Heaven.

Glorious light pierces the darkness, and a thick, heavy cloud of glory saturates the kiln. He directs His angelic host to open the dampers. The fresh wind of God invades the chambers, blasting the dense, sulfuric smoke out the top of the mountain.

"For the Father, the Son, and the Holy Spirit that the Bride may come forth," shouts the warring angelic host. Wielding fiery swords newly released from the Throne Room, they valiantly overthrow the demonic warriors. The sound of clashing swords and pulsating wings fades.

Death howls bitterly and blasphemes Master Potter. His curses are lost in the roar of the escaping black flames. Screeching demons take flight. A frenzy of rage sweeps over Him, and he refuses to back away from Beloved. He raises his gnarled talons in a futile attempt to win the challenge from Master Potter.

But instead of the rage he expects, all he hears is Master Potter chortle. At first it's just a chuckle, but it quickly turns into raucous, belly-gripping laughter and spreads to the angelic hosts and to the vessels as well.

It builds into a glorious crescendo, totally disarming Death. Mortification and shame engulf him, as a holy rush of divine justice renders him impotent. Swirls of fiery glory singe his vile being. The powerful wrath of God hurls him from the mountain in an explosion of righteous anger.

HOLY ECSTASY

More wood is thrown into the fireboxes and the government of God powerfully charges the atmosphere releasing the legacy of heaven. The mountain kiln moves into the high glory fire, and the demonic hordes are banished.

Bluish flames explode in pure white-hot combustion, burning the kiln clean of all the sulfuric debris. Master Potter releases waves of fiery love to wash over the vessels. He reaches down and lovingly sweeps Beloved into His arms. Clutching Him, she weeps, "I knew You would come."

His unrelenting love bathes her in surges of consuming devotion. He holds her in His magnificent embrace and tells her again, "You are my Beloved and will always be so."

She enters into holy ecstasy as she gazes into His fiery eyes. Sweet abandonment sweeps over her in a new revelation of His beauty and holiness. The reality that He has been there all the time, even though she couldn't see Him, penetrates her lovesick soul.

Gently He embraces her again before leaving to visit each of His vessels and bring the same comfort and love. The angels minister grace and peace to the clay pots whose glazes have finally melted into beautiful molten liquid glass.

CHAPTER FIFTY-FIVE

HEAVENLY ENCOUNTER

Beloved sits with her head resting on her drawn-up knees and begins to dream. Or is it a dream? It seems so real. There's Purity walking toward her. Her pretty daughter is now breathtakingly beautiful. Each stride she takes is filled with energy and vitality. She's no longer suffering. Her countenance is glowing with life and health, and her eyes sparkle with light.

But the most wonderful aspect of Purity is happiness. She is absolutely exuberant with life. It literally oozes out of her pores. Such glory! Such beauty!

Beloved is swept into her embrace and holds on tightly, relishing the fresh scent of her hair. It seems to Beloved that every strand is glistening with golden light, and her skin glows with life, so soft and silky to the touch. Purity laughs with pure joy. Finally she draws back to look into her mother's face.

As she peers into her eyes, Beloved begins to weep in a rush of guilt, "Oh, Purity, I wanted to be with you so much. If only I had been there you wouldn't have suffered so much. Maybe you wouldn't have died!"

Purity gently takes her mother's hand, "No, Mom, you've never let me down. You've always done everything you could for me. I always felt your love and prayers."

Beloved's tears flow freely, "But if I'd just been there I could have helped."

"Mom, when I died I saw who Master Potter really is, and I knew I could never leave Him. I love you so much Mom, but that's not enough. He gave me the choice to come back or to stay with Him. I wanted to be with Him. It had nothing to do with a lack of faith or not enough prayer. He's just so beautiful that I couldn't leave Him."

"But we just came together. We lost all those years, and now I'm losing the rest. I've had so many dreams of your destiny, and I wanted to share them with you."

"You will share my destiny when we're together again. There's so much for me to do here. I've never been so fulfilled and happy. It's so wonderful and so much bigger than I ever dreamed. There are no words to express the vastness of

His love. And, even though you can't see me, I can always watch and pray for you along with your mom and Grandma Pearl."

Deep contentment flows into Beloved from the wellspring of her daughter's words. "Master Potter allowed me to come to you in this way so you would know I am all right and that I am fulfilling my destiny in Heaven with Him. Now you must release me so you can be free to complete your earthly assignments. Then we will be together again."

SWEET REVELATION

Purity's destiny being truly fulfilled after death is sweet revelation. The joy and excitement of her essence becomes an overflowing stream of healing to her mother's broken heart. Beloved desperately wants to hold on to Purity, but she feels her daughter's longing to return to Heaven.

Once again their eyes meet and Purity softly says, "Release me, Mom."

The two of them are holding hands and Purity is now at arms length. Beloved can feel the glorious pull of eternity as she tells her daughter goodbye. Ever so slowly, she releases her grip. "One more thing, Mom, Comrade became my very best friend. You need to forgive him." Beloved blinks, and Purity is gone.

She is stunned for a moment as the terrible grief lifts. Then she's overwhelmed with peace and sweet elation. She places her hands over her heart, closes her eyes, and turns her radiant face towards Heaven. Beloved's heart is at rest, for she knows that Death did not hinder her daughter's destiny! Master Potter has made her more beautiful and alive now than ever before.

Death relinquishes his terrible hold over her, and all is well with Beloved's soul.

PART FOUR

THE GLORY FIRE

CHAPTER FIFTY-SIX

GUARDIAN OF GLORY

A s Beloved begins to worship, she feels a presence before her and looks up. "My name is Guardian of the Glory," says an enormous angel standing before her. His entire being shimmers with divine energy.

"Beloved, Master Potter has instructed me to take you on a celestial journey," he says with a mischievous smile. "I think you'll find it will not only encourage you, but it might expand your mind just a little."

He holds out His hand to her. As she takes it, they are lifted together through the blazing pillar of fire over the mountain. She is unsure where the dream ends and this vision begins, but the earth becomes smaller as she ascends through space and time.

A sea of crystal clear glass comes into focus. As she peers into its sapphire blue glory, it becomes a pool of vision and revelation. Eternity has now entered into Beloved's heart as she sees the earth below and galaxies moving beneath her feet.

THE THRONE ROOM

The beauty realm of the Throne Room opens to her with vistas of celestial colors, unfamiliar fragrances, and surges of radiant light. The Father, Son, and Holy Spirit are in a constant swirl of living, creative communication.

Just in front of her, the glorious Son sits on a fiery, sapphire throne clothed in radiant garments of light. A dazzling white purity of unspeakable holiness emanates from Him along with music and messages that change time and eternity. Suddenly, tremendous surges of lightning, peals of thunder, and voices burst forth. These explosions of indescribable splendor and raw transcendent power reflect His fervent passion.

Beloved falls before Him, overcome with holy fear. He stretches His hand out and speaks. His voice is like the sound of many waters: "Don't be afraid, Beloved. It is I, Master Potter! I am alive forevermore and have the keys to Death and Hell."

Peace and strength flood her spirit as He motions her to rise before Him. Holy Spirit manifests as seven torches of blazing fire moving throughout the atmosphere in beautiful symmetry. As far as her eyes can see, glorious angels bow low in worship. Shimmering light reflects from their wing tips, creating a heavenly rainbow in the Throne Room.

Surrounding the great throne are twenty-four elders arrayed in white robes and adorned with crowns. Each elder holds a harp and a golden bowl, representing heavenly worship and intercession.

Guardian tells her, "You've seen these bowls before in the Tent of the Lord. They contain the prayers that you and others have prayed over the centuries. They are still a sweet incense rising to the Father."

Four living creatures full of eyes and blazing with fire guard the throne. These burning ones glisten with dazzling light as they fly around the face of God. Raging infernos of glorious worship, they are alive with the fire of His presence. Lightning and fire flashes back and forth among them in magnificent splendor.

Night and day they never cease their adoration and ministry as they gaze upon and unfold His beauty. Overcome by each revelation they cry, "Holy, holy, holy! Lord God Almighty," and release the new vision of His beauty to the twenty-four elders who fall down and cast their crowns at His feet. They join all of creation in worshipping the One who sits on the throne.

Millions of words and harmonies becomes one magnificent song! A symphony of sounds never heard by human ears resounds throughout the Throne Room.

Beloved begins to comprehend that God is love and that His judgments and His pleasure are motivated out of one all encompassing theme. Love! Love for His creation and love for His Son!

FATHER GOD

Pulsating with tremendous life is a terrifying brightness so huge it engulfs the vastness of the Throne Room. She realizes everything she sees is coming out of this brightness. It's the Father who clothes Himself in garments of light to protect the created order, a light so bright it blinds her eyes and appears as darkness.

Guardian speaks again to Beloved and tells her to look to the sapphire blue expanse. She sees multitudes from every tribe and nation consumed with glorious worship and alive with the fire of His presence.

DANCING IN HIS ARMS

The angel points, and in the distance she sees the graceful form of a couple dancing across the sea of glass, intermingled with fire and glory. The magnificent splendor and beauty of the waltz overwhelm her. She recognizes Purity in the arms of her Bridegroom King as a whirlwind of celestial colors engulfs them.

Tears run down her cheeks as she rejoices in seeing with her own eyes the fulfillment of her daughter's destiny.

This must have been the vision Golden Incense saw.

CHAPTER FIFTY-SEVEN

THE WAR ROOM

Guardian of Glory takes her to an enormous hallway. Glorious weaponry lines the walls as far as she can see. Fervent intercession echoes through the ancient hall. Beloved watches as warrior angels, dressed in military uniforms, take down weapons allocated for specific battles.

He points to a doorway and motions her to enter. She walks over the threshold into a vast room where swirling fire and glory sweep across the floor. Above and all around her are galaxies and stars moving through space. She quickly realizes it isn't space at all, but she's inside a huge pulsating globe of the earth.

The entire room is a living map with continents illuminated on the ceiling and walls. Different nations glow with greater and lesser intensity in the glory of God.

Prophetic time clocks are superimposed on the globe indicating the sovereign releases of historic revival. Outbreaks of glory clashing with demonic forces appear on the map as flashing lights as the two kingdoms battle over souls.

STRATEGIC COMMAND CENTER

Guardian tells her, "This is Master Potter's strategic command center. These maps show the timeline of all the ages. What you see is a global chess game being played out on multilevels that are constantly changing."

Flashing lights move at such incredible speeds she cannot follow them. Fueled by demonic spirits, evil world rulers fight for territory and resources. Astounded, she watches the rise and fall of empires and sees the borders of countries recede or advance. Vessels of wrath and defilement, the power brokers of the unrighteous, plot their heartless schemes for more power and wealth, oblivious to the casualties they cause.

She can see the strategic timing of individuals born with glorious mandates. Righteous men and women rise up in each generation to receive hot, blueprint plans straight from the war room, which affect not only their age but also ages to come.

TWO GOVERNMENTS CLASH

She can make out cities exploding with white light as the government of Heaven invades earth. Divine networking is pictured on the map as brilliant light traveling between geographical areas, forming radiant canopies of His glory.

Pointing to some glaring red lights, Guardian says, "These indicate intense spiritual warfare. Where they connect, evil alliances have been formed to create demonic strongholds over an area. Their purpose is to influence world rulers to imprison and annihilate whole people groups."

At the same time, she sees huge angelic hosts moving over continents and waging war on the demonic forces. She watches as the glory utterly consumes the darkness. Looking into the future, she gasps as she realizes she is seeing the end of the age.

The huge angel tells her, "Watch and see a time when the whole earth will be filled with His glory. As soon as the last brilliant white point of light connects, the earth will disappear into eternity."

GLOBAL WAR GENERAL

It's difficult for her to focus on any one thing, but she's drawn to a large table in the center of the room where another world map is displayed. Unexpectedly the war room is filled with the heavy weight of His presence, as the glorious Son enters. Surrounded by majestic angels in brilliant, golden armor, they discuss divine strategies for different nations. She watches as He moves His beautiful nail-pierced hands across the map. Each movement brings some to life, some to destruction.

Key cities are clearly indicated in a living kaleidoscope of light and color. Historical events flash before her eyes in a moving collage of nations birthed, wars fought and borders changed. She sees the forward movement of troops, both angelic and demonic, over the centuries as the realignment of forces and power take place.

NEW WORLD ORDER

Then the formation of a diabolical New World Order begins to come into prominence. It looks much like a black spider web connected internationally across the globe. As she watches, an angelic warrior touches one part of the web. It causes a rippling effect throughout the dark global network and clearly disrupts demonic communications.

She can also see that the Son has His own timetables and network that sets the kingdom of God into place and releases mantles, weapons, and blueprint plans to individuals opening up cities and regions. So, where the enemy is enslaving and entrapping, God is empowering through the release of new troops.

The Cross is the central focus and source of life in every moment in the realm of time, affecting all of creation in the past, present, and future. Throughout the ages, nothing escapes its power in redemption or in judgment. Its shadow covers the whole map.

Fiery petitions rise as columns of iridescent smoke. Holy Spirit groanings and waves of travail erupt on behalf of cities and loved ones. This marvelous orchestration of fervent prayers from earth flows with Master Potter's hands to activate the angelic troops.

She looks to Guardian, and he walks her closer to get a better view. Stunned, she sees doors open on the map and people walking through from earth. At times angels reach into the realm of time to pull someone through for a divine visitation.

Apostles, prophets, intercessors, and many others travel through these glorious portals to talk with the heavenly war counsel and return to earth with fresh revelation. Different battlefields are highlighted, and secret information is revealed to them.

Guardian speaks to her again. "They are summoned on the wings of prayer and fasting. These people will make divine connections in this heavenly realm. Some of them will meet later on earth at a strategic place in time." Looking at the table, she gets a global perspective and realizes that even though she has a calling to Comfort Cove, it is His will that she will one day go to the nations.

A CALL TO MARTYRDOM

She watches another magnificent angel open a door and a line of people enter the war room. They stand before Master Potter who hands each one a scroll. She knows the scrolls contain judgments and that the recipients will be martyred for proclaiming them. She is surprised to see their faces are radiant. They're smiling, full of joy—and so is Master Potter.

After they are handed their scrolls, they walk through doors into their different nations. She can't understand why they're so joyful! Finally she decides they must not understand that they're being sent to certain death.

As if he can read her thoughts, Guardian tells her, "They are going back to the earth where they will proclaim the scrolls, knowing they will be martyred. They're glad because they're chosen. They love not their own lives even unto death."

Her knees give way, and Guardian reaches out to steady her. She sees Comrade standing proudly in the line. In this heavenly realm, she sees the high calling on his life and the undeniable love in Master Potter's eyes for him. Her face flushes in shame, and her heart fills with love and forgiveness for her old friend. Tears flow. She starts to go to him, desperately wanting to ask his forgiveness, but Guardian stands in her way.

"You can make amends when you return to earth."

CHAPTER FIFTY-EIGHT

COMFORT COVE

Guardian directs her attention back to the table and one area of the map. She recognizes the Formidable Mountain Range and the pillar of fire over the Potter's House. Suddenly the scaly back of a hideous dragon appears superimposed over the rugged peaks.

His monstrous mouth opens in a cavernous snarl as he safeguards his hidden glacial lair. His coiled and deadly tail slowly unwraps to reveal his coveted treasure, Comfort Cove. In the distance, she can see a cloud of darkness rising from the mountain as the dragon's wings unfurl, and he soars into the heavens to meet his swarm of vile troops.

Guardian solemnly tells her, "Look carefully, Master Potter is giving you the dragon's strategies."

HISTORY

As she looks into the past, she sees the founding fathers arriving on ships. The rag-tag group falls on their faces in the sand to give thanks to Master Potter for bringing them safely to these shores. Prayers rise in gratitude for the new homeland where there will be no persecution for their faith.

Fiery mantles of radiant glory are released as Holy Spirit bursts upon the scene. Gusts of glory sweep through the little group, imparting the heart of God for the nations and igniting their prayer mantles. Freshly clothed in heavenly garments of intercession and worship, new sounds erupt from their lips as they praise Him in unknown languages.

Heavenly portals open and angelic choirs join their voices in passionate worship. Guardian angels surround the families in a protective canopy of splendor.

A HOLY COVENANT

The vessels sign a holy covenant decreeing their faithfulness to Master Potter and their commitment to teach the future generations His ways and His love. Heaven responds to the words of life burned into this parchment by activating a line of blessing.

Aroused by their prayers and passionate worship, the territorial strongman is awakened in his icy lair high in the Formidable Mountain Range. He gathers his vile troops and vows, "It will be a cursed land, and I will go after the promised seeds of revival and destroy them and their children."

From the beginning there's a subtle, unseen enemy invasion fighting for dominion. War breaks out, but the vessels stand strong and move in their destinies. A mighty fortress of prayer is established.

She sees the years pass—the first church is built, farms and homes are established, and businesses are launched. For the next one hundred years fervent prayer and fasting never cease. Missionaries are sent out by land and by sea as fiery carriers of the glory. Orphanages and shelters for other new emigrants are built, birthed out of the generous hearts of the people.

As the little community walks out the covenant, Master Potter blesses the land with abundance, and the fishing industry is born. The vineyards and orchards are planted on newly cleared land. The community works together to help one another in times of crisis.

Nostalgic emotions sweep over her as she looks upon the colorful orchards and ancient vineyards planted on the gentle slopes of the mountain. She remembers her journey with Master Potter so long ago and how new and wondrous their first love felt.

Centuries flash before her eyes, and she sees fiery vessels proclaiming the Word of God. Outbursts of radiant lights flash on the living map as revival breaks out and spreads across the sea to other nations. Radical preaching is followed by salvations, miracles and deliverance. The praying church glows on the heavenly map, alive and vibrant with the life of the Spirit.

THE FIRE OF PRAYER DIES

But as time passes, the fire of prayer is lost, compromise sets in, and the church becomes a social club. Powers of darkness ascend on the little village, and its light becomes dim. The ebb and flow of the years speed by on the heavenly timeline.

Beloved can't believe what she sees as a demonic atmosphere of greed and immorality blankets the once godly community. Cloaked in darkness, the strongman infiltrates with deception and witchcraft luring them into compromise. Tears fill her eyes when she witnesses the evil purposes of the dragon being fulfilled in her home village.

Finances once given to help the poor and spread the gospel are hoarded to establish personal wealth and power. Apathy settles over the once fertile land.

Amidst the growing darkness, Beloved notices a flickering light. A small remnant is always praying in every generation, including this one. It cries, "Lord, dress us for battle and send Your mighty angels with the armor and weaponry we need."

A FUTURE GLIMPSE

Familiar faces come into view and pass by as she sees into the future. Heavenly canons go off in the war room, shooting fiery balls of glory into the atmosphere. Hitting their targets they explode, and the wind of the Spirit blows the unleashed fire into a raging revival.

The fishing docks are crowded with hungry people listening to a young man preaching the gospel. Words of conviction pierce hearts and dead men become alive as the heavenly fire touches them. Filled with light, scales drop off their eyes and they're gripped with the desperate need of a Savior.

She sees a tent with the sign, *Revival Fires Tonight*, and people are standing outside because it's so full. The fiery preacher tells them about Master Potter, and they cry out for mercy as they feel the weight of their sins.

Guardian asks, "Do you know who this is Beloved?"

An excitement erupts in her heart, "Why, that's my son, Crusader, preaching! And look, there's Comrade. I knew I recognized that tent. They're working together, winning souls, healing the sick, and performing signs and wonders."

Her heart is bursting with joy as she sees them bringing truth back to her village. "Master Potter was faithful with both my children!" She is unable to contain her tears, "He was faithful to my children, even though I couldn't be there. He truly honored my prayers and delivered them." She fingers the small vial of frankincense around her neck.

THIS IS FOOLISHNESS

But, not everyone is pleased with the revival. It shakes the social and political systems creating a great upheaval to village life. At Comfort Cove City Hall, Mayor Lecherous holds his own meeting. A demonic presence energizes and vile spirits move through the crowd manipulating the people like puppets to incite anger and rage.

The mayor warns the townspeople against the revival on the docks. "This will ruin your businesses and drive customers away. Its foolishness and we must take a strong stand against it. Only the ignorant and unlearned fall for such rubbish."

A FIERY SCROLL

Guardian hands Beloved a fiery scroll of strategies. "There has always been a great battle over Comfort Cove. We have shown you the past so that you can unlock the spiritual heritage of the village. Beloved, eat the scroll; it's a prophetic impartation to commission you."

She puts the scroll to her lips, and it tastes sweet in her mouth. But when she swallows, it becomes a raging fire in her bones.

The mighty angel tells her, "Master Potter is sending you and your team to uncap the ancient wells of revival in Comfort Cove and gather the praying remnant for war. It will be glorious," he looks into her eyes and soberly states, "but also costly."

Her eyes are drawn to the scene below, and she sees a small child seated behind Mayor Lecherous. She's on the stage with a nanny lovingly watching over her. "Who is that child? She's so beautiful. She looks just like Purity when she was that age."

Guardian doesn't answer, but turns to walk away. She looks back at the scene on earth, stunned by the sweet face of the little girl. "How could that be?"

CHAPTER FIFTY-NINE

CHARIOT OF FIRE

Beloved's head spins with revelation and glory! She desperately wants to remember everything, but doesn't know if that is even possible. She and Guardian are standing outside the door of the War Room again.

A blazing whirlwind rushes toward them. Beloved is terrified at its violence and grabs Guardian. In a second it is upon them. Swept into its vortex, she is surprised to find peace. It moves them through the heavens, and she is overcome by worship as she sees the beauty of the galaxies as they pass at the speed of light. Suddenly, a magnificent chariot of fire is in front of them. It is transparent, made of crystal clear glass.

A huge angel dressed in a white military uniform with a golden breastplate holds the reigns to three powerful warhorses. Beloved is awestruck by his majesty, power, and obvious authority. The minute they enter, the fiery chariot takes off leaving a streak of wondrous glory across the heavens.

She sees the sapphire sea surrounding the throne below. A rush of adrenaline sweeps through her body as she realizes the wheels are actually angelic beings. Looking down, she sees the flaming river of fire and water proceeding from the Son, who is once again seated on His throne.

This flaming stream flows onto the sea of glass, igniting orange and yellow flames of billowing passion and unspeakable desire for the human race. Multitudes of tribes and nations stand on the raging sea of glory. They burst forth in intercession and worship.

A RADIANT WHITE DIAMOND

The Son is like a radiant white diamond. His transcendent purity shining forth in unimaginable brilliance. As they approach, a deep red color blazes out from His being, signifying His zeal and passion for justice. Around the throne is a beautiful emerald rainbow of covenant mercy for mankind.

Unfamiliar colors, music, and sounds swirl around them as they fly through the vast, ethereal space. Turning for a brief moment, Guardian tells her she will soon receive revelation of her future life and anointing.

Golden keys in various sizes spin past her. She knows they unlock unrevealed mysteries. Treasure boxes, heavenly jewels, swords, musical instruments, and praise swirl around the chariot. Rods of government and authority wait to be released for the end times!

MANTLES

She's filled with wonder and awe and can't image that there could possibly be more. But suddenly mantles of different textures and anointing emerge. She leans over the edge of the chariot to touch them, but they never quite come within her reach.

Guardian tells her, "Now is not the time for these garments. You'll put them on as you are sent on different assignments. The first mantle is liquid fire and smoke releasing the fragrance of Heaven. When this garment is activated, it will break open the atmosphere over cities and nations. Heaven will come to earth, imparting visions and revelation of Master Potter's glory."

"This one," he tells her, "Is made of pure white linen—the righteous deeds you will perform on earth." Its beauty stuns her. Iridescent light and smoky glory move around the pure white linen garment.

"It's adorned with jewels of salvation, deliverance, and miracles. It glows with resurrection power," says Guardian.

Beloved sees a robe and knows it will be hers in the future. It is a rich, deep blue interwoven with gold threads along the sleeves and bottom. As the wind of the Spirit stirs the celestial robe, nations are revealed in its flowing folds. They are intricately created in precious gems and outlined in silver threads.

Guardian says, "You will go to those nations dressed in this heavenly garment. You will stand before leaders boldly giving testimony of Master Potter."

Immediately after the mantles pass by, fiery scrolls fly through the whirlwind—mandates and prophetic proclamations, hundreds of them! She sees golden letters and symbols imprinted on some. They contain information regarding dates, times, and names sealed according to Heaven's sovereign timetable. These are to be released to thousands of vessels in the future. They are sealed until the appointed time. She watches as her sealed, hidden future flies by.

CHAPTER SIXTY

THE HEAVENLY LIBRARY

Now the chariot slows and enters a vast room with thousands and thousands of shelves containing the books of Heaven. Seated on high stools, angelic scribes record on parchment. As Beloved watches the image before her, she's stunned by the revelation that the words are alive and have eternal power.

Glistening words of the Godhead hang in midair for a moment, and they shimmer with anointing. Streams of pure liquid revelation mysteriously flow into long quills and out through heavenly ink.

Dazzling, vibrant words hang in space like huge banners suspended over time and eternity declaring, "Salvation belongs to Him who sits on the throne. You are worthy, Oh, Lord, to receive glory, honor, and power. You were slain and have redeemed mankind by your blood."

Beloved's eyes focus on two magnificent angels possessing great purity and authority. Working at special pedestals, their hands move quickly across the pages of their enormous books.

BOOK OF DEEDS

Guardian of the Glory tells her, "The angel on the right is the keeper of a vast wing of the library called the *Books of Deeds*. Those books contain a full record of the deeds of everyone born on the earth from the beginning of time. Nothing has escaped the all-seeing eye of God. These records will be used to prove that the works of all men have fallen short of the glory of God at the last day's judgment."

"What's that angel on the left doing? He has only one book."

THE BOOK OF LIFE

"He is the keeper of another book called the *Book of Life*. It's the most important book in the entire heavenly library. It's just a register of names, but if someone's name is not written there, that individual's record of works in the *Books of Deeds* will be used to judge him or her."

Guardian pauses then smiles at her and says, "Your name is written in the *Book of Life*, Beloved. The day you called out to Him in the Potter's Field you were born from above. When you voluntarily gave your heart to Master Potter, we all rejoiced, especially your Grandma Pearl, as your name was written in eternal ink on those pages. You have nothing to fear from the record of your works in the *Books of Deeds*. They will never condemn you."

ARCHIVES OF THE PAST

The chariot moves forward, turning suddenly and takes her to a section marked, Archives of the Past. She sees rows of old, well-used leather books and wonders who reads these books, which are both tall and small—all sizes! Some are engraved with gold leaf letters and intricate designs.

Guardian answers her puzzled look and unspoken question, "These books have the power to bring life and death. Some release powerful truths that have started and stopped wars. Other books contain words that break false religious doctrines and unlock political systems, releasing freedom to enslaved people groups and nations."

Books affecting all aspects of life, with the power of the Cross and the truth of the gospel, are bound in heavenly script. She can feel the glory emanating from them. These books have portals into eternity on their pages with living revelation and impartation.

As they fly down the aisles, she sees angels escorting vessels into the Archive Room. Theologians, historians, and teachers are brought to the heavenly library to experience visitations and research the ancient pathways traveled by the mystics and the saints of old.

Guardian explains, "Some are not even aware they're having a visitation, but their spirits are being ignited with fiery inspiration. With their gifts of writing, they will impart truth from the past, and weave these golden strands for present and future generations."

BOOKS OF REMEMBRANCE

Gesturing to another section, he tells her, "These are the Books of Remembrance. They contain multiplied stories of redeeming love told through all the generations of human history. It is the same story retold countless times, but each has its own unique details.

"These books record the glorious histories of every believer, many of whom were hidden while on earth. Most of them were not great by earthly standards, but in the record of heaven they will be remembered for eternity as true heroes of the faith. Some of these men and women moved with powerful anointing and brought revival fires to the earth. Others stood in simple obedience and faithfulness to the destiny the Son ordained for them. The testimony of their lives unlocks ancient truths, imparting understanding to the next generation."

Guardian pauses and looks at her as he continues, "Beloved, because you are one of His, a *Book of Remembrance* is being written that will tell the story of Master Potter's great love for you. It will record hidden details of your life in God and recount Master Potter's unrelenting commitment to redeem, sanctify, and prepare you for glory. It will tell of all His painstaking effort to make you whole, blameless, and pure before Him. The secret story of how He captured your heart and your affections, so that all your deepest longings were satisfied only in Him, will be told in these pages. One day your life will bear witness to the marvels and mysteries of redeeming love, just as all the other volumes in the Books of Remembrance."

Beloved is shaken by Guardian's revelation of Master Potter's love. To think that her life would be an eternal remembrance in the library of Heaven leaves her stunned. She longs for the day she will linger for hours among the Books of Remembrance and read the stories celebrating the uninterrupted history of Master Potter's love for other earthen vessels. But now, Guardian rushes her along.

BINDERS OF ETERNITY

Traveling back through the passages of time, they return to the present. Angelic scribes are recording volumes dealing with this present age—carefully detailing current issues and events that will impact the future.

Flying over huge tables covered with rolled up scrolls, he tells her, "These angels are called Binders of Eternity. They cut up freshly written parchment and bind them into books and scrolls. They've been given wisdom to discern what belongs in each book and to place the finished books in order on shelves throughout the celestial library. Each of these books in its appointed hour will be used to shape history."

She's fascinated as she watches messenger angels gather scrolls, read them through, and, at the foreordained time, take them to earth. She watches the angels traverse the heavenly portals and deliver the scrolls to earthly vessels. She wonders, but is unable to comprehend, how the wisdom of God is making time the servant of eternity.

She can see time-released books filled with anointing to take people to the next levels of the move of God. These books contain fresh warfare strategies to open gates and bring Heaven to earth in a holy invasion of power affecting cities and nations. They release eternal truths to be made manifest throughout the centuries.

GOD'S WAR BOOK

An angel with perfect vision sits on a high stool looking onto the earth. He is recording in an enormous book titled, *God's War Book*. This book contains the names of battles fought over souls throughout the ages. He records the prayer warriors who enter into the great and terrible wars of the past and the present. He waits patiently, destined to record until the end of time.

PLANS FOR THE FUTURE

Traveling into the Plans for the Future section, Beloved sees books glowing with life and divine energy. The chariot slows down, and she is able to read titles and authors names.

Drawing near, she notices a golden seal imprinted with a Lion and a Lamb on each book, the impression from Master Potter's signet ring. Scarlet and purple strands of silken threads are attached to the seals. At the end of the strands are circular medallions stamped with a date and time, indicating when the books are to be released to earth.

Intrigued by their unusual appearance, Beloved wonders what great exploits are declared within the pages. Reaching out, she runs her hand over a few of them and receives momentary flashes of revelation with each brief touch.

The pace is dizzying, and Beloved is feeling a little confused by what she saw in her glimpse of the future. She saw words and music coming out of boxes. They were animated pictures on something that looked like a long ribbon, a huge, metallic, dish-like machine moving through space transmitting pictures and sounds to earth. *What could these possibly be?* she wonders.

Suddenly she sees a familiar name and turns to Guardian, "Is that my friend, Golden Incense?"

"Yes, Beloved, Master Potter gave her powerful keys in intercession to come against the enemy and open up territories for Him. Do you see those four books on the upper shelf? Let's take a closer look at them."

The chariot rises as he speaks. If Beloved had looked at him, she would have seen him smile at the look of surprise on her face as she sees her own name as the author. She reaches out for them, but they're quickly whisked away.

THE END OF THE AGE

The great angel and Beloved move deeper into the future, and the light grows increasingly brilliant. Guardian tells her they are entering, The Culmination of All Time. Soon the light is so bright she is blinded by it, which keeps most events shrouded in mystery.

A heavily perfumed holiness saturates the atmosphere, and the weight of Master Potter's presence is almost more than she can bear as they travel into greater realms of glory. After a few moments, her eyes are able to make out books and volumes so beautiful they are beyond description.

Glimpses of titles whirl past her: *The Temporal Judgments, The Seven Seals, The Two Witnesses, The Battle of Armageddon, The Great Babylon Has Fallen, The Marriage Supper of the Lamb.* The last one book is bigger and brighter than all the others. It's called The New Jerusalem.

The revelation of how Master Potter has planned every detail leading up to the end of time overwhelms her, and she kneels in the chariot. "I'm not worthy to look at these things. The purposes of God are too marvelous for my understanding, and they are too holy for my eyes."

Guardian lifts her head with his hand and tells her, "These volumes were written before the foundations of the earth were laid. They were in the Father's heart at the beginning and are about to be unfolded at the culmination of earth's time."

Chapter Sixty-One

Miracles Unlimited!

The chariot takes off like a bolt of lightning through huge, ancient doors, and Beloved and Guardian streak through the heavens once again. In the distance is a massive warehouse with the name, Miracles Unlimited, over the enormous doorway. The chariot sweeps into the multilevel structure, passing chariots and celestial traffic.

The height and length of this building are miles upon endless miles. Angelic activity is so varied and numerous that Beloved's mind cannot take in even a fraction of what is taking place. Angels fly one direction with orders and another direction with sparkling packages in their hands!

"Who are they?"

"These are ministering angels delivering miracles to those on earth—pieces of eternity, deposits of love and grace from the Father."

Pointing upward, he asks, "Do you see those flashes of light? Those are angels of glory bringing resurrection life from the Throne Room. Portions of Master Potter's unending life is packaged and stored here until the time ordained for its release. If you look closely, you will see each one is wrapped in a vision showing the person's life and the miracle to come."

RESURRECTION FROM THE DEAD

Guardian takes one of the wrapped up visions and motions for her to look closely. She sees an eight-year-old boy who has just died in a village school in Africa. A dead snake is lying on the ground to one side of the lifeless body. All the school children join together in fervent prayers, which release resurrection power to earth. The little boy sneezes and sits up as his friends run and pile on top of him, laughing joyously.

As other angels pass by, she sees more miraculous dramas unfold as prayers from desperate people bombard the Throne Room. A new heart is given to one, a new leg for another, blind eyes replaced with perfect vision, mutes given a voice, cancers cured—all as result of the special delivery of the heavenly packages.

In a far section of the storehouse, Beloved sees row after row of shelves containing miracles waiting to be released. Names are written over each package of pulsating light. She is profoundly touched by the extravagant love of Master Potter to heal and restore. Tears streaming down her face, she thinks of Purity and Long Suffering.

HEAVENLY SUPPLY CENTER

As they turn down the next aisle, she sees rows of long shelves with a sign, YOU HAVE NOT BECAUSE YOU ASK NOT. These are packages that have not been picked up because no one petitioned heaven for them. Beloved is shocked at how many miracles were ready to be delivered, yet left on the shelves.

Stunning jars of different colors holding glistening oil, line other shelves in this heavenly supply center. Oils of different fragrances are stored in fragile blownglass vessels of hundreds of shapes and sizes.

She remembers the first time she saw Holy Spirit, and how He shimmered with light and power. He was so beautifully wrapped in His celestial garment of fire, wind, and oil.

These must be like the little bottles containing the essence of Holy Spirit. Beloved can visualize people using it to bring faith for healing, while others use it to commission individuals for the purposes of Master Potter. Even others receive emotional healing and the oil of joy for refreshing.

Guardian opens one of the small vials of oil and pours the entire contents over her head. A burning sensation and a sweet fragrance cover her. "If you will use the oil, Beloved, as Holy Spirit leads, then signs and wonders will follow."

When he hands the bottle to her, she is amazed to see that it is still full. He places it in her hands and says, "Holy Spirit's power, majesty, and glory never run out. Keep this vial as a remembrance of your time here and the promise of Holy Spirit to be with you."

FISHING AND TACKLE ROOM

The chariot soars upward and enters the Fishing and Tackle Room. Harpoons, fishinglines, lures, and hooks hang on the walls. Multitudes of angels gather around different tables tying golden cords into fishing nets. These are small nets used to bring individuals and families into the kingdom.

Other angels are flying around the room tying off the huge nets used for territories. All the nets vibrate with the Shekinah glory, and when they are thrown into the dark seas of humanity, they bring in a great harvest of souls.

Beloved is amused to hear the angels share their fishing stories as they busy themselves at their work. They laugh and rejoice with each other, recounting the last great revival and the multitude of souls swept up in their nets.

"My net was used at Pentecost when Holy Spirit fell on the one hundred and twenty and the Church was birthed. Three thousand souls were saved that day!"

"Yes, that was wonderful, but my net brought in five thousand from the next holy invasion of heaven on earth!"

"Look, guys, in the Great Awakening the haul was so big it actually tore my net. It had to be mended before I could use it again, really."

Tackle boxes are filled with colorful lures, fishing lines, bobbers, and hooks. Glowing worms and special scents to attract the different fish are placed carefully into the boxes. Finally golden rods and reels are assembled and the whole kit is packaged for Master Potter's evangelistic fishermen.

THE WEAVING ROOM

Rising to yet another level they enter the Weaving Room. As far as her eyes can see, angelic beings are sitting at looms weaving beautiful garments. The rhythm of the looms creates a war-like cadence of victory and joy that reverberates throughout the level.

Thousands of iridescent, shimmering garments are coming off the looms, and other eager angels pack them into containers ready for delivery. Stickers indicating individuals and nations are attached before they are sent to the supply center via a divine conveyer belt.

GARMENTS OF SALVATION

Pointing to one section, Guardian tells her, "Those are the Garments of Salvation. The gossamer red strands represent His shed blood, and the pure white threads are for His righteousness. All born again believers are wrapped in these garments of light. These garments allow the wearer to come boldly before the Father's throne."

She also sees thick Garments of Righteousness. Coals of fire are contained within the hem of the robes. There are pocket inserts in the folds of these garments holding tools and gems. He tells her that the tools are activated when the wearer moves the garment into the specific situations it was created for.

"As the wearer steps out in faith and moves in his mantle, Master Potter will supply the heavenly assistance. It doesn't come the other way around."

Next, Guardian holds up a royal purple robe and tells her, "Let me slip this around your shoulders."

It looks so regal, so majestic, she thinks.

When he slips it on her, she sees the face of Master Potter. In a flash she is taken to the foot of the Cross and feels the incredible price He paid. She watches His suffering for her. Revelation burns into her being! What magnificence! What great love He has for her!

GARMENTS OF PRAISE

She hears the music of the nations rising from the garments below. Garments of rich color flowing into intricate patterns cover the looms in a beautiful display of the diversity of Master Potter's kingdom.

The very fibers sing with life as they are woven together in a symphony of worship and adoration. All the continents and people groups are represented in a vibrant orchestration of harmony. Thousands of languages mingle together becoming one glorious wave after another. The garment of praise Beloved received from Long Suffering begins to glow.

Beloved's excitement causes Guardian to chuckle. He tells her, "Those are also Garments of Praise given to replace the spirit of heaviness and mourning. You can give this one back to Long Suffering, because I have yours right here."

Over there are the mantles for healing. When they're given to an individual, they have the power to release signs, wonders, and miracles in the earth."

She looks at these beautiful emerald robes with golden threads woven into the fabric and wishes the chariot would get a little closer. Exhilarated by the awesome things she's witnessed, Beloved gushes, "What could be more exciting than seeing people raised from the dead, cripples walking, and blind eyes opened?"

"The greatest miracle has always been, and will always be, seeing a dead soul come to life. Salvation is what brings the most joy to Master Potter. He so longs for His Bride to come forth.

"Sadly, many healing mantles have been returned because people refused the prophetic invitation to wear them. They felt the price was too high. Many of the sick miss out on their preordained healings because these mantles lie dormant."

A PACKAGE FOR LONG SUFFERING

Immediately her heart is gripped for Long Suffering, and she purposes to pray for her healing. The chariot is immediately back in the supply center where she sees Long Suffering's name written on a shelf along with a package containing her miracle under it.

Beloved sees a vision of Comrade and her other friends gathered round Long Suffering, interceding in the fiery kiln. She overhears Golden Incense ask if she's ready to forgive her mom. When Long Suffering nods yes, Beloved hears an audible voice thunder through her being, "Now her healing can be released. She will live and not die!"

As she watches in amazement, their prayers rise in smoky fragrance to the Throne Room, and Master Potter agrees with them, activating an angel who quickly gathers the package, placing it in Beloved's hands. Suddenly an impartation of resurrection power hits her as Long Suffering's miracle is released.

Other angels bring pulsating packages and put them into her hands where they quickly dissolve. More powerful surges of divine energy shoot into her like electrical currents. She receives the revelation that someday she will wear one of the emerald green mantles and bring healing to thousands.

An overpowering yearning to see Long Suffering healed awakens in her heart, and sighing with relief, she clutches the package and offers up a sweet prayer of thanksgiving.

CHAPTER SIXTY-TWO

SPECIAL DELIVERY

When Beloved opens her eyes, she finds herself back in the blazing kiln! *I wonder if I only imagined the whole thing?* Feeling something in her hand, she opens it to see the perfumed vial of anointing oil. Her heart swells with sweet, heavenly confirmation. A tear trickles down her face.

Her senses are still alive with the beauty and fragrances she experienced. *I still feel like I'm there.* Seeing flashbacks of her visitation, she can't help but yearn to go back. Now I understand why Purity chose to stay there.

In her spirit, she hears, "This is only the beginning. You were created to be here and will return often for fresh revelation. What I've given you in the realm of eternity will come forth as you walk out your prophetic journey."

Great logs are thrown into the firebox, and hungry flames devour the wood, accelerating the heat and pressure into the final stages of the high fire. The kiln is now burning so clean that Beloved can clearly see the glory fires blazing throughout the chamber. The white-hot vessels are glowing as their glazes are fused to their surface as molten glass.

LONG SUFFERING'S HEALING

Beloved sees Harvester, Fearless, and other friends crowded around Long Suffering. They are praying fervently for the dying vessel. Long Suffering is wasted and gaunt. Deep lines of pain are etched into her face. Her skin looks thin and stretched over her body. She's hardly recognizable except by her familiar smile as Beloved approaches her.

Beloved is overwhelmed with compassion for her friend and certain that Master Potter is going to heal her. Excitedly she gushes, "I've just seen Purity dancing on the sea of glass with Master Potter. She's so alive and beautiful! It healed my heart to see her, Long Suffering. It's so wonderful there. I didn't want to come back either."

"You don't need to prepare me to go home, Beloved. I was really afraid to die, but I finally gave up all my desires and told Master Potter He could do whatever He wanted. I know I can trust Him. He knows what's best, and I'm ready."

"No! No! Long Suffering, I saw your healing." Looking at the others, she tells them, "I could hear your prayers in the Throne Room. I saw you forgive your mom. I saw Master Potter in His glory! He is so beautiful! He told me you would be healed, and He gave me this package."

The vile spirit of Cancer raises its ugly head and contends with Beloved by throwing Long Suffering into a spasm of pain. She angrily addresses them with her new authority. "Your assignment is finished! I break your power over her life and proclaim she will live and not die!"

Laying her hands on Long Suffering, a powerful surge of electrical current shoots through her and releases the miracle of resurrection life. The fight is over in moments, and Cancer is violently flung into the outer abyss.

Long Suffering's countenance is dramatically changed. Color flows back into her cheeks as strength returns to her body. She stands up immediately, praising Master Potter.

"Here," says Beloved sliding off the garment of praise. "Thanks so much for ministering to me with this, but I want you to have it back. I was given my own, and besides, you've got lots of years left."

Cheers and shouts of joy echo through the high shelves as the news of another great victory over Death spreads.

Golden Incense and her group pass the word to the lower shelves. Faith erupts, prayers are spoken, and heavenly deliveries bring more healings. Celebration spreads like wildfire to all the vessels throughout the entire kiln—except for one little mug named Comrade.

CHAPTER SIXTY-THREE

THE HEAVENLY COURTROOM

Tormenting spirits of Depression and Self-Pity brutally assault Comrade. Cruelly mocking his vulnerability, they use his heart for target practice. "You've lost your ministry, your best friend, and your reputation. Of course it's not really your fault. Master Potter let you down. But, still it's all over for you."

Forgetting to put on his armor, Comrade silently agrees with the lying voices and slips deeper into Self-Condemnation. "Tenderhearted, Purity, everyone I've cared about is gone. Master Potter deceived me! He could have healed Purity! I had the faith! Beloved would have had to apologize and forgive me then."

Anger builds and depression deepens as those near him seem to be doing so well. No longer can he stand to be around Joyful's happy face—and Sweet Adoration spends most of her days in lovesick worship. The rest of the mugs and goblets no longer come to him for prayer. *Who can blame them? If only Purity had been healed!*

THE JUDGMENT SEAT

Forgetting Master Potter's encouraging words of forgiveness, Comrade contemplates his dour future and the injustice of it all. While still in the throws of despond, he is suddenly snatched up before the Judgment Seat. Not sure if he's having a visitation or just a bad dream, he looks around at a celestial room of radiant light.

At first he's relieved, until he realizes he finds himself in a defendant's box with a cruel ball and chain clamped around his ankle. Behind him are row upon row of faceless people who seem angry with him.

Satan enters the courtroom dressed immaculately in a black, three-piece suit. His hair is slicked back, and he's sporting a large handlebar mustache. He commands everyone's attention.

A door opens, and the terrified Comrade watches three figures enter the room. The first and the last are enormous warrior angels in full military regalia, their swords of dazzling light drawn and ready.

The middle figure is wrapped in glorious garments so brilliant Comrade has to look away. The fear of God hits the courtroom, and all fall on their faces as the two angels take their place on either side of the Judgment Seat.

Turning to Comrade, Satan glares with smug confidence designed to terrify him. The look hits its mark in Comrade's heart! Sickening fear rushes through him as he hears the gauntlet fall and a deep voice resound, "This court is now in session, please stand."

To his left, a recording angel transcribes the proceedings in a huge book titled, *Comrade's Book of Deeds*. Just then the Judge asks him to state his name. Hardly able to speak, he can barely mumble his reply.

"C...Comrade, s...sir."

Satan's Case

Immediately Satan pounces with a vengeance. Pointing a long, slender finger, he yells, "This man has abused the healing gift You gave him. He used it to build his own name, his own reputation, and his own ministry. What people thought of him became more important to him than what Master Potter wanted. One might even say he relished the worship and adoration of the other vessels. Bottom line ... that's why he wanted Purity healed."

Comrade stutters, "I...I loved her. I really did!"

"What you really love, Comrade, is yourself! To save your own skin, you blamed the sick when they did not recover. When Purity died, you blamed her and Master Potter."

"But Your Honor, she was too young to die. She never fulfilled her destiny," mutters Comrade.

"Such presumption!" Putting his face into Comrade's, Satan sneers, "Master Potter called her home, and she chose to stay. Isn't that right? You're so prideful that even when Holy Spirit tried to tell you it was Master Potter's will, you didn't listen, did you?"

Turning to address the Judge, Satan howls, "He thinks he knows better than God!"

Comrade blurts out, "No, no, not really."

"What about all those vessels in Precarious Pass? You killed and maimed all those poor, innocent people, just because your lustful appetites were not being satisfied." Turning to address the court, Satan yells, "This man is guilty of murder!"

Condemnation crashes down on Comrade, whisking away all of his arguments before he can utter them. In agony, he cries, "Yes, yes! I'm guilty! I'm guilty of everything!"

Satan tries to gain sympathy with the Judge. "I was thrown out of Heaven for less than this! He should be banished forever. I demand justice!"

The Judge looks down at Comrade's *Book of Deeds*, carefully noting every act of sin and iniquity. Every moment of Comrade's life is before His penetrating gaze. Sadly shaking his head for a long moment before giving his verdict, He asked, "Is there anyone here who can testify for this man?"

Comrade trembles and breaks out in a sweat in the long silence that ensues. Panic engulfs him, and just as he begins to feel he will faint for the fear rising in his chest…

THE GREAT INTERCESSOR

Suddenly the doors are thrown open! Blinding light and awesome power enters the courtroom. Comrade looks up to see the great intercessor, Master Potter. He walks to the Judgment Seat and stands between Satan and the Judge.

Falling in a crumpled heap, Comrade desperately cries out, "Mercy, mercy! I need mercy! Forgive me, Lord!"

As Comrade cries out for mercy, the nail holes in Master Potter's palms and the scars of a thorny crown pushed into His brow begin to glow with divine energy. The weight and authority of the Cross causes Satan to cringe in defeat. He falls backward into a crumpled heap.

Master Potter loudly proclaims, "Father, I paid the price for this man's sins. He stands ransomed by My blood before Your Judgment Seat. He is clothed in My righteousness. His name is written in the *Lamb's Book of Life*."

Instantly, the chains fall off of Comrade. A revelation that his sins, both past and present, have been fully paid for pierces his heart. Weeping with genuine repentance, he cries, "I'm sorry. I'm so arrogant and full of pride. Please change me."

Taking his hand, Master Potter leads him through a doorway called Repentance, and says, "Comrade, I know you loved Purity and were willing to give your life for her, but you need a revelation of My Mercy Seat."

THE MERCY SEAT

Two magnificent angelic beings face each other with wing tips touching. Kneeling, they form a canopy of glory over the blood stained, golden seat. Desperate petitions for loved ones mingled with worship flow into a pure blue flame of His presence rising out from the center of this glorious Ark of the Covenant.

Waves of passionate adoration saturate the atmosphere as countless triumphant worshippers surround the heavenly Mercy Seat. Continuing day and night, the billowing perfumed prayers rise through the heavens.

Speaking gently to the broken little vessel, Master Potter tells Comrade, "You accepted My forgiveness, but refused to forgive yourself. That's why the accuser continued to condemn you with those old issues. You have just learned a valuable lesson. Either you end up at the Judgment Seat or the Mercy Seat. The choice is yours."

"But, I always feel I deserve to be punished. Lord, how can You love me?"

"Comrade, you do deserve to be punished, but in the midst of judgment My love is perfected. Once you understand that in your heart, no fear or condemnation will take you out of my intimate embrace. Instead of running away from Me, you will humble yourself and run to Me in mature love. Your festering wounds then will become glorious scars, giving you ranking and authority in the Spirit."

Comrade sobs uncontrollably, "Lord I repent; please help me."

Suddenly he finds himself sitting on the Mercy Seat in Master Potter's arms engulfed in the blue flames. Master Potter's unquenchable love burns away pride and shame. Freedom penetrates his heart, and for the first time Comrade accepts himself, even in his weak, sinful nature.

Comrade's intense gratitude causes him to fall deeper in love. He longs for intimate relationship as never before. Master Potter has become the magnificent obsession he yearns to pursue more than he desires life itself.

PART FIVE

VESSELS OF HONOR

CHAPTER SIXTY-FOUR

COMMISSIONING

The heavens open and a golden rain of radiant glory takes the vessels by surprise. Books, musical instruments, tackle boxes, fishing rods, golden nets, weapons of war, ancient keys, jars of anointing oil, and fragrant perfume float down in the heavily saturated atmosphere.

Golden flakes and precious gems swirl in gusts invading from the eternal realm. Heavenly songs are released into the blazing inferno. The flutter of wings can be heard as ministering angels descend, carrying armloads of celestial garments. Moving among the shelves, they prepare the vessels for Master Potter.

A fiery figure appears, walking through the chamber walls toward them. A beautiful weight of holiness saturates the mountain kiln, and the vessels are suddenly aware of the presence of God. His entire being radiates dazzling light, and His eyes burn with overwhelming love for them. Transcendent power and authority emanate from the scepter He carries in His right hand.

He comes to each vessel, and with one touch of His scepter He prophetically ignites their destiny. Ministering angels deliver supernatural gifts as He speaks them into being. The gifts mysteriously vanish into the vessels' glazes with a jolt of impartation shooting through their clay bodies.

From the upper shelves, Beloved and Fearless watch together as Master Potter commissions His set of goblets. Turning to the last one, His passionate gaze penetrates Joyful's being.

JOYFUL

She is caught up in a trance and enters into a divine ecstasy of love. "I have created you to be a prophetic singer—one who will take the music of Heaven and bring it to earth. I will give you rhythms and notes that will set captives free and bring great healing to families. You will write songs that will impact generations."

Joyful is adorned with a vibrant garment of praise. Her psalmist robe is a delicately woven symphony of rich color and sound. Beloved hears the music of the nations flowing out of the intricately woven patterns. As Beloved and Long Suffering watch on, a huge angel from Heaven's treasure room places an ancient harp into Joyful's hands. Still in her vision and unaware of her surroundings, she plays heavenly music as she weeps in abandoned love for Master Potter.

Next, he moves on to Beloved's mugs. One by one he commissions Devotion, Loyalty, Generosity, Champion, Mercy, and Kindness. Beloved listens like a proud parent. Her heart overflows with love for all the little mugs.

SWEET ADORATION

"I've have called you to waste your life in extravagant worship and intercession before My throne. You will lavishly pour out the fragrance of your love for Me in prayer both night and day. Your life will be a sweet smelling incense that ministers to My heart."

Angels pour many different fragrances of perfumed anointing oil over her and hand Master Potter a bottle of glistening eye salve. He opens it and touches her eyelids with its contents, "I'm anointing you as a seer to gaze into the heavenlies. You will experience many visitations to my beauty realm."

The little vial tenderly replies, "The secret chambers of Your heart beckon me. Where my heart has been dull, Your voice of love awakens me."

Finally He moves to Comrade.

COMRADE

Tears well up in Beloved's eyes as she hears Master Potter declare, "I call you My friend, Comrade. Many will come into my kingdom through your sacrificial love. I'm clothing you in the mantle of an evangelist. You will fearlessly preach my Word with signs and wonders following. I will use you to help bring the next great revival to Comfort Cove.

Two angels standing on His right and left reach into the open heavens and bring down a scarlet robe. "This is your mantle of miracles, Comrade." Silver threads of redemption are woven into the scarlet fabric. They glisten in the brilliant light. "The scarlet represents My shed blood." Beautiful jewels of salvation, radical deliverance, and miracles are set into the hem of the garment.

"You will do amazing things: The blind will receive their sight, and the lame will walk, the lepers will be cleansed, and the deaf will hear, the dead will be raised, and the poor will have the gospel preached to them.

"You will know persecution and go through many trials as you confront political and financial systems. But, you, My friend, are one who does not love your life even unto death. You are My brave warrior."

Moving to the top shelf, Master Potter turns to the teapot, Golden Incense, and smiles fondly.

GOLDEN INCENSE

Master Potter stops in front of Golden Incense. As He speaks, the angels are busy bringing weapons of warfare, maps, and keys. As He proclaims her destiny, He hands her hot scrolls and tells her, "Eat these."

As she eats them, she sees flashes into the future and how she will intercede to break open different territories.

"The seasons of waiting have prepared you for the golden years ahead. I'm calling you to be a prophetic intercessor for the nations, a freedom fighter! You will repent for the sins of the fathers, uncapping ancient wells of revival to open geographical areas. I am giving you keys to unlock city gates and strategies to break curses from generational bloodlines that affect entire people groups and nations." Turning back to Golden Incense, he says with a smile, "You are very close to knowing your new hair color."

Beloved and Long Suffering watch in awe and excitement for their friends. "Look how He loves her! I hope we get everything she got!"

HARVESTER

Harvester booms, "Now, little squirts, I think you know I'm the only one big enough to contain it all!"

"It's not about size, big fella! It's about our destinies you big, overstuffed canister!" says Fearless standing on his tiptoes to jab him playfully in the ribs.

"I know that! I might be big, but I'm not dumb. It's all so glorious, and we've waited so long for this day. It's hard to believe it's actually happening."

As they banter back and forth, Master Potter laughingly picks him up. "You needed to be big, Harvester, so you can contain the Father's heart I've placed within you."

A glorious mantle of royal blue, servant brown, and majestic purple is placed on His shoulders. A wooden shepherd's staff, glowing with governmental authority, is placed in His right hand.

Taking His golden scepter, the King touches each shoulder commissioning him, and says, "I've called you as a pastor to love and disciple my people. I'm giving you the ability to discern and mentor the gifts I've placed within them. You will be a city gate-keeper, with an anointing to bring unity and restoration to My Church."

"Great balls of fire," says Harvester softly, with tears streaming down his face.

FEARLESS

Fearless begins to tremble when he sees Master Potter heading toward him. He carries a shimmering multicolored robe of scarlet and blue embroidery with golden threads and slips it over his shoulders. The weight of glory resting upon the mantle penetrates his being and takes him to his knees.

Master Potter raises the golden scepter to commission the noble wine carafe with the awesome authority of Heaven. Wave after wave of fiery anointing passes through his body.

"I've called you to be an apostle and help usher in the next prophetic move of God. I will give you new governmental systems for my Church. I've called you to be an architect and builder in the Kingdom, to establish my end-time purposes."

He motions for Fearless to rise as He continues, "I will network you with other apostles and prophets at strategic roundtables for My global plans. You will plant churches and help people find their appropriate places. Many will see the dead raised under your hand as signs and wonders follow you."

Beloved gasps as she sees the anointing and gifts fused into his being: keys, weaponry, blueprint plans, and geographical maps.

"The one gift you asked for above all else was wisdom, and it's now being placed upon your head." A dazzling grace package, a crown from heaven's treasury room, rests on his head.

LONG SUFFERING

Long Suffering asks, "Beloved, I keep hearing that room mentioned. Did you get to go there too?"

"No, but I think I'll start asking for it! Oh, look! He's coming this way!"

She steps back as He gazes deeply into Long Suffering's teary eyes. "Today I change your name to Enduring Love. You have suffered much in your life and allowed it to work a depth of maturity and love in your heart. I have called you to be a prophetic teacher. One who digs up the gold buried in My Word and gives it as treasure to others."

Master Potter places a graduation cap on her head. Smiling, He moves the tassel to the other side to signify her promotion in the Spirit.

"Now this gown will go over the top of the garment of praise." He helps her on with a gown of ethereal splendor with the words of God woven into the fabric on her shoulders. Beloved can see what looks like patchwork squares on the robe, but looking closer, she sees they are living books. Job, Song of Solomon, Isaiah, John, Acts, Romans, Revelation, and many others flow in a living kaleidoscope in this teacher's mantle.

BELOVED

An angel of revelation accompanies Master Potter who carries a mantle engulfed in liquid blue flames and golden smoke. Beloved can feel the weight

of glory as Master Potter turns His attention to her. Looking into His hand-
somely rugged features, she's reminded of the contentment of their first love.
Adoration wells up in her heart as their eyes connect in mutual affection, and
she realizes that first love has matured into a deep, passionate relationship.

Fragrant spices emanate from the anointing oils on this mystical robe sat-
urating the atmosphere. This is the first mantle she saw during her visitation,
and she longed to possess it. Future events, dates, and people move in and out
of the blue flames of His love.

He places the garment over her shoulders, immersing her in smoke and
fire. A spirit of burning moves over her body in waves of impartation. Soon her
bones begin to burn in the sweet pain of surrender. "You're feeling My radical
love to enable you to bring judgment against sickness and sin."

She bows low and kisses the hem of His robe in radical submission and
love. Master Potter places His golden scepter on each of her shoulders and proclaims, "I am clothing you in a new mantle. I am bringing you to a place of great
authority, a place of kingly anointing. My government will back you up.

"I'm calling you to the office of the prophet. I will take you into the realm
of the Spirit that goes into the places of principalities, powers, and dominions
of the air. I will show you strongholds over nations, but first I'm taking you
back to Comfort Cove. You will help usher in the next move of My Spirit.

"The enemy will scatter and tremble with fear as you release My purposes.
I will show you My divine chessboard, and you will prophesy, putting the players into place. You will partner with Holy Spirit to move in signs and wonders,
showing My power and authority. You will be My voice of fire to set the captives free and put the enemy to flight."

Wearing her magnificent mantle for the first time, she feels the same
realm of glory she felt when traveling with Guardian of the Glory. Concealed in
the blue flames of the mantle are visions of cities and nations she will visit in
the future.

CHAPTER SIXTY-FIVE

THE BRIDEGROOM KING

Beloved watches Master Potter moving once again through the chamber, placing a golden ring on each of the vessel's hands. Their countenances change as He intimately whispers to each one, "You survived the high fires. You are worthy to be My Bride."

Heavenly fragrances are poured out as the beauty realm captivates their hearts and senses. Wedding flutes fill the atmosphere with celestial music and heavenly cellos harmonize with angelic voices. Swirling gusts of radiant light surround Him.

Taking Beloved's left hand, He places a golden ring on her finger and passionately whispers, "You are My Bride Beloved, forever and ever. We shall live and dance throughout eternity."

The beauty of His countenance and the power of His affections overwhelm her. The holy ecstasy of divine union pierces her heart, and His fiery love surges through her.

His handsome, rugged face radiates like the sun. Such brightness! His overwhelming beauty enraptures her heart as He transforms into the heavenly Bridegroom King.

He's clothed with a dazzling white garment down to His feet and girded about His chest is a golden band. His hair is white as snow, and His eyes are like a flame of burning fire. On His head are many crowns. A blood-red robe is draped over His shoulders, signifying His awesome sacrifice.

He reaches out to touch her cheek, but she takes His hands in her own and covers them with kisses. Clasping them to her cheeks, her tears spill over onto His lovely hands. She looks at the nailprints in each hand and knows they were caused by His great love for her.

"Lord I love you. You're my life, my very breath! I've never known such intimate passion and felt so loved. I am yours forever!"

"Beloved, I have planned for you to be My Bride from the beginning of time. This betrothal ring brings the sure promise of our future together for all eternity. You will rule and reign with me in bridal partnership forever."

A Glimpse of the Future

As He speaks she catches a glimpse of her future with the Bridegroom King. She is carried away in the Spirit and shown people in a celestial city filled with the light and glory of God. It's a great diamond city made of pure gold like clear glass and adorned with precious stones. Such joy! Such delight!

"Oh, Lord, when will this take place? I so long to be with You! You've ignited such hunger in my heart."

"I died for you and long for you. You are the very one My Father promised Me as an inheritance, but the time is not now. The harvest is ready in the fields, and many others are still tormented in the enemy's clutches. Soon we shall live together forever! I will cause you to shine with the brilliance of My light. This great diamond city was made beautiful by My Father and will be offered to you on our wedding day. He will wipe every tear away, and no longer will there be any pain or suffering."

The Fiery Seal

"In the meantime, I am setting My fiery seal of bridal love upon your heart to strengthen you for the battles ahead. Nothing can break the seal I place upon you, not even death, for our love is stronger than death, and our love is as unyielding as the grave. It is for all eternity…forever and ever."

Reluctantly she lets go of His hand as He turns to address the entire chamber.

"You have suffered through the high fires and enabled Me to burn the dross and impurities out of your lives. You have chosen to love Me no matter what the cost. You have paid a price, and have purchased for yourselves salve to anoint your eyes so you might see as others do not."

Falling on their faces in worship, they cry, "Oh, Lord, who loves as You love? We were the rebellious of the earth, harlots, drunkards, revilers, and demonized! You cleansed and purified us and made our lives beautiful! Such kindness! Such wisdom! Such awesome grace!

"We stand in awe of Your wisdom that penetrates and cleanses the perversion of our hearts. You have power and might to overthrow Satan's kingdom in the hearts of clay vessels! We will go to war with You against his iniquity and unrighteousness. We will follow You even to our deaths."

Heavenly colors waft through the white-hot and pure blue flames of the glory fire. The vessel's melted glazes are beautiful mirror-like surfaces that glow in the blazing heat. Smiling with pleasure, the Bridegroom King says, "Now that I see my reflection shining from each of you ... I will turn off the fire."

CHAPTER SIXTY-SIX

SURPRISING BEAUTY

The temperature in the Mountain of Fire cools slowly. After several weeks it returns to normal.

"What's that noise?" asks Beloved. "It's a scraping sound."

Excitement sweeps through the kiln as the vessels see the bricks that block the doorway being removed, one-by-one.

She remembers how terrified she was in the beginning as she watched the angels stack the bricks that cut off her only escape path. I didn't think I'd make it, but it was worth it. It was truly worth every bit of suffering and dying to be a vessel of honor for His service. A tinge of sadness pierces her heart that Purity is not there, but she is with Him, and, oh, how they love each other.

As the bricks come down, light begins to creep inside the dark kiln. The vessels blink as their eyes adjust. A wave of chatter sweeps the kiln from top to bottom, as they are able to see their friends as finished vessels.

"Great balls of fire! Long Suffering, I mean, Enduring Love, you're beautiful," bellows Harvester. "Before the fire, your glaze was mousy brown with some white streaks. Now you're a blend of rich chocolate brown, black, orange, yellow, and you have gold flecks all over you."

"And Fearless, you look majestic. Oh, Golden Incense, your hair color is just perfect, really it is."

"Do you really like it, Harvester? I can't see it yet."

"Trust me, you look wonderful. It has just a hint of lavender in the silver to match the roses on your side. And you have beautiful golden trim on your lid and spout."

"Oh, it's just like the prophecy Beloved gave me so many years ago."

"And look at all the canisters. Line up guys from small to large; let everyone get a look at us. What do you think?"

"You're a perfect set," laughs Enduring Love.

"How'd my grapevine pattern come out?" asks Fearless.

"It looks almost real," says Beloved. "The purple of the grapes is beautifully intense on that pearl white background."

"Beloved, step into the light where we can see you better," says Enduring Love. "You're dazzling white, with the most delicate blue and golden filigree work on your rim. Now, turn around."

All the vessels gasp, "Oh Beloved. Your angel is exquisite."

"It looks just like Valiant."

"Can I touch it?"

"It looks so real."

"You're radiant. Your finish is flawless."

"Really?" she laughs, "I can't quite see it," she says twisting her head. "I think I need a mirror."

"Trust me," gushes Enduring Love. "You're shiny and beautiful."

"Oh, I wish I could see my matching mugs. I wonder how they all turned out. And Comrade, Oh, dear, sweet Comrade."

UNLOADING THE KILN

When the last bricks are removed, artistic angels enter the cavernous room. They carefully unload the mountain kiln, placing the majestic pots of every conceivable size and shape, along with their sets, into Master Potter's wagons. Stunning glazes of golden yellows, crimson reds, sapphire blues, emerald greens, burnt oranges, bronze, silver, and gold, shimmer in the sun.

Angelo and Rembrandt admire the vessel's finished glazes and reminisce about how plain the little pots were as bisque ware. "What a difference suffering has wrought in their lives."

Rembrandt picks up Beloved and admires his handiwork "Well, Beloved, I wasn't sure if I'd ever see you glazed as a vessel of honor, but you paid the price, and you are worthy to be called His Bride."

"Oh, thank you Rembrandt. Thank you for painting me so beautifully. I haven't seen it yet, but everyone says my angel is beautiful."

"It was the Father's design from before the foundation of the world. Now close your eyes, we're about to step outdoors. It's a bright, sunny day, the beginning of spring, and you haven't seen that for a long time."

He sets her gently into the wagon. She opens her eyes slowly, shading her face with her hand. Looking around she sees her seven mugs waiting. "Oh," she says catching her breath. "Devotion, Loyalty, Mercy, you've each got angel wings. Generosity, Champion, Kindness, I'm so proud of you all," she says, looking at each mug and giving them a huge hug.

RECONCILIATION

The last mug in the row is Comrade, looking rather tentative and uncomfortable. Finally, her gaze rests on him, and their eyes lock for a moment.

"Comrade, oh, Comrade," Beloved cries, running to him. She grabs him in an enthusiastic embrace, and they gently sway back and forth. He motions for her to sit beside him and makes room as she slips her arm around his shoulder. She softly tells him, "Comrade, please forgive me. You truly have been my faithful friend, even when I rejected you. You stood by my Purity when I could not. Can you ever find it in your heart to forgive the awful things I said to you? I'm so sorry."

Silent tears trickle down his cheeks, and he whispers, "I forgive you, Beloved. I just want you to know that I would have died in her place. I really did pray from my heart!"

"I know you did. Now I realize that she was given a choice, and she chose to stay with Him. I miss her so much, but I can't blame her. I'd have made the very same decision.

"Did you know, I saw her dancing with Him as the Bridegroom King on the sea of glass?" Her silent tears mingle with Comrade's as they embrace each other again. The six little mugs gather around.

Harvester and the canisters, Fearless and his wine goblets, and Golden Incense and her cups and saucers all excitedly examine their friends. Praising Master Potter for His faithfulness, they chatter and recall the harrowing events of the high fire.

Enduring Love and Sweet Adoration are the last one's loaded.

"Oh, it's so good to get out in the fresh air," says Enduring Love.

"I can't wait to get some perfumed oil," says the delicate Sweet Adoration as she pulls out her stopper. "No offense boys, but that kiln smelled like a locker room!"

RETURN TO COMFORT COVE

Master Potter leans over the edge of the wagon, "I am so proud of you all. You are all My vessels of honor, filled with My love and glory. Because you suffered through the high fires—you loved Me no matter what—you are all worthy to be my Bride.

"Today, you are beginning an exciting time of spiritual espionage against the enemy. I will lead each one of you on your prophetic journey. You were built for great exploits," He says gently touching Harvester and the other canisters. "I came to empower you to destroy the works of the devil."

"That's us, team," shouts Harvester, raising his hands over his head.

"Many of you will be reunited with family," He says, winking at Beloved and Comrade.

From whom is Comrade separated? Beloved wonders.

Master Potter walks to the other side of the wagon. "Look how beautiful she is," He says holding Enduring Love up for everyone to see. "She's dazzling!"

"I send you out to a hurt and dying world to gather other broken vessels." He pauses at Sweet Adoration and inhales deeply. "What a heavenly aroma follows you, precious one. It makes Me feel like I'm in the Throne Room right now.

"The kingdom of Heaven is at hand." He looks directly at Comrade and then to Beloved and her team. Pointing to each one of them He firmly commands, "Heal the sick, cleanse the lepers, raise the dead, cast out demons: freely you have received, freely give.

"Today you return to Comfort Cove. Go and make disciples, baptizing them in the name of the Father, the Son, and the Holy Spirit, teaching them to observe all things whatsoever I have commanded you; and lo, I am with you always, even unto the ends of the world."

BIOGRAPHY

Jill Austin founded Master Potter Ministries over 25 years ago and has traveled nationally and internationally as a conference speaker and prophetic voice in the Body of Christ.

As an award-winning potter, she combines music, drama, and art to depict Jesus as the Master Potter in dramatic presentations throughout the world. Jill retired her potter's wheel 15 years ago when God transitioned her into a fiery preacher with a powerful prophetic voice. What began as a performing arts ministry quickly changed as the Holy Spirit began to move powerfully in her meetings, bringing renewal and awakening destiny to individuals and churches.

She has appeared on The 700 Club, PTL, TBN, and numerous radio shows and has published articles in *Women of Destiny Bible*, *Last Day's Magazine*, *SpiritLed Woman* and *Kairos Magazine*. Jill is currently on the teaching staff of the Forerunner School of Prayer in Kansas City, MO, under Mike Bickle's leadership.

Her vision is to train and equip people to move in the power of the Holy Spirit, not only in the church, but also in the secular marketplace with a demonstration of signs and wonders following.

Her first book in this series is *Master Potter*.

Master Potter's Jill Austin has traveled extensively for over 25 years as a conference speaker and teacher. If you would like to have her speak at your conference or church, please contact us at **info@masterpotter.com**. Jill's powerful teaching tapes can be ordered online at **www.masterpotter.com** or by using the form provided in this book.

Desperation, Visitation & Anointing (2 tape or 2 CD album)

Are you desperate for a visitation from the Lord? Have you had radical encounters with Him, only to be confronted with an onslaught of persecution or misunderstanding? Do you want the anointing so badly that you are willing to climb the mountain once again for a fresh visitation and meet the Lord as a friend, face-to-face?

Many years ago, Jill was ministering in the performing arts with a Master Potter drama called The Empty Cradle, which dealt with the issue of abortion. During this time she encountered heavy spiritual warfare, leading her to desperately cry out for a touch from God. As the story unfolds you will gain confidence that even when heavy opposition comes against you, God will open up the heavens above and deliver you.

Jill had a 21-day visitation after this warfare, which dramatically changed her personal life and ministry. It was an encounter in which the Holy Spirit manifested himself in many different ways. From three in the afternoon until six in the morning, for three weeks in a row, eternity visited earth in her living room as she saw visions into God's glory realm. The Lord showed Jill how to move in the anointing, in a way she had never experienced, and set a foundation through prophetic revelation and biblically sound teaching for her ministry today. Through the impartation of this teaching, you will be inspired to cry out for a visitation of your own!

Master Potter's Jill Austin has traveled extensively for over 25 years as a conference speaker and teacher. If you would like to have her speak at your conference or church, please contact us at **info@masterpotter.com**. Jill's powerful teaching tapes can be ordered online at **www.masterpotter.com** or by using the form provided in this book.

Intercession & Divine Encounters
(2 tape or 2 CD album)

Changing History through Radical Prayer

Outside the palace walls Mordecai stands, a strategic gate-keeper, crying out in prophetic intercession to stop the demonic decrees to exterminate the entire Jewish nation. From the inner courts, in her royal robes, Queen Esther summons her people to fast and pray for a miracle. Two hands join and the destiny of a nation is changed forever. In this teaching, Jill powerfully and prophetically preaches on how God is fulfilling the Malachi 4 mandate, bringing two generations together in radical prophetic intercession to save His people. This tape will empower you to be one who stands in the counsel of the Lord, possessing governmental authority in the heavens, to battle both in the courts of heaven and of men, reversing the decrees of death over your life, your family and your nation.

When the Lord Breaks In…

Do you feel unqualified or unworthy for a visitation? Jill's teaching shatters illusions and misunderstandings by revealing how God visits His people, not based upon their goodness, but because of His own. She sheds light on the supernatural by offering live clips from interviews and incredible testimonies of men and women, much like you, who experienced life-changing visitations. In this tape, you will journey to the throne room of God, marvel at the four living creatures, stand in amazing awe of your Maker and gain greater desperation for God.

A favorite among the Master Potter staff, this album offers two radical tapes for truly radical believers. Warning to listener: The Lord will break in suddenly!

Master Potter's Jill Austin has traveled extensively for over 25 years as a conference speaker and teacher. If you would like to have her speak at your conference or church, please contact us at **info@masterpotter.com**. Jill's powerful teaching tapes can be ordered online at **www.masterpotter.com** or by using the form provided in this book.

The Dawning Revolution (2 tape or 2 CD album)

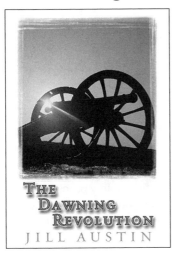

Joshua: A New Generation Emerges

Jill Austin ministers in powerful prophetic preaching and impartation to release God's call to raise up a Joshua Generation. This teaching will give you courage to be one who seeks God's divine strategies to tear down walls and strongholds, bringing freedom to the captives. You will be challenged to go beyond the four walls of the church, moving in radical exploits for God. Prophetic proclamations release impartation, enabling you to start walking out your prophetic destiny as part of God's New Generation – the Joshua Generation. Whatever your gifting or calling, whether from the platform of a church, a place in the media or the floor of the Stock Market, this tape will raise up the Joshua in you.

Elijah: The Revolutionist

Has intimidation, manipulation and control caused you or your church to shut down? Has your God-given governmental authority been usurped by the Jezebel spirit? Jill unveils the plots of the enemy to cause you to abort the purposes of God in your life.

The Holy Spirit is working in this hour to bring forth the new revolutionists who move with fire and unction in His Spirit. The Lord is bringing forth a new generation – one which will yield to the leading of the Holy Spirit to rise up against evil in these last days. Like Elijah, can you call down the fire of God? Does the government of the Lord back up your words with demonstrations of a heavenly magnitude? Are you willing to join the ranks and be a modern day history maker, taking the world by storm for the Glory of God?

Master Potter's Jill Austin has traveled extensively for over 25 years as a conference speaker and teacher. If you would like to have her speak at your conference or church, please contact us at **info@masterpotter.com**. Jill's powerful teaching tapes can be ordered online at **www.masterpotter.com** or by using the form provided in this book.

Vessels of Fire (4 tape or 4 CD album)

These classic teachings, once sold as individual tapes, are now available in this four-teaching set. A perfect addition to your audio teaching library, this album also makes a great gift!

Passion and Fire

Caution: this teaching is full of fire! Revelation and impartation are released as Jill makes prophetic proclamations. Are you willing to be a history maker full of fire, boldly proclaiming the Word of God? Your heart will be gripped with a desire to surrender to God's will and prophetic destiny for your life.

Are You a Cracked Pot?

This challenging allegory traces the transformation of a broken clay vessel, shaped by the Master Potter, into a beautiful vessel of honor for His use. This profound message will give you understanding and insight as you continue your own prophetic journey.

Carriers of the Glory

Like Peter, is your shadow dangerous? Does the glory of God radiate from you, confronting darkness around you in everyday life? This dynamic tape gives powerful keys to carrying His presence outside of the walls of the church to a hurt and dying world.

Do You Want a Visitation?

Do you hunger for a demonstration of the Holy Spirit in your life? Is there a cry in you to know God more intimately and to experience His fiery presence? Hear accounts of Jacob's ladder experiences, radical encounters with the Lord and magnificent angelic visitations.

Newest Teachings 2 Tapes 10.00 / 2 CDs 12.00

The Beauty of Brokenness
Jacob: A Deceiver Redeemed
Joseph: From Prison to Palace
The Dawning Revolution
Joshua: A New Generation Emerges
Elijah: The Revolutionist
Intercession & Divine Encounters
Changing History through Radical Prayer
When the Lord Breaks In...
Holy Spirit: Preparing the Bride
Holy Spirit: Best Friend of the Bridegroom
From Brokenness to Bridal Love
Radical Forerunners
Mary: A Radical Forerunner
Esther: Extending the Golden Scepter

Two-Part Teachings 2 Tapes 10.00 / 2 CDs 12.00

Hearing the Voice of God
Moving in the Anointing
Taking the Prophetic to the Streets
Desperation, Visitation and Anointing
The Prophetic Voice of an Eagle
The Price Behind the Anointing

Four-Part Teachings

Abba Father:The Heart of Forgiveness 4 tapes 20.00/4 CDs 24.00
Visitations Series Volumes 1 – 4   4 tapes 20.00/5 CDs 24.00

Classic Albums (Formerly offered as single tapes)

Show Me Your Glory
available on 2 tapes for 10.00 or 2 CDs for 12.00
Moses:Getting God's Fresh Revelation Face to Face
Joseph: From Dungeon to Destiny

Is the Master in Your Midst?
available on 2 tapes for 10.00 or 2 CDs for 12.00
Is the Master in Your Midst?
Governmental Keys from the Life of David

A Call to Radical Christianity
available on 3 tapes for 15.00 or 3 CDs for 18.00
Radical Exploits Around the World
Carrying the Banner of the Lion and the Lamb
Walking Flames of Fire for the Harvest

Vessels of Fire
available on 4 tapes for 20.00 or 4 CDs for 24.00
Passion and Fire
Are You a Cracked Pot?
Carriers of the Glory
Do You Want a Visitation?

Keys to the Anointing
available on 4 tapes for 20.00 or 4 CDs for 24.00
Keys to the Anointing
Prophetic Birthings that Opened the Heavens
Fresh Oil in the Land
Opening Spiritual Eyes

*Please visit **www.masterpotter.com** for descriptions and photographs of each tape album.*

Please use this form for ordering audio teachings or order online at **www.masterpotter.com**

Qty.	Title	Price Each	Total
		Sub-Total	
		Shipping	
		Donation	
		Total	

Please mail completed form to:

Master Potter Ministries
P.O. Box 9803
Kansas City, MO 64134
(816) 767-9955

Shipping Charges
Please include $3.95 plus 10% of your product total to cover shipping and handling costs. This rate is for orders shipped within the United States only. For international orders, please call us to place your order.

Method of payment: ☐ Visa ☐ MasterCard ☐ Discover ☐ American Express ☐ Check/Money Order

Credit Card Number: ___ ___ ___ ___ - ___ ___ ___ ___ - ___ ___ ___ ___ - ___ ___ ___ ___ Exp. ___/___

Name _____

Address _____

City _____ State _____ Zip _____

Phone _____

Email _____

_____
Cardholder Signature

Thank you for supporting the work of Master Potter Ministries!